DARK CHANT
IN A CRIMSON KEY

By George C. Chesbro

The Mongo novels

Dark Chant in a Crimson Key
The Fear in Yesterday's Rings
In the House of Secret Enemies (novellas)
The Language of Cannibals
Second Horseman Out of Eden
The Cold Smell of Sacred Stone
Two Songs This Archangel Sings
The Beasts of Valhalla
An Affair of Sorcerers
City of Whispering Stone
Shadow of a Broken Man

Other novels

Bone
Jungle of Steel and Stone
The Golden Child
Veil
Turn Loose the Dragon
King's Gambit

Writing as David Cross

Chant
Chant: Torture Island
Chant: Code of Blood

DARK CHANT
IN A CRIMSON KEY

A MONGO MYSTERY

GEORGE C. CHESBRO

THE MYSTERIOUS PRESS
New York · Tokyo · Sweden
Published by Warner Books
A Time Warner Company

Mysterious Press books are published by
Warner Books, Inc., 1271 Avenue of the Americas, New York, NY 10020.

w A Time Warner Company

Printed in the United States of America
First printing: April 1992

10 9 8 7 6 5 4 3 2 1

Library of Congress Cataloging-in-Publication Data

Chesbro, George C.
　　Dark chant in a crimson key / George C. Chesbro.
　　　　p.　cm.
　　ISBN 0-89296-463-4
　　I. Title.
PS3553.H359D3　1992
813'.54—dc20

91-58020
CIP

DARK CHANT
IN A CRIMSON KEY

CHAPTER ONE

In a just world the commission of good deeds would bestow upon the charitable in our midst commensurate physical beauty and social grace, and Emmet P. Neuberger would not look like a pumpkin-in-progress with a complexion to match, nor act like the buffoon at the dinner party who desperately wants to make a good impression but who can't stop telling bad jokes in a loud voice and whose tie somehow always manages to end up floating in the soup. He had pale green eyes which always appeared to be out of focus, as if they had been set wrong at the factory, and he looked like a man who would smell bad, although he didn't. The obsequious manner in which he dealt with most people only made matters worse.

I considered my aversion to Neuberger to be a character defect on my part, but I took some comfort in the fact that even my brother Garth, quintessential defender of underdogs and buffoons, studiously avoided the man, not only in our business dealings with him but also at the numerous New York charity balls and other assorted galas to which the oft-incredulous but

1

undeniably renowned Frederickson brothers were asked to lend their good offices and presence.

I certainly respected what Neuberger did, which accounted for the fact that somewhere along the way we had gotten on a first-name basis. His grandfather had been one of the more ruthless of the nineteenth-century robber barons who had amassed fortunes in both coal and the railroads to transport it. Before he died, the patriarch, perhaps to assuage a measure of guilt at the lives he'd crushed and twisted out of shape to acquire his treasure horde, had set aside a goodly portion of his gargantuan estate to establish the Cornucopia Foundation, a philanthropic organization with a primary, if not exclusive, task to finance both scientific and emergency relief efforts to assuage hunger, disease, and malnutrition in the world. Emmet P. Neuberger was the current elder scion of the clan carrying on the family tradition of administering the multibillion-dollar philanthropic entity for a salary of a dollar a year. Frederickson and Frederickson often accepted generous fees to run routine investigations on presumably saintly individuals and famine research or relief organizations upon whom or which the board of directors of Cornucopia was considering bestowing some of its legendary largesse, and I occasionally did some *pro bono* work for them. Neuberger's heart was certainly in the right place, and under his ten-year stewardship the Cornucopia Foundation had enhanced an already impeccable reputation. I wished both Garth and I liked him better personally than we did.

He was in my office on this sunny summer Monday morning to ask me to go to Zurich, because the man who was universally conceded to be the world's most wanted criminal, an individual who specialized in what might be described as terror-driven confidence scams and extortion, had ripped off the Cornucopia Foundation to the high-pitched tune of ten million dollars, and subsequently burned out the eyes and cut out the heart of a hapless Interpol inspector who had presumably gotten too close to his prey, perhaps even seen his real face.

"But why?" I asked.

Emmet P. Neuberger stared at me with his out-of-focus gaze for a few moments, nervously pulled at his pendulous lower lip, shook his head. "Why?"

2

"Why do you want me to go to Zurich, Emmet? Just what is it you expect me to do there?"

He smiled tentatively, took his fingers away from his mouth, and proceeded to tug at the end of his too-wide tie. "I'm surprised you should even ask, Mongo. Surely you've read that Interpol and the Swiss authorities report they have this Chant Sinclair trapped inside Switzerland, and that it's only a matter of time before their net closes in on him. I would think that a man of your accomplishments and interests, an ex-professor with a Ph.D. in criminology, connoisseur of the bizarre, and world-famous investigator, would at least want to be on the scene when they catch this legendary criminal. I would think it would be like a football fan receiving free tickets and an all-expenses-paid trip to the Super Bowl."

"Very colorful, Emmet. But just because I've been involved in some strange cases doesn't make me a connoisseur of the bizarre, as you put it. At heart I'm really just a simple farm boy from Nebraska. And I'm not a journalist, which means that whatever is going on over there is none of my business. Besides, if I had a buck for every time Interpol or some other police force somewhere in the world announced they were about to catch Sinclair, I could fly to Europe in my own private jet."

"It's different this time. The Swiss Army is being used to help seal off the borders."

"Hell, nobody can even agree on what he looks like now; the last photograph taken of him is twenty-five years old. I know you're anxious to recover Cornucopia's ten million, Emmet, but I wouldn't hold my breath waiting for anybody to catch Sinclair."

Emmet P. Neuberger again fixed me with his eerie, out-of-focus gaze. There was a good deal of anxiety and tension in his pale green eyes. "And you say you're not intrigued by the unusual? You obviously know a great deal about Chant Sinclair."

"No more than what anybody who reads newspapers and watches television would know."

What those readers and watchers were likely to know was that "Chant" was a nickname that John Sinclair had picked up in Vietnam, although nobody seemed to know how he had acquired it, or what it might mean. He'd been a U.S. Army captain in

3

Special Forces, and a highly decorated war hero after two and a half tours of duty. One day he'd apparently just got up in the morning and decided to desert. On his way out of the country he'd managed to kill five highly trained Army Rangers, no less, who had been unlucky enough to have received orders to go after him. Nobody knew how he'd managed to get out of the country with the Viet Cong, North Vietnamese, *and* the U.S. Army all on his case, but he had. Nobody knew where he went, or where he lived now. About the only thing everybody did agree on was that within five years after he walked away from the war he'd established a reputation as a master criminal who'd stolen millions from various individuals and companies around the world, usually by means of often very elaborate con games. But he was no white-collar crook; very messy, sometimes bizarre, violence was a kind of signature trademark of his, as with the missing eyes and heart of the Interpol inspector. He seemed to like people to know when he'd been in their neighborhood.

"He stole ten million dollars from us," Neuberger said tersely. There was a good deal of anger in his voice, but I thought I saw an equal measure of fear reflected in his eyes.

"How?"

He blinked and smiled at me, as though I'd said something especially pleasing to him. "Actually, it's rather complicated. Are you sure you want me to explain it to you?"

"Well, Emmet, I don't know," I replied, glancing at my watch. "If it's all that involved, maybe it had better wait until—"

"He somehow managed to gain access to one of our fund depositories in Europe."

I suppressed a sigh, leaned back in my leather-covered swivel chair, placed my hands behind my head. "You make it sound like a transaction at an automated teller machine."

He thought about it, nodded. "Actually, the analogy is not inappropriate—but only to a degree. You see, at the level of finance at which we operate, in dealing with our investments as well as the organizations and individuals Cornucopia wishes to back financially, money never actually changes hands."

"How do you pay salaries and buy paper clips?"

"That's mere housekeeping," he replied with a dismissive wave of his pudgy right hand. "Those kinds of administrative details are handled through separate accounts which are maintained and administered by regional directors around the world, the same as with any global corporation. These accounts are, of course, routinely audited, as with any business. However, our business is the dispensation of many millions of dollars to worthy causes. Although we do occasionally give grants to individuals, most of our dealings are with corporations, and sometimes with national governments. In our philanthropic disbursements, and in the management of our investments, dozens of different currencies are involved."

"Emmet, this is all very interesting, but I really don't have the time to—"

"In a single hour on any given day, hundreds of millions of dollars may be moved from one investment activity to another, from one country to another. This is done by our own team of investment bankers, using computers and what are called electronic keys, which are similar to the numbers you are assigned for your savings and checking accounts at your bank. One must be authorized to make such a transfer between accounts, of course, but it is not unusual for any large corporation to have a dozen or more investment bankers, working under close supervision, authorized to make such transfers."

"But we're not talking cash here."

"Precisely. We are talking only about numbers, like the listed value of a stock, essentially symbols of value that can only be used when converted into some currency. The actual conversion of credits into currency is done by the recipient of the grant, be it the International Red Cross or some enterprising scientist, *after* the organization or individual receives it. The credit, if you want to call it that, is transferred to the recipient's account by means of a special electronic key created for that single transaction. Such a key cannot be created without the signed authorization of three individuals—our chief financial officer, one member of the board of directors, and myself. To create a special electronic key, transfer credits to the new account, and then be able to actually convert the credits into cash without any sort of authorization along the way is theoretically impossible."

5

"So much for theory. John Sinclair made it happen."

Emmet P. Neuberger's pumpkin-shaped face took on an extremely soulful look, as if he were getting ready to cry. "Yes. Essentially, what he did was to open up his own personal checking account with ten million dollars of our money, and then empty it. To accomplish that, he had to defeat the most sophisticated electronic security system in the world."

"Maybe you'd better have a heart-to-heart talk with your people in Zurich."

"Oh, the police and Interpol have interviewed all our staff people over there thoroughly, although I could have told them they were wasting their time. Hyatt Pomeroy is the executive in charge of our western European operations, but he couldn't possibly have been involved in the crime."

"Why not?"

"He doesn't have the authorization to transfer funds, and I doubt he even understands the complex procedures involved."

"Just what is it Pomeroy does?"

"He administers our Zurich office. He has access to some funds, of course, but only to run the office, pay staff, that sort of thing. We maintain offices around the world to take applications and interview potential recipients of grants."

"But he must have talked with Sinclair, even if he didn't know it was Sinclair."

"Presumably," Neuberger said in a slightly absent tone. "The money this man took was funds marked for emergency famine relief in the Sudan. In a very real sense, the Interpol inspector isn't the only person Sinclair has murdered. Untold numbers of men, women, and children may now starve to death because the relief funds that would have been provided will not now be forthcoming."

I grunted, inclined my head slightly, and stared at Neuberger, who stared anxiously back at me. Finally, I said, "Just what is it you want me to do, Emmet?"

He blinked rapidly, seemingly surprised. "I thought I'd made that clear. I'd like you to go to Zurich."

"You've told me where you want me to go, not what you expect me to do once I get there. My P.I. license is no good in

Europe. I have no franchise to operate as an investigator over there, and I really don't think either Interpol or the Zurich police would be too eager to even buy a glass of *zinferdal* for a private citizen they'd have to perceive as a smart-ass American who'd arrived on the scene to look over their shoulders and second-guess them."

"You're internationally known and respected, Mongo. They'd talk to you."

"About what? I wouldn't know what questions to ask. I don't have the financial or computer expertise to even begin to get a fix on how Sinclair did what he did. You certainly know more about your own operations than I ever will. You already have a city and international police force, not to mention the Swiss Army, working on your behalf. I really don't fancy wasting my time or Cornucopia's money."

"I will be paying you personally, Mongo," Neuberger said quickly, leaning forward in his chair. "None of the people you mentioned work for me; they don't report to me, and all of the information I get is secondhand. All I want is a report on what has happened and the progress of events from someone who has Cornucopia's interests in mind. A report, Mongo; that's all I want. And if you can't find out anything more than I already know, that's all right. All I'm asking is that you go over as soon as possible and take a look at things. Please. I can't tell you how important this is to me."

"I can see that," I said, suppressing a sigh. "Look, Garth is in Brussels taking care of some business for another client. He'll be finished in a day or two, and I'll have him swing through Zurich on his way—"

"No, no, Mongo!" he said sharply, almost plaintively. When I looked at him, somewhat taken aback by the vehemence of his reaction, he continued quickly, "Garth isn't you, Mongo. I mean, he doesn't have your tact. He can be quite abrasive with certain people, as I know you're aware. I'm not sure he could get the job done."

"Damn it, Emmet, that's an insult to Garth. He's a professional, and he's every bit as well known and respected as I am. Besides that, he's an ex-cop; the Zurich police and Interpol could be a lot more impressed by him than by me, and they might extend him professional courtesies they would deny me. Garth may stand a better chance of getting the job done than I would, and he's already in Europe. It will not only save you money, Emmet, but it makes more sense."

Neuberger leaned forward even farther in his chair, clasped his hands in his lap, and bowed his head, allowing me the privilege of studying his bald spot and pronounced dandruff. He made a strange, muffled sound deep in his throat, and when he looked up, I was startled to see that his pale green eyes were misted with tears that puddled in his puffy lids, then rolled down his round cheeks. "But Garth doesn't like me, Mongo. You know that. Not many people do. You may not care much for me, but at least you treat me with courtesy and respect."

"I like you just fine, Emmet," I said lamely, looking away in embarrassment.

"Even as a child, I was never able to make many friends, no matter how hard I tried. Having a lot of money wasn't enough; it just led people to try to take advantage of me. I wanted to *do* something, to *be* somebody. Cornucopia has given me the chance to make my life meaningful. The foundation *is* my life. This may sound odd to you, Mongo, but what John Sinclair did to Cornucopia makes me feel personally violated. I just want to feel as if I have some measure of control, or at least that I'm being kept properly informed about events concerning my . . . child. Having you personally go to Zurich to prepare this report would give me a great measure of relief. Please, Mongo. As a personal favor, would you do it for me?"

"Emmet," I said quietly, hoping my exasperation didn't show in my tone, "I have personal reasons for not being able to go over to Europe right now. I have a lady friend whom I haven't seen in a long time coming into town, and—"

"Miss Rhys-Whitney," he said, smiling broadly. "The snake woman. Such a *lovely* lady. I met her at the Museum of Natural History benefit, remember?"

"Harper and I were planning on spending some time together, Emmet. We've been looking forward to it."

"Then spend it together in Switzerland! She can meet you

there. I'll pick up all expenses, so you can think of this as a paid vacation if you like. It shouldn't take you long to meet with the people you'll want to talk to. You can fax me your report, and then the two of you can be on your way."

Actually, the thought of a European vacation with Harper was not unappealing; we had talked about going off somewhere for a couple of weeks, but hadn't decided where it was we wanted to go. "I don't accept paid vacations from clients, Emmet. But I'll go over to Zurich and poke around a bit, if you insist you want to spend your money that way."

Emmet P. Neuberger positively beamed. "I can't tell you how much I appreciate this, Mongo. Just tell me when Miss Rhys-Whitney is scheduled to fly in, and I'll make all the arrangements to have her flown on to Zurich."

"Don't worry about it, Emmet. You let me take care of Harper. I'll bill you for what I think is fair. I'll do the best I can to provide you with a clear picture of what's happening, but I want it clearly understood that, no matter how much of my time and your money I spend, it's unlikely that I'm going to find out much more than you knew before you walked in here."

"If that's the way it turns out, so be it," Neuberger said, rising and reaching out to pump my hand. "At least I'll know it's the truth, and I won't be depending on strangers, or on subordinates who may have something to hide. I can't tell you how much I appreciate this, Mongo."

"Right."

He walked quickly to the door, then turned back and smiled tentatively. "Will you be . . . leaving right away?"

"No, Emmet, I will not be leaving right away. I have appointments and other business to take care of. But I will be there by the end of the week."

He flashed a broad grin, nodded eagerly, then turned and walked out of the office. There was a decided bounce to his step.

CHAPTER TWO

Veil Kendry was a friend of mine, and a most unusual man with a midnight-dark past whose secrets Garth and I were privy to, a past which could one day conceivably blow up in our faces and ruin a lot of lives as well as the increasingly strong presidency of Kevin Shannon. Most of the world knew Veil as the painter he was, an artist who in the past few years had received international acclaim for his decidedly eerie "dream paintings," very large-scale works comprised of any number of smaller, individual canvases which existed on their own as works of art, and were sold separately. I was probably one of the few people in the world who had actually seen one of the "master paintings" whole, with all of the component canvases hung together in neat rows and covering all of one wall in Veil's spacious loft in a building he owned on Manhattan's Lower East Side.

Garth considered this man with the long yellow hair and glacial-blue eyes a very dangerous man, which was right on the mark. My brother didn't much care for Veil, his enmity going back to a time when I had been drawn into the mist of Veil's hidden past, and we had all nearly lost our lives. But in the end, the journey we had taken had enriched all our lives. Many, if not all, of the friends and connections Garth and I now had in Washington had come to us as a direct result of my leap into the history of this man who had once been known and feared as the deadly "Archangel," combat soldier *extraordinaire*, martial arts master, and one-time point man in the CIA's secret war in Laos.

Indeed, the more I thought about it, the more it seemed to me that Veil's background as a soldier had much in common with what I knew of John Sinclair's military record. Both men had been highly decorated combat soldiers in Vietnam, both had been officers, and both had departed from the service under unusual circumstances—Sinclair as a deserter, and Veil after being branded a traitor and subsequently cashiered as part of an insidious plot to destroy him concocted by his CIA controller, the man who, decades later, would have been shaping the nation's foreign policy had it not been for his obsession with killing Veil, and incidentally Garth and me. Both men were capable of extreme violence—Sinclair obviously by design, and Veil as a result of brain damage suffered at birth; Veil had sublimated his penchant for violence into high art, while Sinclair had parlayed his into a career as a master criminal and what might be termed the art of commercial terror. Both men had unusual names, albeit "Chant" was a mysterious nickname, while Veil's name had been given to him by his parents as a kind of prayer for deliverance from the smothering caul that had enveloped him at his birth. Sinclair was a legendary hand-to-hand fighter, arguably the world's most accomplished martial arts master, and part of the mystique surrounding him was that he possessed special powers acquired as an acolyte of a secret society of Japanese masters. It was the sort of item that Garth, with his long-standing disdain for any kind of fighting that wasn't done with fists, would term a typical "ninja bullshit story," and I sort of agreed. I was highly skeptical of all the "special powers" business, and in fact I suspected that a great deal of what was reported about John Sinclair was pure myth, "ninja bullshit stories," but I had no doubt that he was a formidable warrior, even now in middle age.

As was Veil. Veil was the most accomplished street fighter and martial arts master *I* had ever seen. While Sinclair had reportedly begun formal training as a young child in Japan, where his father had been a State Department official, Veil was completely self-taught, his fighting style eclectic, a mixture of many oriental martial arts disciplines laced with not a few devastating moves he'd developed himself. I had a black belt in karate—the fruit of natural physical skills, quickness, and a few thousand hours spent practicing *kata*. My karate skills had served me extremely well in any number of difficult situations, but all of my knowledge, talent, and skills were insignificant compared to Veil's, and he had become my teacher. We worked out two or three evenings a week, using the mats and equipment set up in a corner of Veil's loft.

As usual, we started off the evening practicing *muzukashi jotai kara deru*, a loathsome practice of Veil's invention which could be loosely translated as "extricating oneself from knotty situations," and which I found boring and time-consuming. However, since Veil was the teacher and I the student, I did what I was told, keeping my impatience to myself in the face of Veil's insistence that "muzu," as he called it, was a handy thing to know.

I was happy when we moved on to the more traditional physical stuff, and we proceeded to practice stick-fighting skills, with long poles of split bamboo taking the place of the heavier *kendo* sticks we sometimes used. We used the poles to train for quickness and agility, and the exercise primarily consisted of taking turns flailing away at each other; while one attacked, the other sought to escape a painful whack by blocking or moving out of the way. We wore no padding to slow us down, since—unlike working with *nunchaku* or *kendo* sticks—there was no real danger of injury; a smack with the bamboo pole could leave a painful welt, but broke no bones.

I was pretty good at this business, rarely taking a full hit—but then, I wasn't exactly a looming target. Veil, at six feet, made a right fine target when he was standing still, but when you swung at him, he was always someplace else by the time the pole sliced through the space where he had been standing only a moment before. On defense, he rarely bothered to use his pole to block or parry. His evasive skills were extraordinary, to say the least, and it seemed he could effortlessly hop over, duck under, or spin away from just about any blow, delivered from any angle. He occasionally had another of his students videotape one of our sessions, and I always found it breathtaking to watch him on tape; he resembled a ballet dancer.

We'd been at it for ten minutes since our last water break, with me assuming the attacking role. It was unarguably more taxing to keep leaping out of the way than it was to slash with the light pole, but I was the one getting sweaty and out of breath as I kept slicing up the air around Veil's constantly dodging and weaving body.

"I've got Mets tickets for Thursday night," Veil said as he leaped high into the air to avoid my swipe at his knees. I followed up with a chop at his head, and he spun away. "Want to go?"

"I can't," I wheezed, hacking at his right shoulder and missing as usual. "I'll be in Switzerland."

"Business or pleasure?"

"Going to Switzerland is always a pleasure." Puff puff.

"You got that right."

I feinted a blow at his left thigh, then spun around and swung at the space where his midsection should have been. I missed by a foot; Veil always seemed just out of reach. "I plan to take care of a little business and a lot of vacation." Puff-puff. "Harper's coming over on Saturday."

"Sounds good to me. What's cooking in Switzerland that requires the attention of the senior partner of Frederickson and Frederickson, if I may ask?"

"The senior partner of Frederickson and Frederickson isn't really sure what he's supposed to do in Switzerland," I said as I abruptly leaped forward and launched a vicious series of short chops aimed at Veil's head and shoulders. He retreated, and I went after him, moving him smartly around the loft, but never landing a blow. "As close as I can figure it, my client"—puff-puff—"simply wants me to go to Zurich and ask Interpol to grade themselves on their progress in the hunt for a very kinky crook by the name"—puff-puff—"of John Sinclair, who nipped a foundation my client operates for a cool ten million. Since I can't believe he believes Interpol and the police over there will

13

say much of anything except that they're doing a wonderful job, I consider my mission a bit foggy." Puff-puff.

I swung hard at Veil's head, and to my utter astonishment the splayed end of the pole landed square on his right cheek with a loud *swonk*. Because I was so accustomed to having Veil avoid anything I could throw at him, I had swung with all my might. But he had suddenly and unaccountably stopped dead in his tracks a moment before I had launched my strike, and now the end of the pole had sliced his flesh. His deep blue eyes registered neither surprise nor pain, but blood welled up over the edges of the two-inch-long cut, then rolled in a scarlet sheet down his cheek.

"*Jesus*, Veil!" I cried, throwing the pole to one side and hurrying over to him. "I'm sorry!"

"Not your fault," Veil said somewhat absently as he walked over to the matted area. He picked up a towel, pressed it to his slashed cheek, then headed for the partitioned-off living area at the far end of the loft. "You expected me to get out of the way, and I should have. I slipped, lost my footing."

Feeling queasy and guilty, I followed him into the living area, through the small, spartanly furnished bedroom into the bathroom, where he turned on the tap, leaned over the sink, and began to flush the cut with cold water. It hadn't looked to me like he'd slipped; he'd simply stopped moving. "You want help?" I asked anxiously.

He shook his head as he opened the medicine cabinet above the sink and took out a gauze compress, which he pressed against his cheek. Then he turned, fixed me with his ice-blue eyes. "I'm all right, Mongo. It's just a superficial cut." He paused, and shadows seemed to move in the depths of the bright eyes that continued to stare at me. Finally, he continued, "You mind if I ask you a question about your business, Mongo?"

It seemed an odd question, coming from Veil, and there was an uncharacteristically terse tone to his voice. "When have I ever minded you asking me about anything?"

"What's your—or your client's—interest in whether or not Interpol captures John Sinclair?"

"Are you kidding me? I already told you."

"Indulge me, Mongo. Tell me again, in detail, if you will."

"Sinclair used a little financial wizardry, which I don't understand, to rip off ten million dollars of funds earmarked for famine relief in the Sudan. The director of the philanthropic foundation that provided the money is just a bit pissed off about it. He's taking it personally, and he wants his own man on the scene to report to him on what's going down. I don't expect to find out anything he doesn't already know, but it seems he'll be perfectly satisfied just to get an independent report with my name on it. It's such a milk run that I'm embarrassed. I should be finished by the weekend. Harper's meeting me over there, and we'll split for Zermatt."

Veil grunted softly, then turned back to the medicine cabinet. He removed the compress, washed the cut with hydrogen peroxide, then applied an antiseptic salve. "How are Garth and Mary?" he asked in a flat tone.

"Just fine," I replied, staring at his reflection in the mirror. I had the distinct impression his mind was elsewhere. "Mary has a new album out and climbing the charts, and Garth's in Brussels taking care of some business for a client." I watched him apply a clean, smaller compress to the wound, tape it in place. "You might want to go for some stitches in that cut. It could leave a scar. You want me to drive you over to the hospital?"

He turned around, placed his hand gently on my shoulder. "Let's have some juice."

We went into the kitchen, and I sat down at the small, painted wood table. Veil set up two glasses, then retrieved a frosted pitcher of fresh grapefruit juice from the refrigerator. He poured for both of us, then sat down across from me. He sipped his drink, studying me over the rim of the glass.

"What's on your mind, Veil?"

Veil drained the glass and set it back down on the table. He sighed, shook his head slightly. I had the feeling he'd made some kind of decision—one he was not particularly comfortable with. "I'd like to offer you some gratuitous advice."

"You know I value any advice you have to offer, my friend. What is it?"

He poured himself more grapefruit juice, again fixed me with his steady gaze. "Steer clear of anything whatsoever that involves John Sinclair."

Suddenly, I felt a slight chill. I wasn't sure if it was an aftereffect of the exercise, or from the sudden rush of excitement I was experiencing. "Hey, you know this guy?"

Veil shifted his gaze to the glass in front of him, shook his head.

"Ever met him?"

"No. I just know what I read in the newspapers." Now he looked up at me, and I again had the impression that he was uncomfortable and that he was struggling with some private dilemma. "But I hear things too. I wish I could be more specific, but I can't. It's just a feeling. I know you think it's an easy job, Mongo, but maybe you should pass on this one. Don't go to Zurich."

My friend's uncharacteristic reticence was beginning to make me uncharacteristically annoyed with him. "Wow," I said, my tone just a millimeter or two short of sarcasm. "Now, there's some pretty straightforward gratuitous advice, Veil. I shouldn't go to Zurich because you hear things, and you have a feeling."

"Mongo—"

"Just what do you hear that I haven't heard, Veil? What's the word on the street regarding John Sinclair? Is there something even more awful about him I should know, aside from the fact that he'll starve children to line his pockets and that he has a nasty tendency to torture, maim, or kill anybody who gets in his way?"

"Mongo," Veil said in a slow, measured tone, "if you go to Zurich to investigate this matter—"

"I'm not investigating anything. I don't have a franchise to investigate anything outside of New York State. I'm going over there to politely ask Interpol and the Zurich police about *their* investigation."

"—you're liable to find yourself in a hall of mirrors instead of on any milk run. In that hall nothing may necessarily be what it seems to be. In fact, I'm suggesting to you that nothing you may have read or heard about John Sinclair is necessarily true."

Veil's words, as well as his sincerity and obvious concern in giving me such a clear warning, intrigued me. I knew I probably should be patient and allow him to explain his somewhat mysterious approach in his own way, but my irritation at the fact that he seemed to be withholding information that would back up his warning won out. "What the hell are you talking about, Veil?" I asked, somewhat surprised at the sharpness of my tone. "What can't necessarily be true? The man's got an M.O. and track record going back twenty years. He's a big-time thief and a murderer of sometimes unbelievable cruelty. If you have something else to tell me about him, why not just come out and say it? Why the hell jerk me around like this?"

"You're angry with me," Veil said evenly, leaning back in his chair and smiling thinly. "You feel I've stuck my nose in your business. I'm sorry. I didn't mean to offend you."

"I'll tell you what offends me, Veil. Certainly not that you care about me, or that you're concerned for my safety. I take that for granted. But you seem to be playing some kind of game here, and *that* offends me."

"Mongo, I—"

"For Christ's sake, Veil, you and I share some history. You know the types of situations I've been in, and you know what I can handle. You, Garth, and I have faced up to some pretty dangerous people together. Now I casually mention that I'm off to Europe to do nothing more than ask for a progress report from the authorities, and you issue a ringing warning for me to avoid anything involving John Sinclair. That clearly tells me you *do* know something, and you won't tell me what it is." I paused, took a deep breath. Suddenly, I realized that what I felt even more than anger was hurt. Perhaps I was overreacting, but it seemed to me that Veil's obvious reticence in discussing all he knew or suspected about John Sinclair implied that, despite everything I knew about Veil, and other confidences we had shared over the years, he did not completely trust me. That came as a shock, and gave me a decidedly empty feeling. "You damn well do know something more about Sinclair," I continued quietly. "Earlier, when I mentioned his name, it startled you, and you lost your concentration. That's why I was able to whack you. But you won't tell me what it is you know. This isn't like you at all, Veil. You know me well enough to know I don't pry, but *you're* the one who brought up the subject in the first place."

"I'm sorry you're angry, Mongo," Veil said, looking away. "I'd take it as a personal favor if you'd let me come along with you."

"Thanks for the warning and the offer, Veil," I said coldly, abruptly standing, "but at the moment I can't see how either is of much value. I'm going to Zurich to take care of my business, then I'm going to spend a few days in the mountains with Harper, and then I'm coming home. I'll send you a postcard."

I waited, still hoping that Veil would say something more, or at least explain *why* he wouldn't say more. It wasn't so much that I thought I needed the information to accomplish what I still could not conceive of as anything more than a minor errand, but because I felt that in a space of only a few minutes, with words that had—or had not—been exchanged, a friendship that I valued beyond what any words could describe had been irretrievably damaged.

When Veil did not reply, I turned and headed for the freight elevator that would take me down to the street.

CHAPTER THREE

I emerged out of Customs into the main terminal at the Zurich airport and was startled to see a figure in a fabulously ill-fitting chauffeur's uniform holding up a sign with what might have been my name had it not been misspelled, with two *k*'s. He was a very tall man, well over six feet, whose physical grandeur was marred by a crippled left leg and what appeared to be a permanent stoop. His blue serge uniform looked like it had been put together from spare parts; although the cap precariously perched on top of his head was at least one size too small for him, the rest of the outfit had the appearance of being hastily cut and sewn together from some enormous blanket with no other purpose in mind than to simply drape his large frame. There was an anxious, almost furtive air about him as he peered over the heads of the people around him in search of his fare. Pushing my luggage cart ahead of me, I veered off to my right, heading for a side exit where an array of gleaming silver and blue buses were parked at the curb.

"Dr. Frederickson! Dr. Frederickson, please wait!"

It seemed the man with the sign had been waiting for me after all. I stopped and turned as the big man lurched toward me, leaning heavily on his stout cane and half dragging his crippled leg after him. He was decidedly short of breath by the time he reached me, and it took him a good thirty seconds to get his wind back. This accomplished, he pulled himself as erect as his damaged body would allow, then tugged at the tails of his coat and brushed some imaginary lint from his lapels. Despite his comic-opera outfit, there was a distinct, touching air of dignity in the way he presented himself.

"I am Carlo at your service, Dr. Frederickson," he said in English laced with a heavy Italian accent. "I am to be your driver during your stay in Switzerland."

I smiled up at the man with the craggy face with permanently weathered flesh, coal-black eyes, and unkempt, silver-streaked black hair flaring out from beneath his cap. "It's nice to meet you, Carlo, but I told Mr. Neuberger I didn't want a chauffeur. It's nothing personal; I just believe in public transportation. Have a nice day, and tell your boss I said thanks anyway."

I proceeded toward the exit, stopped again, and heaved a little sigh when I heard Carlo's cane thumping behind me on the tile floor. "Dr. Frederickson, please wait!"

Once again I waited for him to catch his breath, hoping he wasn't going to have a heart attack.

"I don't know this Mr. Neuberger, sir," he finally managed to say. "I was sent by my superior at Cornucopia here in Zurich. I have been ordered to make sure you are made as comfortable as possible."

"I understand, Carlo, but I really do not want a chauffeur. Being waited on makes me nervous."

He repeated his curiously dignified gesture of pulling himself up and tugging at the tails of his coat. He turned his head to one side and swallowed hard. When he looked back at me, I was startled to see that his ebony eyes were moist. The air of anxiety about him I had first noticed was now even more pronounced. "What's the matter, Carlo?" I continued. "I told you it was nothing personal. I just don't want to have to wait around for a chauffeur to come when I want to go someplace, and I don't want one hanging around when I don't. Like I said, it makes me nervous."

He planted his cane on the floor in front of him, leaned down as far as he could, whispered, "You don't understand, *signor*."

"Please stop leaning over like that, will you, Carlo? You're going to throw out your back. What is it I don't understand?"

His response was to lean down even closer to me and whisper, "I'm Italian."

"Really?" I said, suppressing a smile.

He shook his head. "It's so embarrassing."

"Being Italian?" I asked incredulously.

"No. It is my situation. I am Italian-Italian, not Swiss-Italian."

"So what?"

Now he straightened up, but continued to gaze down at me with his soulful black eyes. "The Swiss allow me to work for good wages, which I can use to support my family back in Italy, so I do not mean to sound ungrateful. But I must speak the truth if I am to make you understand why it is so . . . important that you use me. The Swiss are a very rich people. There are jobs for all Swiss who want them, and it is not necessary for any Swiss to do menial jobs like collecting garbage or cleaning streets. For those kinds of jobs they hire foreign workers like myself who cannot find jobs in our own countries. But they are very strict about certain things. For example, they do not allow foreign workers to bring their families with them. More important, they issue only temporary work permits that are good for staying in this country only as long as you are working. If you lose your job or quit, you must leave the country immediately."

"Carlo," I said, starting to feel more than a bit impatient, "are you telling me that you'll lose your job, you'll be forced to leave the country, and your family will starve just because I don't want to use you? Cornucopia must have somebody else for you to drive around. Listen, I'll be happy to call your boss and explain the situation."

"No, *signor*," he replied quickly, opening his eyes wide. "That would only make matters worse. You see, there isn't anyone else to drive around; there hasn't been for weeks. Cornucopia has

21

been very, very good to me. They originally hired me as a janitor ten years ago. Then I hurt myself, and they saw that it was difficult for me to do the heavy physical labor sometimes required of me. Rather than dismiss me, they gave me this job of chauffeur. This is work I can do, *signor*; it is the best job I have ever had. But I know they are thinking there really isn't that much need for a chauffeur. I am afraid of being let go. Please, *signor*, you look like a kind man. If you would let me serve you, and then—if you are satisfied with my service—perhaps say a kind word about me to my boss, I would appreciate it very, very much. I promise not to get in your way, and I will always be close by when you need me."

Carlo might be old and crippled, but he was no slouch when it came to presenting a case. Cornucopia should have hired him as a lawyer. I grunted, pointed to his crooked left leg. "You can, uh, drive all right with that leg?"

"Oh, *si, signor*. The car has automatic transmission. You will find I am a very good driver."

.   .   .

He was right. Despite my protestations, he had insisted on using his free hand to push my luggage cart out of the terminal to a special-permit parking lot where a gleaming black Mercedes-Benz was parked off to one side, and from the ease with which he tossed my luggage into the cavernous trunk, I knew he was not a man I would have wanted to annoy when he was younger. Behind the wheel of the Mercedes, he drove along the highway into Zurich, and then through the city's streets, with confidence and skill, and—despite his Keystone Kops uniform—an air of professionalism that made him appear as if he'd been a chauffeur all his life. As if fearing to invade my privacy, he'd rolled up the window separating the front seat from the rear *salon*, which seemed to me only slightly smaller than a handball court. There was a bar, television, and a selection of about a dozen newspapers and magazines. There was also a thermos of hot coffee. I opted for the coffee, pouring myself a cup of the nutty, chocolate-laced liquid, leaning back in the soft, rich-smelling leather that surrounded me, and enjoying the view out the windows as we made our way to the Hilton.

I told Carlo to wait for me while I checked into the hotel. I was amused to find that Neuberger had booked me into one of three "honeymoon suites," since the Presidential Suite had already been booked when he'd called. If the car's *salon* had been big enough for a game of handball, the hotel suite was more suitable for jai alai. After an initial twinge of guilt at being the proximate cause of so much wasted money, I reminded myself that my expenses were coming out of Neuberger's very spacious pockets, and not funds meant to feed starving children; if he wanted to spend his money this way while I looked into what might have happened to the funds that had been meant to feed starving children, I wasn't about to complain. I'd already done that.

It was four o'clock, local time. I was tired, of course, but my experience with jet lag told me that I wasn't going to be able to wind down and sleep for hours, and so I might just as well get right to business. I called Hyatt Pomeroy at Cornucopia's branch office in Zurich, announced who I was and why I was there, and asked if I could come over to talk to him. Pomeroy, who spoke with a pronounced Australian accent, didn't sound exactly thrilled at the prospect of having his day capped by me, but he'd been expecting my call, and he didn't object. I jumped into the shower, put on fresh clothes, and went out to find my chauffeur waiting for me at the curb.

•   •   •

"He totally misrepresented himself," Hyatt Pomeroy announced in his high-pitched, nasal voice virtually the moment I stepped through the door into his office. He sounded like he believed this was new information to me, and that it would explain everything.

Hyatt Pomeroy, the executive in charge of Cornucopia's operations in western Europe, made much the same negative impression on me as Emmet P. Neuberger, despite—or perhaps because of—the fact that he was a polar opposite in both appearance and demeanor. While Neuberger was obese and obsequious, Pomeroy was rail thin and haughtily austere; Neuberger was warm, if that was the word, to the point of nausea, while this man with the piccolo voice and Australian accent was ice cold. Neuberger, despite his enormous wealth, wore clothes that looked like they had been hastily snatched off some pipe rack at a fire sale while the fire was in progress, while Pomeroy's suit, shirt, Hermes tie, and Gucci shoes were all top-of-the-line. Although he had insisted that I sit in the straight-backed chair placed in front of the desk in his cramped office, he remained standing, like a man ready to make a quick getaway. I could tell he was not overjoyed to see me.

"How so, Mr. Pomeroy?" I asked evenly.

"Let me be frank with you, Dr. Frederickson," he said, shoving both his hands into the pockets of his suit jacket. "I resent you being here—or rather, I should say I resent the fact that Mr. Neuberger has seen fit to send a private investigator here to question me. Not only does it betoken a complete lack of trust and confidence on my employer's part, but I consider it insulting. I've been thoroughly interrogated by both Interpol and the Zurich police—a number of times. Every scrap of paper from this office has been confiscated. I can't even authorize the payroll for staff until this bloody business is finished. How could Mr. Neuberger possibly think I had anything to do with this theft?"

"I'm not here to investigate you, Mr. Pomeroy."

That took him by surprise. He stared at me for a few moments, slowly blinked. "What, then?"

"All Mr. Neuberger wants is a comprehensive report bringing him up to date on the investigation. My being here is in no way a reflection on you."

Pomeroy sniffed. "I talk to him on the phone at least once—and usually twice—a day. What's the matter with the reports I give him?"

"You'll have to ask him that question, Pomeroy, because I don't have an answer for you. I've told you what my job is. If you don't want to talk to me, fine. I'll just include that in my report."

Hyatt Pomeroy thought about that for a few moments, then abruptly walked behind his desk and sat down in the swivel chair there. He brushed some imaginary lint off his lapels, then leaned forward and clasped his hands together on his desktop. "The man whom authorities say is actually John Sinclair was known to me as Michael Radigan," he said evenly. "We met four times over a period of six weeks. He sat right there where you're sitting."

"What did he look like?"

"What difference does it make? I'm told he's a master of disguise, and that nobody is certain what he really looks like."

"I'd like to know anyway. It should be in my report."

Pomeroy shrugged. "He was a big man, over six feet and powerfully built, but he came across as rather effeminate."

"How so?"

"I don't know; some of his gestures, the way he talked. I just got the impression he might be homosexual. Some of those big hunk-types are, you know."

"Is that a fact? I'll be damned. Go ahead."

"He had blue eyes, thinning red hair. He claimed to be French-Canadian, and he spoke English with a French accent. He dressed adequately, by which I mean that his clothes were expensive but not necessarily well selected; he didn't have the taste he thought he did." Pomeroy paused, wrinkled his nose. "He actually wore an earring, which absolutely ruined the businesslike appearance he was trying to project. He had a sort of sallow complexion and a persistent smoker's cough. He also wore thick glasses that made his eyes seem very large."

I grunted. "Sounds like quite a costume."

"Yes," Pomeroy agreed. "You could say he was an imposing figure, but the overall impression was negative."

"How did Cornucopia become involved with him?"

"The same way we get involved with all individuals representing private groups. This office received a proposal for a project and an accompanying request for a grant."

"What was the proposal?"

"It involved a genetically altered strain of wheat that would be highly drought-resistant and grow rapidly in a wide variety of climatic conditions. Radigan-Sinclair claimed to represent a group of businessmen in Quebec who were seeking to establish a large laboratory to research, and eventually produce seeds for,

25

this particular strain of wheat. They had already raised a certain amount of money, and they were supposedly looking for a matching grant."

"Like ten million dollars?"

"Oh, heavens no. The amount they were requesting was really not much more than—literally, if you will—seed money for architectural surveys and printing brochures to try to attract more money. If this initial phase was successful, they would have been free to approach us for a larger grant. Actually, the proposal was excellent, and I signed off on it."

"Meaning you authorized the grant?"

"No. I'm not empowered to authorize grants. I merely express approval of an application, if that's the case, and recommend that the grant be awarded. The awarding of grants is executed in New York, as is the actual transfer of funds. Authorization requires the approval of Mr. Neuberger, the chief comptroller, and a member of the board of directors. The authorizing directorship is rotated every month, since it is considered an honor."

"Just what is it you do, Mr. Pomeroy?"

"I thought I had explained that. This office serves as a clearinghouse for applications that originate in western Europe and sections of North America, including Quebec Province. Based on what we find out, we—I—pass judgment on whether or not a grant should be authorized, and this is usually based on the nature of the proposal. We process thousands of applications every year."

"And you investigated this Michael Radigan?"

He stiffened. "Yes, to the degree that we investigate any applicant. It's easy to second-guess this office now, but his credentials, and those of the organization he claimed to represent, seemed impeccable at the time."

"Even though it was all phony."

"Dr. Frederickson, if John Sinclair was not capable of erecting such exquisite inventions, he wouldn't be the master criminal he is, now would he? I did my job, and Interpol tells me that the cover he invented would have survived a much more thorough investigation than the ones we routinely conduct."

"Mr. Neuberger tells me New York never authorized the grant."

"Of course not; they never had the time. And if they had, it would have shown up in bank records."

I was experiencing a growing sense of frustration and a feeling of inadequacy. Another feeling I had, and it was only a feeling, was that Hyatt Pomeroy was withholding something—perhaps something important—but I just didn't have the information or expertise to adequately grill him.

"Will that be all, Dr. Frederickson?" he continued, responding to my silence.

"Look, Mr. Pomeroy, Sinclair didn't rob you with a gun, he robbed you with a number. This whole damn thing is about numbers. What I know about encryption of data codes and electronic transfers of funds wouldn't wet the bottom of a thimble, but I sure as hell know that Sinclair wouldn't have gone to all the trouble of setting up dummy corporations and inventing a phony identity to get in here, and he wouldn't have wasted six weeks of his time to meet with you on four occasions, if he didn't need something from this office, from *you*. What did you give John Sinclair that he needed to fleece Cornucopia, Mr. Pomeroy?" I paused when I saw the change of expression on his face, and I felt a tiny surge of exhilaration. And suddenly, I thought I knew the answer. "A number. You gave him a number. You may not be authorized to award grants or transfer funds, but you do assign certain numbers. Is that it, Mr. Pomeroy?"

In only a matter of seconds, Hyatt Pomeroy had gone from looking defensive but self-assured to downright glum. "Mr. Neuberger is well aware of the encryption process used by the organization his grandfather founded and which he now directs, Dr. Frederickson. He also has all the pertinent data, as does Interpol."

"Well, it apparently slipped Mr. Neuberger's mind to give me the information I'm looking for now, and I didn't know enough to ask. But he obviously wants me to have it, or he wouldn't have sent me over here to prepare a report. So let me ask you again: What did Sinclair get from you that he needed to pull off the scam?"

Pomeroy heaved a long, heartfelt sigh, then abruptly wrote something down on a slip of paper, which he shoved across the desk toward me. "A file number," he said tersely.

"Ah, now we're getting someplace," I said, glancing at the seven-digit number he had written down before putting the paper into my pocket.

"Not really, Dr. Frederickson," he replied in the same brusque tone. "While it's true that he required a file number, he also required a good deal more that he didn't—couldn't—get from this office. Don't assume that just because I find it humiliating to have to rehash all this bloody business for the hundredth time it means you've wrung from me some earth-shattering discovery. The file number forms the base for the final encryption code, but twelve more numbers—digits—are required to construct the electronic key he needed to get at the money. It's all very complex, and it can only be accomplished with computers operated by people with proper authorization codes. What he did should have been impossible."

"Your boss agrees with you. But the fact remains that Sinclair used the file number you gave him to manufacture his very own encrypted electronic key, upped the ante to ten million dollars, bypassed all the built-in security procedures, transferred the ten million to an account he had created, withdrew the money, and walked away."

Pomeroy nodded curtly. "Apparently."

"Definitely. You have any idea at all of how he might have done it?"

"None whatsoever."

"You have any notions at all about this bloody business that you'd care to share with me?"

"None whatsoever."

It was looking like the business part of my trip to Switzerland was going to take even less time than I'd thought.

•   •   •

The first thing I noticed when I walked back into my hotel suite was a distinct and unpleasant medicinal smell. I assumed the odor was from some kind of disinfectant, but everything had seemed in perfect order when I'd checked in, and I couldn't understand why the maid would be cleaning a clean bathroom so late in the day. I opened all the windows before going down to the hotel dining room to eat. When I returned, the odor was gone. I closed the windows, turned on the air conditioner, and went to bed. I fell asleep almost immediately and dreamed of making love to Harper by a roaring fire in a chalet somewhere high in the Alps.

CHAPTER FOUR

My anxiety at the possibility of being stonewalled by Interpol turned out to be completely unfounded. Before leaving New York I had called Interpol's headquarters in Geneva, identified myself and my purpose, and asked for an appointment. It was not quite three o'clock on Wednesday, my second day in Switzerland, and I couldn't think of another thing I had to do, except actually prepare my report, which I could easily dictate to one of Cornucopia's secretaries for mailing to Neuberger. I was sitting in the silence of my chauffeured limousine, gazing out at the chocolate-box landscape, as we sped back to Zurich from Geneva. As I went over my notes and sipped at a Scotch, I decided that being driven around in a stretch Mercedes wasn't such a bad experience after all, and I made a note to myself to give Carlo a generous tip.

I had feared resentment on the authorities' part over my gratuitous appearance on the scene, but that had not been the case at all. Carlo had delivered me to the entrance of the great, cathedral-like building that was Interpol headquarters promptly at eleven o'clock, and I'd been met at the door by one Pierre Molière, their public relations officer. I'd been made to feel like an honored guest and had even been asked to sign a few autographs before being ushered into a spacious conference room for a briefing—complete with maps and charts—that had lasted nearly two hours. Without any prompting on my part, I'd been informed of everything I could possibly have thought to ask about John Sinclair and the theft of the ten million dollars—and more.

Interpol was especially aggrieved over the brutal murder of Inspector Bo Wahlstrom, who it seemed had become something of a legend in their ranks for his dogged pursuit of John Sinclair over the years. Indeed, Wahlstrom was given a good deal of credit for refurbishing Interpol's image and reputation, which had suffered mightily over charges of collaboration with the Nazis during the Second World War.

Interpol has only an investigative franchise, not enforcement powers, but Bo Wahlstrom had apparently been an investigator *par excellence*. Beginning sometime in the late seventies, Wahlstrom—then a low-ranking officer—had begun receiving some remarkably precise and damning information about John Sinclair and his various criminal activities. It seemed that a key to Sinclair's success, the reason why his hand in matters was so often able to escape detection until it was too late, was the fact that so many of his individual and corporate victims, with the notable exception of Cornucopia, were corrupt, or engaging in criminal activities, themselves. As a consequence, Bo Wahlstrom, although always a step or two behind Sinclair himself, had managed, along the way, to advance his career considerably simply by sweeping up after Sinclair—acting on information of criminal activities engaged in by the individual or organization brought to light during the course of one of Sinclair's operations. As often as not, Sinclair's victims—if they were still alive—would wake up the morning after Sinclair had taken their money to find the police, acting upon information supplied by Wahlstrom, waiting at their door with a warrant for their arrest. According to Molière, nobody in Interpol was quite sure where Wahlstrom had gotten his information, but it was assumed he'd had an informant highly placed in Sinclair's organization. For the past few years, Bo Wahlstrom's sole responsibility had been to pursue John Sinclair.

Then Bo Wahlstrom had apparently closed the distance between himself and his longtime quarry, and that burst of speed had proved fatal, ending in his brutal murder by torture. According to Molière, in the days just before his death Wahlstrom had been particularly excited about something, and it was now generally assumed that the Swede had stumbled across some particularly telling piece of information that had led him to his death at the hands of the man whose real face was a mystery. What that information might have been also remained a mystery. The case file, presumably containing whatever it was Wahlstrom had uncovered, had been in the possession of a young Greek Interpol officer by the name of Nicholas Furie, whom Wahlstrom had taken on as an administrative assistant six months before. The young officer had been at a mountain outpost near the Italian border where Sinclair had reportedly tried to cross and been turned back but not captured by the Swiss Army. Furie had been murdered in his bed—his eyes burned away and his heart cut out—the morning of the day I'd arrived, and the case file was missing.

So that was it, I thought. The secret of what it was Wahlstrom had discovered that had finally enabled him to catch up with John Sinclair had probably died with him and Nicholas Furie. But now, according to Interpol, Sinclair was trapped inside Switzerland, and the net was gradually tightening around him.

Right.

As far as I was concerned, things seemed to be proceeding apace. There was no mystery about what Sinclair had done, only the mechanics of how he had managed to construct an electronic key on his own and then execute the command for Cornucopia to cough up ten million dollars into his account. Now every available resource was being used to pursue him. That was what I had come to hear, and that was what I would report. My own opinion was that John "Chant" Sinclair was no closer to being caught this time than in the past and that he had probably already slipped across the border. But that wasn't my concern.

Harper wasn't due in until Saturday afternoon, but as far as I was concerned, my job was finished, except for actually writing the report. When we arrived back at the hotel, I gave Carlo a good-sized tip. Despite his protestations that he was supposed to remain at my service until Harper arrived, I told him I didn't need him anymore and that he should use the time he would have spent with me to visit his family in Italy. He said he couldn't do that, but he thanked me profusely for the money, then got into the Mercedes and drove off, waving goodbye as he did so.

I glanced at my watch, calculated that Neuberger was probably at home. Feeling a bit guilty at how little I was having to do to earn this particular fee with a European vacation thrown in to boot, I went up to my room and placed a call to Neuberger's mansion on Long Island, figuring my client might appreciate a prompt verbal report on what was going to be in my written report.

Neuberger's butler, Peterson, usually answered his telephone, but the man's voice on the other end of the line definitely wasn't Peterson's. The voice was somehow familiar, but I couldn't identify it in the context of Emmet Neuberger's household.

"This is Dr. Robert Frederickson," I said. "I'd like to speak to Mr. Neuberger."

"Mongo?"

"Who's this?"

"Barry Stone."

I felt a tingling at the base of my spine, and I sat down on the edge of the bed. Barry Stone was a Long Island homicide detective, a friend of Garth's and mine. "What the hell are you doing in Emmet Neuberger's home, Barry?"

"First I have to ask why you're calling here, Mongo."

"Neuberger's a client. I'm doing some work for him."

"Where are you calling from?"

"Zurich."

"What kind of work are you doing for him?"

"Come on, Barry, it's your turn. What's going on there?"

"It could be a while before you get to speak to your client again, Mongo—if ever. He was snatched sometime last night, apparently by a guy named John Sinclair. I assume you've heard of him?"

"I've heard of him," I said tersely, suddenly feeling slightly short of breath. "How do you know it was Sinclair? I didn't think kidnapping was his thing."

"We can't be positive, because Sinclair changes his handwriting like other men change shirts, but there was a note left with his name on it. Also, every servant in the house was killed with something sharp and hot through the eyes and into the brain. Now, that *is* something Sinclair might do."

I swallowed, found that my mouth was dry. "How much money does he want, and who does he expect to pay it?"

"The note didn't mention money, and it wasn't addressed to anyone. It just said he'd be in touch. Now tell me what Neuberger sent you to do in Switzerland."

I did. I talked for twenty minutes, struggling with feelings of distraction and disorientation, briefing the homicide detective on just what it was Neuberger had wanted me to do and what I'd learned from Hyatt Pomeroy and Interpol. After I'd finished I gave him my number at the Hilton, and he gave me a number where I could reach him if I found out anything else at my end. He thanked me and hung up.

I poured myself a stiff drink from the bar in the suite, sipped it as I stared out the window, thinking. One thing seemed clear: my much-anticipated vacation with Harper was going to have to be postponed. Although I had fulfilled my professional obligation to my client, and while there was no reason why I couldn't traipse off to Zermatt with my beloved while Interpol and the Long Island police went about their respective business, I knew I couldn't. It seemed somehow inappropriate, and I was surprised to find that I had a somewhat proprietary feeling toward the hapless Emmet P. Neuberger, who had not only had his family charity ripped off for ten million dollars but was now likely to have his life ripped out of him. I knew I was going back to New York, not because there was anything I could contribute, but simply to stand vigil in a way for a well-meaning but vaguely obnoxious man whom nobody, including me, much cared for.

I tried to call Harper at her home in Palmetto Grove, Florida, but she was out, and her answering machine was off. I was just getting ready to call the Zurich police and Interpol to ask them if they knew that the man they were so certain they had penned up in Switzerland was busy in New York killing and kidnapping people when there was a knock at the door. Surprised, I replaced the telephone receiver in its cradle, went to the door, and opened it.

The man standing in the doorway was about six feet tall, well dressed in a three-piece suit off Savile Row. He was whippet thin, with pale brown hair and eyes. An angular, rodent-like face was made to seem even more angular and rodent-like by a wispy moustache. However, the most striking thing about the man was the strong antiseptic smell, perhaps skin or scalp medication, that he exuded. It was precisely the same odor I'd detected in my room the day before.

"My name's Duane Insolers, Dr. Frederickson," the man said, producing a slender, well-worn leather wallet which he flipped open to reveal a very official-looking violet and gold card with his photo on it. "I'm with the Central Intelligence Agency, and I'd appreciate a few minutes of your time. May I come in?"

I stayed in the doorway. "None of the spies I've ever met have gone around flashing ID cards. I hope you're not here to try to sell me a set of encyclopedias, or something."

The man who had identified himself as Duane Insolers smiled wryly. "Ah," he said, scratching his left ear, "I've been told that you and your brother know more than a little about the intelligence community, and that some of my colleagues have made a bad impression on the two of you in the past. I can assure you that I don't shoot people, and I don't go skulking around trying to overthrow unfriendly governments. I'm really just a functionary, a bureaucrat."

"Sure you are. *Now* you're starting to sound like a spy."

"If you want more convincing, the last ten digits of that very large number at the bottom of my ID card is an eight-hundred number for a direct line to Langley. They'll verify that I am who I say I am."

"What do you want, Insolers?"

"To speak with you."

"About what?"

"May I come in?"

35

"How'd you know about me?"

"Well, to say that your reputation precedes you anywhere you go in the world is an understatement. Interpol told me you were coming to town to make inquiries about the matters involving Chant Sinclair. Interpol and the CIA cooperate on many things, but we're especially cooperative when it comes to hunting Sinclair."

"You may not skulk around trying to overthrow unfriendly governments, Insolers, but you're definitely a skulker. If you didn't want to give me a bad impression of you, why did you search my room yesterday? What the hell did you expect to find?"

He reacted. He caught himself quickly, but not before I had seen the glint of surprise in his pale brown eyes; it occurred to me that, as skillfully stealthy as Insolers might be, he was actually not aware of the odor he carried and left in his wake like an olfactory fingerprint.

"Really, Dr. Frederickson. Even if your room was searched, what makes you think it was me?"

"Is that a denial, Insolers?"

He studied me carefully while he considered his answer. "No," he said at last. "I'm usually pretty good at these things, and I'll be damned if I saw any detection devices. You must know some tricks I don't."

"I'm a veritable magician. What were you looking for?"

"I wasn't sure, Frederickson. That's the truth." He paused, shrugged. "I guess old skulking habits die hard."

"Forget it," I said, turning and walking back into the suite, casually motioning for him to follow me. "You can skulk around here all you want, and it won't make a damn bit of difference. You, Interpol, the Zurich police, and the Swiss Army are all wasting your time. Sinclair took his show back out on the road. He's an ocean away, butchering and kidnapping people in New York."

I stopped and turned, expecting to find him right behind me. But Duane Insolers was still standing in the doorway, looking positively stunned and making no effort to mask it. "What are you talking about?" he asked in a tight voice.

"I just finished talking on the phone to a Long Island cop who

36

tells me Sinclair kidnapped Emmet P. Neuberger last night—motive unknown, since he didn't ask for money in the note he left. I was about to call the authorities here to see if they knew, when you showed up."

"Just because there was a note with Sinclair's name on it doesn't mean he did it."

"He left a calling card; he killed all of Neuberger's servants, burned out their eyes. That does seem to be his preferred method of murder these days."

Insolers had obviously discovered the hidden bar with its complimentary supply of booze during his earlier visit to my rooms, because that's where he headed now. He opened the cabinet, took out a bottle of malt Scotch, and poured himself a serious drink.

"Make yourself at home," I said evenly. "Maybe you'd like a drink?"

He turned around and sipped at his Scotch, staring somewhere over my head, as if he hadn't heard me. "No," he said at last, setting the half-finished drink down on top of the liquor cabinet.

"No, you wouldn't like a drink?"

"No, I don't think Sinclair snatched Neuberger and killed his servants."

"Why not?"

It seemed a simple enough question, but it took him a long time to answer it. Finally, he said, "I have my reasons."

"Which are?"

"One of them is that even Sinclair can't be in two places at once, and there's very good intelligence, from a number of different sources, to indicate that he's still in Switzerland."

"Maybe he had his people do it."

Insolers dismissed the suggestion with a wave of his hand. "Sinclair always works solo, regardless of the odds. It seems to be a point of pride with him."

"Well, there's little likelihood of a copycat killer at work. This is basically a European story, and it hasn't gotten much play in the American press."

"The Swiss have the borders sealed off," Insolers said distantly. "He couldn't have gotten out."

"Just like he couldn't have gotten out of Vietnam twenty-five years ago, right?"

"Ah," Insolers said, fixing me with his pale brown eyes. "You know about that."

"It's in the public record, part of the legend. What do you want from me, Insolers?"

The CIA operative picked up his drink, walked across the room, and sat down on a beige sofa. "If Sinclair really did get out of Switzerland," he said carefully as he slowly rotated his tumbler on an open palm, "I'm not going to be the only one surprised; not a few people are going to be downright disappointed. Zurich is beginning to resemble a convention center for a lot of different kinds of espionage types. So far, I've counted operatives from six different countries. It's another of the reasons why I don't think Sinclair did the Neuberger thing. These other people have been getting the same signals I have, maybe from different sources. The word is that he's still in Switzerland, lying low someplace."

"Why are all these intelligence types interested in Sinclair? What's your interest? Sinclair's a murderer and con man, not a spy."

"My interest is to find out what their interests are. My assignment is to try to sort out the players."

"That's just double-talk. If you don't want to tell me anything, that's fine, but I still don't understand what you think you can find out from me."

Insolers sipped at his drink while he studied me over the rim of the glass. After he had drained the tumbler, he resumed turning it in the palm of his hand. "Does the term 'Cooked Goose' mean anything to you, Frederickson?"

He had tried to make the question seem almost casual, but I was certain I detected an underlying tension in his voice. I thought I was beginning to understand how Alice had felt when she'd tumbled down the rabbit hole. "Insolers, somehow I sense that you're not talking about food, or the usual slang usage of the term. Am I right?"

"Level with me, Frederickson," the other man said quietly. "Do you know what it is?"

"I do not. You tell me. What is Cooked Goose?"

"I don't know," Insolers replied evenly. "I actually thought you might. It's well known that the Frederickson brothers have friends in very high places. I'm told that, over the years, the two of you—as well as your friend Veil Kendry—have picked up all sorts of . . . interesting information."

"Mr. Insolers," I said, walking over to him and putting out my hand, "if you'll be so kind as to give me that ID card of yours, I do believe I'll call that number at the bottom after all. I know you're jerking me around, but for the life of me I can't think what you're hoping to gain. Maybe Langley will tell me—if that really is a number for Langley."

"Cooked Goose was the reason John Sinclair packed up his career and medals and deserted," the man with the medicinal smell said evenly, ignoring my outstretched hand. "It was why he walked out of Vietnam, leaving five dead Rangers in his wake."

"I take it the army was really serious about trying to stop him."

"Oh, yes. And the reason for such concern had to have been his involvement with—or knowledge of—Cooked Goose. It was the code name for a secret operation, obviously, but I don't know what that operation was, or whether or not it was actually ever executed. Very few people know what that operation was all about, and I'm not one of them. It still carries the highest classification. I think Cooked Goose is the reason there are so many intelligence operatives milling around here at the moment; they all want a shot at him, some of them quite literally. Sinclair has make a lot of enemies, embarrassed a lot of very powerful people and organizations, including the Mafia, and not a few of these interested parties would love to claim the credit for killing him."

"Now we're talking about assassination, not capture."

I suddenly became aware of a distant *thwap-thwap-thwap* sound, which was rapidly coming closer. Insolers and I both glanced out the window as an olive-drab Swiss Army helicopter zoomed past. A few seconds later the sound died, as if the craft had landed close by, perhaps on top of one of the buildings.

"We're talking here about individuals, organizations, and governments with different agendas," Insolers said, turning back to face me. "There's no doubt some of these parties would like to kill him for revenge, but I think others want to capture him because of what he knows about Cooked Goose. To be perfectly honest with you, I don't believe the CIA much cares what I find out here. I think I'm being used as a front man to throw the people watching me off the track while some free-lancer they've hired accomplishes what they really want, which is to kill Sinclair. If Cooked Goose is so sensitive that it still carries the highest classification even after all these years, it's reasonable to assume that they certainly don't want him captured by some other intelligence outfit, or thrown into some foreign prison where he could use what he knows to bargain for his freedom, or maybe kick back and write his memoirs. No. The CIA definitely wants him dead, and I strongly suspect they've had a contract out on him for more than two and a half decades."

I stared at Insolers in utter astonishment. When I realized that my mouth was actually open, I closed it. My throat was dry, and I swallowed hard, trying to work up some moisture. I had the distinct feeling that something bad was happening to me, and I didn't even have the slightest idea what it might be. "Jesus Christ, Insolers," I said in a rasping voice. "Aren't you spook types trained to withstand gruesome torture, or even encouraged to take a cyanide pill, before giving away the kinds of information you've just imparted to me in this casual little conversation? Why the hell are you telling me this stuff?"

"Because," Insolers said, his voice low and very intense as he leaned forward on the sofa, "I asked you to level with me, to trust me, but I gave you no reason why you should. Now I have. You appreciate very well how badly I could be hurt if you ever breathed a word of what I've just told you to anyone else." He paused, leaned back on the sofa, crossed his legs. "You see, I'm quite convinced you're keeping secrets of your own about your real reasons for being here, and I'm equally convinced I haven't told you anything you didn't already know."

"You couldn't be more wrong on both counts, Insolers. I have never heard of Cooked Goose, and I had no idea anybody but law enforcement officials were after Sinclair—until now."

Insolers abruptly rose from the sofa with a suddenness that startled me. In an instant, his whole demeanor had changed: His pale brown eyes had gone icy, and his casual air had completely disappeared. At that moment I understood that Duane Insolers could be a very dangerous man. "Are you a player in this game, Frederickson?" he snapped. "If you are, I want to know right now, while there's still time to affect the outcome of all this. You have to read between the lines, know that you can trust me. Consider the possibility that you and I share an identical agenda."

Suddenly I was afraid—not of Insolers, but of being caught totally off guard in a situation that thrummed with danger, but which I didn't begin to understand; I was being casually fed information that had to be classified top secret, being asked questions that had no meaning to me, all because some CIA operative who smelled like a medicine cabinet seemed to think I might have a hidden agenda concerning a monstrous human being who had no pity. I didn't want to die by accident, and I vividly recalled Veil's warning about finding myself trapped in a deadly hall of mirrors. "I don't know what you mean," I said tightly.

"I'm asking if you have a . . . relationship . . . with John Sinclair." He paused, then continued in a softer tone, emphasizing each word. "Frederickson, I guarantee you no harm will come to anyone as a result of you telling me the truth. I need to know."

I pulled myself up very straight, as if that would lend weight and credibility to my words. It was suddenly very important that I make this man believe me. "I don't know what you're talking about or trying to get at, Insolers. I don't think I want to know. I told you why I came here."

"That's bullshit," Insolers said casually as he went to the bar to fix himself another drink. "I can appreciate why you might be reticent to confide in a man you've just met, but you don't have to insult my intelligence. I mean, this city is filling up with intelligence operatives and assassins, and I'd be very surprised if there was even one of those people who hadn't heard of Dr. Robert Frederickson. They're all aware of the kinds of cases you've been involved with over the years, and they are definitely going to assume there's a link between you and John Sinclair. They're probably not yet aware that you're in town, but when they do find out, they're going to be all over you. Nobody is going to believe the story that the world's premier private investigator flew all the way to Europe just to ask the law enforcement officials how they thought they were doing. I doubt Interpol believes it. It's a very weak cover; you must have been in a big hurry to get here, or you'd have come up with something better. The fact that Neuberger has been kidnapped may mean your cover is already blown."

"Insolers—"

"Don't assume we have different goals, Frederickson. You really can trust me."

"Insolers, what I told you just happens to be true. Do you understand? It's *true!*"

He looked at me long and hard, shadows moving in his pale brown eyes. "R. Edgar Blake," he said at last, raising his eyebrows slightly. "I was there. I know. The countess will vouch for me."

Insolers was a man who wouldn't take I-don't-know for an answer; incredibly, he still seemed to be trying to cue me to say something he very much wanted to hear. Thoroughly baffled, I raised my hands in a gesture of helplessness and shrugged. "Insolers, I don't have the slightest idea what you're talking about."

The hard look of skepticism on his face and in his eyes slowly gave way to one of incredulity, and I knew he finally believed me. "You jumped into the middle of this thing just to ask Interpol for a report card? That's insane."

"I'm not the one paying the bills. Just what is it I've jumped into the middle of?"

Duane Insolers shook his head in apparent disbelief. His manner now seemed brusque, hurried, as he set his untouched second drink back down on the bar. "Here's a little something you can add to your report," he said in a clipped tone. "It's an item I'm certain Interpol neglected to mention. Sinclair may have pulled off a neat bit of financial and electronic wizardry to raid Cornucopia's coffers, but he wasn't the first to do it. That bucket already had a hole in it. Money's been secretly draining out of Cornucopia for a long time—probably for fifty or more years, since the day it was founded. I doubt anybody would have found out about it if Sinclair hadn't come along, and I'll bet the ranch he didn't figure out this scam on his own. He stumbled across this little secret, how money was illegally skimmed from this tax-exempt foundation, and he simply repeated the trick."

"A back door," I said distantly.

"Right."

"Whoever designed and programmed the original computer security codes left open a back door for their own use in the electronic network. All of the codes could be bypassed."

"Precisely. Everybody talks about how complicated the security codes are, and they're right. But Sinclair never broke the codes; all he did was find the electronic back door to the vault somebody else had been using, and he went in the same way."

"Jesus, Insolers, it wouldn't make sense for Neuberger to steal from his own foundation. Would it? I mean, he's got billions of his own. What would be the point?"

Insolers shrugged as he glanced at his watch. "What can I tell you? If Neuberger is a crook, so were his daddy and granddaddy. This computer back door has almost certainly been there from the beginning, and it's remained open through a whole hell of a lot of advances in computer science and encryption theory. Somebody—and it's probably more than one person—tends to it, maintains it. It could be that it has nothing to do with Neuberger. The answer is probably somewhere in the past, with the grandfather's associates. Incidentally, this information was uncovered by Bo Wahlstrom, the Interpol inspector who was killed. He passed on the general information to his superiors, but all of the financial records—the proof—he had are missing. Sinclair probably has them."

"Why are you telling me this, Insolers?"

"Because there is no harm in you knowing, and because I want you to owe me," the CIA operative replied evenly. He strode quickly to the door, opened it, then turned back. "You've convinced me you're not a player in this game, Frederickson. You're not involved in any way, but you do have a reputation for finding out things."

"I don't plan on trying to find out anything I don't already know, Insolers. In fact, I have this sinking feeling that I already know too much."

"Your track record shows that events and situations tend to gel around you, Frederickson. You and your brother always seem to end up in the center of the action, whether you mean to or not. Information may come your way. There's the whole question of Neuberger's kidnapping, what the motive may have been. You may not trust me, but I've given you no reason not to. I've given you a lot of very sensitive information, and I've made myself vulnerable by doing so. All I'm asking in return is that if information does come your way, you keep me plugged in; you can always reach me through Interpol. In the meantime, forget the money, and forget your investigation, or whatever it is you think you're doing here. This matter isn't about money at all. There's something very heavy coming down here, and it's my job to find out what it is. There's nothing more for you to find out here, but a lot of nasty people are likely to figure the way I did—that you're a player. These people won't ask you questions in a friendly manner. If you're smart, you'll go home."

CHAPTER FIVE

How smart I was seemed most arguable at the moment, but under the circumstances, going home seemed like an eminently sensible idea. I called the airport to see what flights were available and learned I just had time to catch one to Newark, if I hurried. I hurried. First I called down to the desk to say that I was checking out, and noted that the clerk sounded curt, tense. I packed my bags, then tried Harper's number one more time. She still wasn't home. I picked up my bags, went to the door, and was startled to find Inspector Pierre Molière and a Zurich policeman standing out in the hallway. Molière, who had been about to knock, lowered his hand. The faces of both men looked grim, and I assumed it had to have been Molière in the helicopter that had flown past the window. I had left him only a few hours before, and I wondered what could have happened in the interim to cause him to fly to Zurich to see me, as opposed to just picking up the telephone.

"I would like to speak with you, Dr. Frederickson," the gaunt Interpol inspector said in a tone that was decidedly less friendly than the one he had been using with me earlier.

"Of course, Inspector," I said, glancing at my watch. "But I had planned to go home, and I have a flight to catch. Would it be presumptuous to ask for a ride out to the airport, and we could talk on the way?"

"It is better that we talk here, Dr. Frederickson," Molière said coldly.

So much for the flight into Newark. "Come in," I said, setting my bags to one side and stepping out of the way. "What's the problem?"

Molière and the policeman stepped into the room, stopped just inside the doorway. Molière was actually frowning as he looked at me, and his tone had grown even colder. "Do you have anything to tell me, Dr. Frederickson?"

I took some time to think about it—probably a mistake in itself, but I had to consider the implications of an Interpol inspector and a Zurich cop showing up on my doorstep barely ten minutes after a veritable chatterbox of a CIA operative had left after giving me a large store of highly sensitive information that I had neither needed nor wanted to know. I wondered if Molière was waiting for me to tell him about Insolers' visit, and if so, what I was expected to say. But if Molière wanted to know what I had been doing with the operative, he could have simply asked, and so I decided that Insolers probably wasn't the issue, and it might only muddy the waters to bring him up.

"Look, if you're talking about the nasty business in New York, I only just found out about it, and—"

"How did you find out about it?"

"I tried to call Neuberger to give him a report on my conversation with you people, and I got a cop who's a friend of mine. He told me."

"I am not talking about the nasty business in New York. I am asking about your business here in Switzerland."

"You know about my business in Switzerland."

"We have reason to believe you have not been completely forthcoming with us, Dr. Frederickson."

"Look," I said, half turning and gesturing toward the large room beyond the foyer, "maybe we should go in and sit down."

Molière ignored my suggestion. Now I noticed that beneath

his suddenly cold and hostile demeanor, there seemed to be an air of disappointment, resentment, and perhaps betrayal. "Two hours ago a message for you was telephoned to the desk of this hotel. I would like you to explain it."

"Two hours ago I was having lunch with my chauffeur in a quiet little restaurant in a quiet little town between here and Genève. And the desk clerk hasn't informed me of any message."

"No, she did not, because she was instructed not to. When the call came in, she quite properly called the police. The police called me, which is why I am here."

"What did this message that I wasn't given say, Inspector?"

"The caller said you should be told that you had been warned. He identified himself as John Sinclair."

Suddenly, I felt slightly dizzy. I sat down on my suitcase and stared at the floor, trying to think, searching for a link between the message and anything else that had happened, perhaps Duane Insolers' visit or the things he had told me. I suspected now I should have mentioned Insolers to my current visitors at once, but felt that bringing him up at this juncture could only make matters worse. "I don't understand what it means," I said at last, looking up to meet Molière's accusing gaze.

"Have you ever been in contact with John Sinclair, Dr. Frederickson, either before or after your current visit to Switzerland? This is a gravely serious matter, and I advise you to think very carefully about your answer."

"I know it's a gravely serious matter, Inspector, and I don't have to think about my answer. No, I have never been in touch with John Sinclair, nor with anybody representing him, which is why I don't understand what the message could mean."

"I see your bags are packed, and you yourself told me you were on the way to the airport. Yet, earlier today you cheerfully informed me that you were looking forward to the arrival of a lady friend and a vacation in Zermatt. Then a message for you is received from a man identifying himself as John Sinclair; the message says that you have been warned—and now you are on your way to the airport. If you have not spoken with Sinclair or his agents, how do you explain this?"

"I see your point," I said with a small sigh, and I knew that it was no longer possible to avoid the subject of Duane Insolers. "I had a visit from a CIA man just before you arrived, and he made me very nervous."

The Zurich policeman spoke for the first time, in perfect English. "Why did you not tell us this before?"

"I didn't think it was important," I replied lamely. "It was Duane Insolers, whom I believe you know, Inspector. He was interested in what I might know about John Sinclair. I told him I didn't know anything but what I'd read in the newspapers or seen on television. Nothing of what he said made any real sense to me, but the conversation convinced me that I was in danger of becoming involved in something here that was way over my head. That's why I was leaving."

"Indeed," Molière said archly, drawing himself up very straight. "I do not believe you, Dr. Frederickson. I believe you came to Switzerland under false pretenses."

"Look, Inspector—"

"Something important has happened in the short time since you left my office, sir. Two corpses have been found on a riverbank just outside the city. Both men were murdered, and maimed, in the same manner as Inspector Wahlstrom and Nicholas Furie. Both men are unidentified, but a note was found on one of the bodies. The note said that Robert Frederickson would be meeting with the man and his partners at the prearranged time and place and that you would have the money with you." The tall man paused, sighed, passed a hand over his eyes. "What have you involved yourself with here, Dr. Frederickson? What was your real reason for coming to Switzerland? Why did Bo Wahlstrom, Nicholas Furie, and these other men have to be tortured and killed by this monster, Sinclair?"

"I want you to listen to me very carefully, Inspector," I said, getting up off the suitcase and standing very straight, my arms at my sides. My voice was steady, and my legs no longer felt wobbly. I was certainly still very confused, but I had willed the confusion to contract, back off, and sit quietly in a corner of my mind while I struggled to straighten things out. What was perfectly clear to me, the only important thing at the moment, was that, whether I liked it or not, I had become one of Duane

Insolers' "players" in a game where I had no rule book. I did not want to be run over and crushed by events over which I had no control, leaving as my legacy a final case where I had ended up pawn and village idiot. "I have *not*, repeat *not*, lied to you at any time. I came to Zurich for the express purpose I explained to you, and for none other. I do *not* know about any meeting or any money. I *do* know that somebody has set me up; they're using me, or my name, and I don't know why. I propose that we help each other find out the answers. Let me work with you."

"I simply do not believe you, Dr. Frederickson," Molière replied coldly. "I find it incomprehensible how a man of your professional stature could have allowed himself to become gratuitously—if you are to be believed—involved in a matter such as this in the first place. Now you choose to lie in an attempt to cover your tracks. I would ask my colleague from the Zurich police to arrest you right now, but I don't care to deal with the furor and distracting attention of the international media I'm sure that would cause. There are already far too many foreign interests meddling in this affair." He paused, knit his brows, and glared at me. "What I will do is take steps to make certain you will remain available should you have a change of heart and choose to cooperate."

It was the policeman who put out his hand. "I will take your passport, sir. And you will please confine your movements to the city of Zurich. If you do not, you will be arrested, despite Interpol's wishes."

•   •   •

Interpol and the Zurich police weren't the only disgruntled campers in Switzerland. I was seething as I made my way to the elevator. Even another village idiot would have been able to figure out that this village idiot had been set up by the man for whom I had been so willing to stand vigil only a short time before. At the moment I wanted nothing more than to get my hands on Emmet P. Neuberger, but, since John Sinclair had apparently beat me to him, I was going to have to settle for a substitute. It was time for another chat with Hyatt Pomeroy, and if he didn't have some of the answers I wanted, he was going to wish he did.

I strode through a spacious, marble-floored lobby crowded with American tourists filing off a fleet of gleaming silver and red buses lined up at the curb just outside the entrance. As I headed for the desk to order up a cab, I was surprised—and not displeased—to see a familiar figure in a ridiculously ill-fitting chauffeur's uniform, only partially hidden by a huge potted plant, sitting very erect in a straight-backed chair set against a wall near the main desk. Carlo spotted me, bounced up from his chair, and limped over to me, his untipped wooden cane tapping loudly on the stone floor.

"Forgive me, *signor*," he said, gasping for breath as he reached me. "I know you told me I should go, but I was ordered to stay with you until Saturday. I was hoping you wouldn't mind if I just sat here in the lobby during the day in case you needed me after all. I hope you're not angry."

"I'm not angry with you, Carlo," I said, stepping to one side to avoid being crushed by a large knot of people elbowing their way toward the main desk. "In fact, I'm glad to see you. I have to go back to the Cornucopia offices."

The big, crippled Italian nodded eagerly. "I have the car parked in back. You wait outside. I won't be a minute."

As Carlo hobbled off toward a rear exit, I pushed through the glass revolving doors at the entrance, picked my way through more men, women, and children who were standing by their luggage as they waited for the crush inside to ease, and took up a position at the curb behind the last bus in line. Suddenly, a hand roughly gripped my shoulder and yanked me around, nearly pulling me off my feet. I found myself staring up into the craggy, unshaven face of a man, probably American, who looked to be in his early thirties. He also looked as if he hadn't slept in days, and he smelled terrible. There was a look of desperation, even terror, in his wide, bloodshot eyes.

"What have you done?!" he screamed at me, his foul-smelling spittle flying in my face. "Why didn't you meet us like you said you would! Furie, Henry, and Jacques are dead! Why weren't—?!"

The terrified man with the haunted eyes stopped in midsentence as he suddenly looked up at something behind me in the driveway. His mouth dropped open and he gagged, as if he wanted to scream but couldn't. The expression on his face had climbed a notch or two above terror; this was a man looking at his own death—and maybe mine. It seemed a good time to part company. Without wasting time to turn to see what had attracted his attention, I dropped to the sidewalk and rolled to my left a split second before a swarm of bullets from a sputtering automatic weapon ripped through the space where my head had been and into the chest of the American I had left behind. The deadly steel spray also cut into the flesh of the men, women, and children from the tour group who had been standing nearby, and my own howl of disbelief and horror mingled with their screams. I stopped rolling, looked back in the direction from which death had so suddenly appeared.

A gray Peugeot was stopped in the center of the driveway, and a man wearing a black hood and wielding an Ingram MAC-10 machine pistol was standing, legs slightly apart, by the open door on the passenger's side.

"*Nooo!*" I screamed as the man swung the machine pistol in my direction, knowing that a single squeeze of the trigger would mean the extinguishing of even more lives in the crowd of hysterical, terrified people milling around on the sidewalk to my sides and behind me, still in the line of fire.

I rolled again as the gunman fired, howled again with horror, rage, and dismay as the spray of bullets ricocheted off the area of concrete sidewalk where I had been and into more of the screaming people around me.

Horror upon horror; the cost of my trying to stay alive was the rising death toll of the people around me—including, I had to assume, at least one infant I had seen being carried in its mother's arms.

I kept rolling until there was a bus between the gunman and me, then sprang to my feet and darted into the narrow space between that bus and the one parked in front of it. The space might well turn out to be a death trap, but I felt I had no choice but to stay there; the logical thing to do was to keep moving in and around the buses until I could make a break for the lobby of

51

the hotel, but that would only make me an elusive target moving against a backdrop of dozens of not-so-elusive targets, and I could not bear the thought of any more innocent people being killed or maimed because of me, simply because they had been in the wrong place at the wrong time.

I inched forward in my narrow, open-ended steel coffin and peered out from between the buses. The gunman immediately saw me, brought the machine pistol around, and pulled the trigger. I dropped to the ground as bullets smacked against the buses, some penetrating the steel skin, others ricocheting back and forth above my head. When the firing stopped, I looked up; the gunman had ejected an empty clip and was reaching into the baggy pocket of his jacket for another.

The odds were heavily against my being able to get to the man before he inserted the second clip, but that was the only acceptable option I had. I got to my feet and was about to sprint forward when I heard the screech of tires off to my left. An instant later my huge, black limousine with a grim-faced Carlo at the wheel came careening around a corner of the service driveway leading to the back of the hotel. The car hit a speed bump, sailed into the air, landed in a shower of sparks as its frame scraped the concrete. It kept gathering speed as it approached. The assassin's driver must have seen the oncoming juggernaut in his rearview mirror, for the Peugeot suddenly shot forward and veered sharply to the left, bouncing up over a curb and chewing up sod as it sped across the hotel's spacious lawn toward the street beyond, abandoning the gunman.

The assassin realized his peril a moment too late. He had just finished inserting the fresh clip into his machine pistol and was preparing to resume firing when his driver had sped away. Confused, he started to wheel around, and managed to squeeze off one brief burst of fire that went harmlessly into the air just before the limousine hit him. There was a sound like a ripe melon bursting, and then the gunman, minus his gun, shoes, and jacket, was thrown through the air a hundred feet or more, landing down the driveway with a dull thump, shattered limbs pointing in all directions at odd angles.

Feeling both numb and cold, with the screams of the dead,

dying, and terrified echoing in my ears, I slowly walked forward to examine the corpse of the man who had been willing to kill so many others in his effort to kill me.

The articles of clothing not left behind in the driveway had been shredded by the forces of impact and scraping on the concrete. The man appeared to be Japanese, or perhaps Korean. On his bare back, clearly visible even among the framing carnage of bloody flesh and splintered bone, was what appeared to be a large tattoo that had been applied not only with needles and ink but perhaps with a branding iron as well. The combination of tattooed skin and scar tissue formed a grisly picture of tongues of jet-black flame erupting over his back and across his shoulders.

And then Carlo was beside me. He laid one huge hand on my shoulder, as if he sensed that I needed some steadying. "*Signor*, are you all right? I heard the gunfire while I was bringing the car around. I saw what was happening, and . . . I did not know what else to do but what I did."

"You saved my life, and probably the lives of a lot of others," I said in a hoarse stranger's voice as I looked up into the soulful black eyes of the Italian. "I owe you."

I glanced once more at the assassin's corpse with its burn-tattoo of black flame, then turned around and started back toward the sidewalk to see if there was anything I could do to help the gunman's real victims. The air was filled with a cacophony of wails, both mechanical and human. There was a blur of movement all around me, but off to my right I glimpsed Pierre Molière and the policeman who had been with him urgently directing the driver of the first ambulance that had arrived toward the bodies that were strewn on the sidewalk near the spot where I had been standing when the gunman had first opened fire on me. I headed toward the two men, suddenly feeling oddly distanced from the horror that was all around me, although I was filled with a bitter sorrow for the people who had died this day simply because they had been standing too close to me. But beneath the sorrow was a deep, white-hot core of abiding rage I knew would now govern my every action, consume every waking moment, and which would not be extinguished until I found a way to do what I now knew had to be done.

CHAPTER SIX

Veil, it's Mongo."

"Mongo! Jesus, I've been trying to reach you for the past three hours. That massacre at your hotel is all over the news here. What the hell's going on over there? Are you all right?"

"No, I'm not all right," I replied, looking down at the front of my shirt and slacks still spattered and smeared with blood. I had lost track of time. First there had been my feeble efforts to help the victims, and then the hours spent in a police station being grilled as Pierre Molière had looked on, anger and suspicion in his eyes. I was certain Molière and the police were convinced, as Insolers had at first been convinced, that I was concealing important information about my role in events, and I had been surprised when they'd finally let me go. But they still had my passport, and I had acquired a not-so-subtle tail comprised of two plainclothes policemen in a pale blue Volvo. "The bullets that killed those people were meant for me."

"Get out of there now, Mongo," Veil said tightly. "When you hang up, go straight to the airport and—"

"The police took my passport."

There was a short pause, then, "I'll be there as soon as I can, Mongo. I'll bring you false identity papers."

"You'll bring me nothing, Veil," I replied, noting that I sounded even colder than I'd intended, and I'd certainly intended to sound cold. "False papers wouldn't do me much good, now would they? I'm not exactly inconspicuous. Besides, I wouldn't leave now even if I could. It's too late for that."

"Mongo, listen to me—"

"No, Veil, you listen to me, because I have a few things I want to say to you. You may or may not be willing to talk about Chant Sinclair now, but if you are, I don't care to hear any of it. It's also too late for that. I don't know what's going on over here, and I don't know if I would have acted differently if I'd had more information, but it occurs to me there's a possibility that if you'd leveled with me at the beginning concerning what you knew or suspected about Sinclair, instead of giving me a half-baked warning you must have known I'd ignore, a number of men, women, and children would still be alive, and another man wouldn't be sentenced to spend the rest of his life in a wheelchair. I don't care how many people have been looking for Sinclair, or how many years they've been looking; I intend to find the sadistic, murdering son-of-a-bitch, and I intend to kill him before he kills me, or kills anybody else who just happens to be in the line of fire. Any information I need, I'll get myself. I no longer consider you my friend, and I want as little to do with you as possible. Is that straight enough for you?"

"I hear you," Veil answered in a flat tone. "May I say something now?"

"Not quite yet. Now that you know how I feel about our relationship, I'm going to ask you to do something for me. I'd like you to touch base with Mary, reassure her. I'd call her myself, but she must have heard about the killings by now, and I'm not sure how she's handling this. I'm just not ready to talk to her yet, and I'm not sure she'd be able to concentrate on what I have to say. I need certain things done. I'm in pressure city here, and I'm just a bit strung-out. What I need on that end is someone who can keep a clear head in a heavy emergency, and you have the clearest head under pressure of anyone I know. If you don't want

55

to do it after the things I said, just say so. I wanted to be honest with you up front."

"I'll talk to Mary," Veil said in the same flat tone. "What else do you require?"

"I thank you for that," I answered curtly. "Got some paper and a pencil?"

"Just tell me."

"After you talk to Mary, get in touch with Harper in Florida. Hold her off. She's supposed to land here Saturday, which I think is the day after tomorrow, and there's no way I want her anywhere near me. Just tell her I'm safe and that I'll call her as soon as I can."

"Harper's not going to go for it, Mongo." Veil paused, then added drily, "I can hear her now. She's going to call you a recidivist sexist pig for trying to stop her from helping you. You should call her yourself, no matter how strung-out you are."

"I don't need advice, Veil!" I snapped. "Just action! Simply tell her I don't want her around, okay?"

"I'll tell her. How long has it been since you've slept?"

"I really don't know. I'm a little foggy on time right now. I tried to call Garth, but he'd already checked out of his hotel, which means he's probably already in the air. He's due to arrive in a couple of hours at JFK, TWA flight two ninety-one from Brussels. He hasn't heard about what happened, or he'd be here. When he does hear about the massacre and finds out it happened at the hotel where I'm staying, he's going to figure I'm involved, and he's going to hop on the first available flight to Zurich. I would dearly love to have Garth here, but I need him there. I want you to meet him at the airport, be there when he gets off the plane. Mary's supposed to pick him up, so you'll have to coordinate things with her. I'm not sure how you're going to want to handle that, but I'd prefer that you talk to Garth first about the details, so that he understands the situation."

"I'll take care of it, Mongo."

"I think he'll want to stay in New York at the brownstone, because he'll need New York's research facilities. He may also have to call in a lot of IOUs to get the information I need, but he'll know to do it. I need absolutely every scrap of information on John Sinclair he can get, and I don't mean just the stuff that's been printed in the newspapers over the years. He should call Mr. Lippitt and ask him if he can tell us anything about a secret military operation in Vietnam code-named Cooked Goose, and Sinclair's possible involvement in it. In fact, if he can manage it, he should try to get hold of Sinclair's complete military record. Make certain there's nobody around when you talk to Garth about this, and Garth should make certain he calls Lippitt on a secure line. I think we're talking dangerous data here."

"Okay."

"The gunman at the hotel was probably Japanese. He had a big mark on his back that looked as if it had been made by tattooing over and around burn scar tissue. The tattoo was of black flames. It could be a yakuza mark, and I'd like Garth to see if he can identify it."

"Okay."

"You don't want me to repeat anything?"

"That's not necessary. Where can I reach you?"

"There's one other thing. Tell Garth to find out all he can about a man by the name of R. Edgar Blake, and make a note of any countess he may come across in the course of his research endeavors."

"I've got it. Anything else?"

"Not that I can think of offhand."

"Where can I reach you?"

"I'm not sure. I plan on keeping an even lower profile than usual. If the police will allow it, I think I'm going to move to a different hotel; obviously, the wrong people know I'm in this one. But until you hear differently, you can call or leave messages for me here. Just be careful what you say, since the desk clerk is reporting my messages to the police. My phone will probably also be tapped, if it isn't already; I'm making this call from a phone in the hotel lobby. I'll get back to you. Leave your machine on."

"If I go out, I'll make sure there's someone I can trust here to answer the phone; that person will always know where to reach me."

"Yeah." I sighed. The anger and resentment toward Veil had

drained out of me, and I was now grievously sorry for the words I had spoken to this man to whom I owed so much, including my life. I wished now I could retreat a few steps back along that crooked, pitted road of venomous words, but I didn't know how. "Thanks, Veil," I concluded wearily.

"I'll take care of things on this end, Mongo. I'll call Mary now and ask her to pick me up on her way to the airport, and I'll make sure Garth gets your message. If you move out before you hear from either of us, make sure you leave a number where we can reach you."

"Right."

"May I say something now?"

"You may say something now."

"I want you to go to the Amnesty International offices in Geneva and talk to a man there by the name of Gerard Patreaux. He's an A.I. regional director."

"He a friend of yours?"

"No. Unless he's familiar with my paintings, my name won't mean anything to him. But I know who he is, and I have reason to believe he can tell you things about John Sinclair nobody else can—if he chooses to do so. My suggestion is to tell him everything that's happened and then see what he has to say. And get some rest. Remember that you're not the one who killed those people."

"All right, Veil," I said quietly. I paused, swallowed hard. "Look, I want to say—"

"Keep your head down, Mongo," Veil interrupted, and hung up.

It seemed like his way of telling me the bridges of our friendship I'd burned couldn't be rebuilt.

•   •   •

A few hours of sleep gave me a second wind. John Sinclair wasn't a subject I wanted to discuss over the telephone with a man I'd never met, so I called the Amnesty International office in Geneva and, in my fractured French, asked for an appointment with Gerard Patreaux. Fortunately, Frederickson and Frederickson had, over the years, done a sizable amount of good works, *pro bono*, for the global human rights watch group, and—more fortunate still—Patreaux knew it. Patreaux, who spoke English with virtually no accent, said he would be delighted to meet with me and graciously invited me to his home that evening for dinner at eight. Despite the restrictions on my travel, I said I'd be there and wrote down the directions.

In the car, I told Carlo I wanted to be in Geneva within two and a half hours; the problem was how to elude my watchers in their pale blue Volvo while I was being driven around in a half-block-long limousine. Carlo's simple yet effective solution was to drop me off at the entrance to a chic restaurant known for its good food and leisurely dining. I went in, said *"Ciao"* as I walked right past the startled maître d', kept going through the dining room into the kitchen, where I waved to the surprised cooks before proceeding out the back door, where Carlo was waiting for me in the narrow driveway used by delivery trucks.

At ten minutes to eight, Carlo was pulling the limousine up to the curb in front of Gerard Patreaux's modest stone house in a modest neighborhood just outside the Geneva city limits. Although Carlo insisted he had already eaten a large lunch earlier in the day, I knew he had not. I tried to get him to take some money to go and buy himself something to eat, but he refused. Gerard Patreaux suddenly appeared in the doorway of his home and solved the problem by inviting Carlo to come in and have a meal in the kitchen. This offer Carlo accepted. With my chauffeur ensconced in the kitchen and being served by a cook, Patreaux and I proceeded into his small study for drinks.

The Swiss was a slight man, five feet six or seven, with a gentle, caring face and expressive, light blue eyes. He poured himself a glass of wine, while I asked for a Scotch on the rocks. We chatted for a few minutes in the book-lined study, and I seized the first pause in the conversation to get to the reason for my surreptitious journey.

"Mr. Patreaux," I said carefully, setting my drink down on a stone coaster on the stone table next to me, "I have a reason for being here that I didn't want to mention over the phone. As a matter of fact, I could use your help."

He smiled, shrugged. "But of course. How may I be of service to you?"

"I need to talk to you about John Sinclair."

It seemed to me that the question startled him for just a moment. He set his drink down, patted his mouth with a paper cocktail napkin, then stared at me quizzically. "You mean John Sinclair the terrorist?"

"The same."

He continued to stare at me, his face revealing nothing more than puzzlement. "I'm afraid I don't understand," he said at last.

"I was told by a friend of mine that you might have vital information about Sinclair that I could use. It's very important to me."

Gerard Patreaux shook his head. "Who is this friend?"

"His name's Veil Kendry."

He thought about it, said, "I don't believe I know a Veil Kendry. It's an unusual name. I would remember."

"He said you didn't know him."

"Then why should he think I would know anything about John Sinclair that could not be found in the newspapers?"

"Mr. Patreaux, I don't have the slightest idea."

"Are you certain he meant me?"

"He definitely meant you."

The Amnesty International official thought about it some more, then raised his arms in an elegant gesture of helplessness. He was beginning to look slightly pained, and I was beginning to feel more than a little foolish. My anger toward Veil was beginning to build again.

"Did this friend of yours give any indication of *what* it was that he thought I could tell you?"

"No, sir." And he damn well should have.

"Perhaps he was playing a joke on you?"

"No," I said, my renewed anger at Veil now blending with frustration at the thought that I was probably wasting my time in addition to risking arrest and incarceration for violating the ban on my traveling outside Zurich.

"May I ask why gathering information about John Sinclair is important to you?"

60

I proceeded to fill Gerard Patreaux in on the sequence of events that had occurred since I had acquiesced to Emmet P. Neuberger's plea that I come to Switzerland to check on the investigation into the theft of his foundation's money. Then I told him about the death I was leaving in my wake. I had rather hoped that my narrative might jog his memory, but the only emotions apparent on the man's face were pain and pity when I described the bullet-ripped bodies of the people at the hotel who had taken the bullets fired at me. He had been sitting very straight as I spoke, his eyes cast down. After I had finished, he sighed heavily, then looked up into my eyes.

"Dr. Frederickson," he said softly, "I can appreciate the grave circumstances which brought you here, and your present state of mind. The events are . . . so recent. You must be in a state of great shock. I deeply regret that your friend was misinformed."

It was my turn to shrug. "Yeah, well, that's not your fault."

"But you will still share a meal with me?"

There was a sour taste in my mouth and a knot in my stomach the liquor had done nothing to ease. I wasn't hungry. The fact of the matter was that I wanted nothing more than to go back to my hotel and go to bed. However, I was unwilling to offend the kind and gracious man who was my host, and so I resolved to try to be a gracious guest. I said that of course we would share a meal, and we rose and went into his dining room.

The fine dinner was built around thick veal chops, and I found I had more appetite than I'd thought. Soon we were on a first-name basis, and I was glad I had come, despite my disappointment at not getting what I'd come for. I enjoyed the company of this man, and the meal and conversation provided a welcome respite from the tension and vivid memories of violent death that waited for me back in Zurich. Throughout dinner, as we chatted about the work of Amnesty International and other things, I thought I caught the other man watching me with an intensity that was incongruous with the relative lightness of our conversation, as if he were gauging, perhaps judging, me.

"Mongo," Patreaux said to me as he poured coffee for both of us, then lit a French cigarette of aromatic black tobacco, "if I may say so, I still don't quite understand why you are so intent on investigating Sinclair. This is clearly a police matter, and I'm told that Interpol, the Zurich police, and even the Swiss Army are pursuing the man with utmost vigor. What do you expect to accomplish that those combined forces can't?"

"They just want to catch him. I . . . have something else in mind."

Patreaux dragged deeply on his cigarette, then blew a thin stream of smoke out the side of his mouth as he raised his eyebrows slightly. "Ah," he said in a curiously neutral tone, as if he did not wish to insult me by pointing out how ridiculous I must have sounded. "But how can *you* ever hope to find him in order to accomplish this 'something else' you have in mind?"

"Gerard, at the moment I don't have the foggiest notion. But the fact is that I'm highly motivated, since he seems to want to kill me. I don't know why, but I have the feeling that the key to understanding everything that's happening is in his past. If I can find out more about that past, it may give me the answer to the question of why he wants to kill me, and it may also give me some insight into how and where he may be vulnerable. It's a pretty faint hope, but it's the only one I have. I don't much care for playing the role of passive target, so I'm trying to find some way of going on the offensive. Poking around in his past is the only means of attack I have right now. If I can understand more about him, maybe I can find a way to defeat him."

"I see," Patreaux said distantly as he gazed over my head, as if there were something or someone behind me. He drew in another lungful of smoke, then abruptly stubbed out his cigarette, looked up at me, and smiled brightly. "Well, then, perhaps you would care for some brandy?"

"Thank you, Gerard," I said, rising from the table, "but I'm going to pass on the brandy. I think it's time I went home. You've been a wonderful host, it was a lovely meal, and I thank you."

I turned and started toward the kitchen to get Carlo, stopped when Patreaux said, "It's occurred to me just now that I may know what it was your friend was referring to when he said I might be able to tell you something about Chant Sinclair."

"Really?" I said, turning back to face the other man. The dinner, liquor, and talk had mellowed me, but now the tightness in my stomach had returned; but it was the kind of tension that hope can sometimes bring, and it was not unwelcome. "And what would that be?"

"You will have some brandy, then?"

"Sure," I replied in a neutral tone as I returned to my chair and sat down, watching him now as carefully as I thought he had been watching me all evening. "I'm not driving."

Patreaux rose and went to an antique, carved wooden sideboard, opened it, and took out a decanter filled with a dark amber liquor. He poured the brandy into two balloon snifters, handed one to me. He did not sit back down at the table, but stepped back against the wall next to the sideboard, where his face was half hidden in shadow.

"What occurred to me is that there's a story about Sinclair you may not have heard," Patreaux said casually. "As a matter of fact, it involves Amnesty International. I don't know how much of it is true, but it does contradict the general belief that Sinclair has never been captured. I can't verify the veracity of the story, and I frankly can't see how it could be of any use to you."

"I'd still like to hear it, Gerard."

The slight man now emerged from the shadows near the sideboard, sat back down across from me. He sipped at his brandy, then set the snifter down to his right. "One of Amnesty International's chief concerns is, of course, the abuse of human rights—especially the use of torture. Torture is a common practice in many countries, but what is confounding is that today there are upwards of fifty-five countries with governments that *officially* sanction the use of torture by the police and armed forces. Adding to the horror of this situation is the fact that, in most cases of torture, the aim is not to extract information, but to break the bodies and minds of dissidents; torture becomes a tool of political terror and oppression. The secret police will pick up a known dissident, break him or her beyond repair but still living, and then release that individual back into society, where the condition of the victim's body and mind will serve as a warning to other dissidents of what could happen to them if they do not mend their subversive ways."

The Swiss paused, either to gather his thoughts or to give me a chance to ask questions. I remained silent, watching him. I knew more than a bit about torture and its long-term effects, perhaps even more than Gerard Patreaux, but I didn't care to talk about it.

Patreaux took another sip of brandy, continued, "But there are, of course, cases where the purpose of torture *is* to extract information the authorities feel is vital to state security, or whatever, from an individual who feels it is equally vital to keep the information *from* the authorities, and would much prefer to die rather than talk. For these people, the perceived emotional anguish they would suffer from talking is greater than the physical agony they are suffering at the moment. If such a person is trained to resist torture, if he or she can successfully evade and dissemble under great duress, then the authorities and their torturers have a real problem. Such a person may very much wish to die, especially after the torturers' first pass at him or her, and this desire can often speed up the process. There is only so much agony the human mind and body can endure at one time before the nervous system begins to shut down, resulting in unconsciousness or a general numbing process. This kind of situation can be even further complicated when the authorities, for one reason or another, must eventually exhibit the victim to the outside world, and it cannot be obvious that the victim has been tortured. This is the problem faced by some renegade police departments in your Western democracies: torture may be used to extract confessions, or sometimes merely to punish, but care must be taken not to leave marks on the victim that could prove embarrassing at a subsequent hearing or trial.

"For these difficult cases, the average torturer—one who knows only how to break bones, burn flesh, or tear out fingernails until the victim talks—just won't get the job done. Since the torturers cannot risk the premature—from their point of view—death of the victim, a specialist is often brought in, someone who can manage to keep retuning the victim's nervous system to register a maximum degree of pain while keeping the victim alive. Very often this person is a specially trained physician. We call these people torture doctors.

"The most successful and notorious torture doctor was a man

by the name of Richard Krowl, a renegade Harvard Medical
School graduate who, at one time, was considered a brilliant
researcher into the causes and treatment of chronic pain. He
ended up a torture doctor after he was barred from both research
and general practice as a result of conducting secret, unethical,
and illegal research experiments at some university. Apparently,
he really believed he was conducting important research that
could be done in no other way." Patreaux paused, shook his head
in disgust. "You know, it's really quite remarkable how some
people can rationalize virtually anything they do, no matter how
vile."

"Indeed," I agreed quietly.

"After his teaching credentials and license were lifted, Krowl
started free-lancing as a torture doctor for various Central and
Latin American dictatorships. He ended up with his own special
torture institute, if you will, a training facility for torturers located
on an island twenty miles off the coast of Chile that was financed,
for the most part, by the right-wing governments he was working
for. We called it Torture Island, and it was there that Krowl and
his staff of resident torturers carried on his so-called research into
pain to his heart's content, using as subjects political prisoners
his backers had sent there for no other reason than punishment
and death. It was also used as a training school for would-be
torturers sent there by the sponsoring countries. Krowl would
also, on occasion, accept responsibility for extracting information
from difficult subjects sent to him by any government or government agency willing to pay his reportedly very high fee. In fact,
we have reason to believe that Krowl's services were contracted
for, on more than one occasion, by such unlikely and mismatched
clients as MI5, the Mossad, the CIA, and the KGB."

"But you could never prove it."

"Correct. Ironically, not a few of the torturers on Krowl's staff
were former police officers from various countries who had been
trained in interrogation techniques in the United States as part of
law enforcement exchange programs. Americans, on the whole,
aren't all that much interested in torture, as long as it's the citi-
zenry of some other country who are being tortured. Your Congress routinely votes financial aid to right-wing governments

widely known to employ torture as a means of political repression. For that reason, in a very real sense Torture Island was largely financed by the recycled tax dollars of American citizens. We felt the situation would change if we could obtain incontrovertible evidence that American citizens had been delivered into the hands of foreign torturers by an agency of their own government. We believed that the outcry in the American media would be sufficient to force the offending governments to withdraw their funding—and use—of Richard Krowl and thus shut down Torture Island.

"The problems involved in obtaining proof were formidable. Because he fancied himself a serious researcher, it was assumed that Dr. Krowl kept voluminous records on the island, but Torture Island was twenty miles offshore, in shark-infested waters, surrounded by jagged coral reefs, with sheer escarpments on all sides. In short, it was inaccessible by any means of transportation except helicopter. There was one scheduled helicopter run per week, to bring in supplies and ferry prisoners, and the skies were carefully watched the rest of the time by heavily armed guards."

"What about the testimony of former prisoners?" I asked, intrigued by this story of Richard Krowl and Torture Island, but wondering what any of it had to do with John Sinclair.

"The identity of any prisoner sent to Torture Island was always a carefully guarded secret. Many, probably most, of the victims sent there for interrogation were subsequently murdered, probably fed to the sharks. Those marked for return to their societies, even had we been able to identify and find them, would have had their minds so mutilated by the experience that their testimony would have been useless. So, for years, all we were left with were the persistent rumors."

Patreaux had finished his brandy, and he rose to pour himself another. I waited, increasingly impatient to hear some mention of John Sinclair, but reluctant to interrupt the flow of his words with questions. He poured more brandy into my glass, then began to slowly pace back and forth, his face passing in and out of the shadow cast by a standing lamp next to the sideboard.

"There was one outsider who did manage to get on the island," he continued in a tone so soft I had to strain to hear him. "According to the story, he got there by posing as a student sent there for one of Krowl's torture seminars by a Latin American government. In fact, he was an American investigator for Amnesty International. Reportedly, he was actually able to steal a large number of Krowl's files, and he somehow managed to escape from the island with this documentation. Unfortunately, he never got a chance to pass on any of it. He was captured by Krowl's security forces before he could get out of Chile. He was taken back to the island and tortured to death—not to gain information, of course, but to punish, and for use as an object lesson for any other investigator who might be tempted to try the same thing. Amnesty International received his remains in a sealed vacuum container—Krowl wanted us to be able to determine the details of what had been done to him before the corpse deteriorated. An autopsy revealed that he had taken a very long time to die. He had been partially devoured, eaten alive, and the bite marks were human. There were signs of crushed bones, charred flesh, punctured organs, unnatural surgery; so many unspeakable things had been done to him, and all as a warning to the rest of us who wanted to put Krowl and his torture institute out of business. Rumor had it that the man tortured to death was a friend of John Sinclair's."

I sat up straighter in my chair. "What was the man's name?"

"Harry Gray," Patreaux replied as he abruptly stopped pacing and turned to face me.

"This isn't just a story, is it, Gerard? This actually happened."

"I present it as a story, rumor, because there are so many details that can't be confirmed. Yes, there really was an American A.I. investigator by the name of Harry Gray, and yes, he was tortured to death and his remains returned to us in a vacuum container. Gray had been after Krowl for years. Obviously, A.I. would never authorize one of its investigators to place himself in such a perilous situation, so the notion that he got on the island by posing as a seminar participant is pure speculation, as is the rumor that he was a friend of Sinclair's. The rest of the story, if you care to hear it, also falls into the category of pure speculation, rumor. There is no way to corroborate any of it."

"I'm sorry I interrupted you, Gerard. I definitely want to hear the rest of it. Please go on."

"There was a rumor that not only was Harry Gray a friend of Sinclair's but that, for years, Sinclair had been providing him with both information and documentation concerning human rights abuses around the world."

I thought about it, shook my head. "I'm sorry, but I don't think I get the picture. Why would Sinclair do that? Talk about human rights abuses; Sinclair is a torturer and murderer himself."

"Obviously, I have no answer for you; I am simply repeating the rumors. However, if it's true that Sinclair, for whatever reason, did want to pass on information about other people's criminal activities, he would certainly be in a position to do so. Allow me to make a few observations. While it's true that all of Sinclair's activities seem cloaked in violence, violence does not appear to play a key part in the operations themselves. As with his theft of the Cornucopia funds, he virtually always seems to rely on treachery and deceit, not force, to accomplish his primary goals."

"You're saying he kills people because he feels like it, as a kind of celebration for pulling off another successful scam, not because he needs to."

"That would seem an accurate assessment. His operations are very carefully planned, meticulously executed. Often, the victims are themselves corrupt. He seems to purposely choose targets— be they individuals, groups, corporations, or even entire governments—that have something to hide. Because of the nature of the way he initially sets up his operations, through infiltration, he is usually in a position to find out about others' criminal activities and to obtain incriminating documents. Why he would choose to pass on such information to someone like Harry Gray, or anyone else, is a question probably best left to the psychiatrists.

"In any case, the rumors surrounding this incident say that when Sinclair learned of his friend's death, he vowed vengeance on Richard Krowl and the rest of the torturers on that island. To that end, so the story goes, he managed to get himself on the island, just as Harry Gray had done."

"By masquerading as a participant in one of Krowl's torture seminars?"

"No. After the Harry Gray incident, screening procedures for participants had been tightened considerably."

"But you said the island was virtually impregnable."

"He had himself delivered."

"Delivered?"

"By the CIA—so the story goes. You see, there is a lot of speculation that Chant Sinclair is privy to a great many secrets he's not supposed to know, and that the CIA is desperate to make certain Sinclair never shares those secrets with anyone. That's one theory. Another theory is that the CIA wants to know Sinclair's secrets. If we assume the first theory to be the correct one—the CIA knows what Sinclair knows, and wants to make certain the information never becomes public—then it stands to reason that, if Sinclair were captured, the CIA's first priority would be to find out if Sinclair had indeed shared his secrets with anyone, or if there might be a cache of pertinent documents that could surface after his death. Naturally, Sinclair couldn't be expected to just tell them what they wanted to know, and he is a very tough man. The CIA would probably be perfectly willing to torture him themselves, but they couldn't be certain they were up to the job of getting the truth out of him before they killed him. They would require the services of a top expert interrogator-torturer if they hoped to break Sinclair. The point is that Sinclair wanted to get on Torture Island, and he correctly guessed that the CIA would pack him up and send him there if they ever got their hands on him."

"Jesus Christ," I said softly. "You're saying he engineered his own capture, knowing he would almost certainly be sent to a place where he would be tortured?"

"So the story goes, Mongo. In his judgment, it was the only way he could get on the island and infiltrate Krowl's organization—as a prisoner. Supposedly, the man who actually arrested him was an Interpol inspector by the name of Bo Wahlstrom."

"The same man Sinclair tortured to death?"

"The same."

Connections. Wheels turning within wheels within wheels behind clouds of smoke. A hall of mirrors. I raised my brandy snifter to my lips, found it was empty. Patreaux produced the decanter, came around to my side of the table, and poured me a generous refill. After he had finished, he lit another cigarette and stared at me, as if he were waiting for me to ask a question. I obliged.

"Supposedly, nobody knows what Sinclair really looks like, so how did he manage to get himself arrested? Did he just walk up to Wahlstrom and say, 'Here I am'?"

"Hardly. That would have raised suspicions in some people's minds that Sinclair was up to something. As a matter of fact, Sinclair arranged for Wahlstrom to arrest him by prevailing upon a friend to inform on him."

"What's the friend's name?"

"I've never heard it mentioned. If there's any truth at all to the story, the identity of the friend who informed on him must have died with Bo Wahlstrom."

I stared into the amber depths of my brandy, pondering the kind of courage it would take to risk not only death but prolonged, indescribable pain administered by the world's most accomplished torturers, in the incredible hope that he could somehow manage to turn the tables on these men, despite the shackles on his wrists and ankles. Now *that*, I thought, was self-confidence.

I found Gerard Patreaux's tale very odd and disquieting. A man who would risk so much to avenge the death of a friend and shut down a torture factory would not seem a likely candidate to go around burning out the eyes of innocent people, or send a gunman to shoot up a hotel sidewalk crowded with men, women, and children. Yet, this was the first time I had ever heard anything said about John Sinclair that even remotely hinted that there might be another side to him; all of the stories I'd read or heard focused on the death and torture for which *he* was responsible.

Which also led me back to the big question of where Veil, who had suggested I come here, had heard the story, if such was the case, and why Veil hadn't told it to me himself.

Finally, there was the elaborateness and detail of the story, which somehow made me doubt Patreaux's claim that he had thought of it only as I was leaving. I now believed he had been carefully watching me all evening, vetting me in his mind, trying to determine if I was worthy to hear this account. It was almost as if I'd had to pass some kind of test; having succeeded, being told this bizarre story about John Sinclair was my reward. It was all very strange.

Wheels within wheels. *Nothing will be as it seems.*

"There's a simple way to verify this story," I said quietly. "If Sinclair actually was arrested by Wahlstrom, then Interpol would have a record of it."

Patreaux smiled thinly, shook his head. "If such a record does indeed exist, I would not count on ever seeing it."

"Why not?"

"Because it would be so intensely embarrassing to many of the involved parties, on any number of counts. First, you must remember that Interpol is still trying to live down the fact that it virtually served as an arm of the SS during the war. They would certainly not want it known that they voluntarily, and secretly, turned an international criminal, one who is wanted in dozens of countries, over to the Americans as a kind of special favor. For its part, the CIA would certainly not want it suggested that they even condone torture, much less that they turned over someone—even a man as vile as John Sinclair—to specialists like those who worked on Torture Island. Finally, none of the parties involved would want it known that they had once actually had Sinclair in their clutches and had allowed him to escape. If the story is true, and we will probably never know for certain, it seems Sinclair accomplished everything he had set out to do. I can report to you as fact that Richard Krowl is dead, and Torture Island no longer exists; and we all know that Chant Sinclair, at least for the moment, is alive and well, running all over Switzerland giving various law enforcement and intelligence agencies of the world fits."

I put my hand over my glass as Patreaux raised the decanter to offer me more brandy. "Is that it, Gerard?"

"That's it. Like most of the legends surrounding Sinclair, virtually none of the important parts can be substantiated. Now, may I ask if you think that hearing this little tale can be of any help to you?"

"I don't know, Gerard," I replied absently, trying and failing to see through the clouds of smoke what engine, if any, the turning wheels were running. "I just don't know."

I rose, thanked him again for the fine meal and conversation, and he escorted me to the door. My belly was full, but my mind felt empty; I felt sure I was missing things, not seeing connections I should be making. Veil's behavior still baffled me, and I felt I was leaving something important behind me in this house, with this man. I had the distinct feeling that Gerard Patreaux had been trying to tell me even more than he had—or that he had told me and I'd missed it.

The Amnesty International administrator opened the door for me, but I didn't move; I stood in the doorway, looking out into a night aglow with pale moonlight. Carlo was sitting in the limousine, reading a magazine by the car's interior light. He seemed to sense my presence; he looked up and saw me, put aside his magazine, and turned on the car's engine. The haunting feeling that Gerard Patreaux had left something vital out of his story had grown overwhelming.

I slowly turned back, asked, "Are you the friend Sinclair prevailed upon to inform on him, Gerard?"

Shadows moved in the man's expressive blue eyes, but he did not otherwise react. If anything, he almost gave the impression that he had been expecting the question and was vaguely surprised that it had taken me so long to ask it. "You are, of course, making a joke," he said, and laughed.

"If it's true, Gerard, why can't you just come out and tell me? If Veil knows about these things, why couldn't *he* just come out and tell me?"

"Perhaps your friend didn't want to waste your time repeating what may be only fairy tales and gossip," the other man said evenly.

I started to protest, stopped when Patreaux raised his hand. "Mongo," he continued, "even if what I told you is a fairy tale, like most fairy tales it may have a moral. The moral of the story I told you about John Sinclair risking his life on Torture Island to avenge a friend could be that you shouldn't believe everything you read or hear about this man. Things aren't always what they seem."

"I'll bear that in mind, Gerard," I said, shaking his hand once more before going to the car. Before getting in, I looked back toward the house, where the slight figure of Gerard Patreaux was silhouetted in the open doorway, black against light. I waved, but the figure remained still. I got into the limousine, and Carlo drove off into the night.

CHAPTER SEVEN

There was a message waiting for me when I returned to the hotel; it was brief, succinctly to the point, and both Garth and Veil had put their names to it. The message said, *Stay put*.

I found Garth and Veil's little communication to be off-putting and pretentious; I needed information, not orders. I considered calling one or both of them, then decided against it. It was almost midnight, too late anyway to consider moving to another hotel before morning, and I reasoned that Garth would have asked that I call if he'd had anything to report. I double-locked the door, jammed a straight-backed chair up under the knob, then went to bed.

Although I was exhausted, I slept only fitfully. My dreams were filled with violent, vivid images of branding irons, racks, electric generators, pincers, and cattle prods, and the blurred face of a mysterious man who could at once countenance the slaughter of innocent people, and who was a torturer himself who burned out men's eyes, but who would risk his own torture

74

and death to right a wrong. That seemed a contradiction. John Sinclair himself was emerging as a contradiction, a paradox, a very dark and dissonant Chant in a crimson key of blood, pain, and death.

I awoke in the morning still tired, restless, and anxious, haunted by a sense of foreboding, convinced that still more terrible things were waiting to happen. I was in the eye of a maelstrom, and could see neither faces nor motives in the black winds that swirled around me. I picked up the phone, gave my credit card number, and called Garth's private number at the brownstone. There was no answer, and his answering machine was not on. That annoyed me. Next, I tried Veil's loft, and a voice I recognized as belonging to Lee Miller, one of Veil's students, answered in the middle of the first ring.

"Lee, it's Mongo."

"Mongo! Are you all right?"

"Yeah. Where are Veil and my brother?"

There was a short pause at the other end of the line, then: "They're due to arrive at Zurich airport at eleven this morning, your time."

I said, "Shit."

"They said that if you called I should tell you that they're coming directly to your hotel, so just stay there, in your room. They have a lot of things to tell you. You should do absolutely nothing, and talk to no one, until they get there. They said to tell you that you're in a deep pile of shit."

"Wow. That's really great, Lee. It's precisely the kind of information I was hoping Garth could dig up for me. What flight are they on?"

"Swissair seventy-six, out of Kennedy." The other man paused, then added, "Mongo, you should know that Harper is with them. She insisted."

"*Shit!*" I said, and slammed down the receiver.

I'd asked Veil to ask Garth to do some digging for me, and what I was getting was a reunion, complete with the woman I loved. Three more potential targets for Chant Sinclair to aim at. It was just the kind of news I needed to start off my day.

• • •

I saw Garth, Veil, and Harper before they saw me. The three of them, striding briskly, emerged from the mouth of the wide corridor leading from Customs looking like two and a half grim-faced gunfighters marching down Main Street to face off with the bad guys. Garth and Veil, with their tall, lithe bodies and powerful physical presence, looked the part, but Dr. Harper Rhys-Whitney, the snake- and dwarf-charming love of my life, was barely five feet tall, and she looked very small and frail walking between my brother and Veil. I knew better. This small woman with the maroon, gold-flecked eyes and long, soft, silver-streaked brown hair was, in her own way, every bit as deadly as the two men who accompanied her. I wondered if she had declared to Customs the tiny, deadly krait she carried everywhere in a small wooden box in her purse. I doubted it.

This petite, explosive charge of a woman had spent many years with the Statler Brothers Circus, where I had met her, as a head-liner like myself, a fearless snake charmer. Now she was a research herpetologist, a world-renowned expert on venomous snakes who kept a thirty-four-foot reticulated python as a house pet. I loved her to absolute distraction, and the depth of my feelings, the loss of control over my own fate that implied, frightened me. I was still trying to figure out what to do about it.

Finally, Harper saw me. She came running across the terminal, threw her arms around me. As always, I had an instantaneous physiological reaction as I felt her lips on mine, her large breasts pressing against me. "Hello, sweetie," she whispered in her low, husky voice that always seemed so improbable in such a small body. "What nasty business have you gotten yourself into this time?"

It was a very good question. I was deliriously happy to see Harper, to be able to hold her in my arms, but I felt guilty for it, as if I were indulging my pleasure at risk to her life. "Harper, Harper, Harper," I murmured into her ear. "What the hell are you doing here?"

"You must be joking, Robby," she replied, releasing her arms from around my neck. "When I heard about the hotel massacre,

I just *knew* you had to be on the scene somewhere, probably being shot at. You need help. I was getting ready to fly over here on my own when Veil called. I just told him to wait for me. I flew my own plane to JFK, then came over here with him and your brother. Did you think I was going to just sit around in Florida while you were in trouble over here?"

"Foolish me," I said evenly, resisting the impulse to roll my eyes toward the ceiling. I satisfied myself with casting a grim and accusatory glance at my brother and Veil as they approached.

"I appreciate your wanting to keep me out of harm's way, Robby," Harper said, just the slightest edge to her voice, "but that's typical of your sexist thinking. Didn't I come in handy during that business with the loboxes and the circus?"

"Harper, I—"

"Since I've already saved your life once, I just thought you might like to have me around. I guess I'm the one who's foolish."

"Harper, I didn't want *any* of you here. There's nothing to do here but duck."

"Garth and Veil have important information."

"That's why phones were invented."

She tilted her head back slightly, sniffed. "Veil and Garth didn't argue when I insisted I was coming along. They both agreed they could use all the help they could get in handling you."

Garth and Veil had taken up positions on either side of us, and were standing very close as their gazes swept over the other people in the terminal. Seeing the two men together like this, working as a team to guard Harper and me, it would have been impossible for anyone else to detect the animosity that existed between them. Both of them had shoulder-length hair tied back in a ponytail, and they were about the same height; they might have been brothers.

By way of greeting, Garth put a large hand on my shoulder and squeezed gently. Veil offered me a curt nod, then went back to surveying the people around us.

"Handling me?" I said, looking up at Garth.

"You heard right, brother," Garth replied gruffly. "True to your character and track record, it looks like you've executed a perfect swan dive into one deep pile of shit."

"That was Lee's line. So, naturally, you and Veil had to dive right in with me, bringing Harper along for the ride. Why couldn't you just do what I asked? I don't need handling."

"Mongo, right now you need handling more than anyone else in the world I can possibly imagine. You shouldn't have come to the airport."

"I made sure I wasn't followed."

"There are a lot of things you don't know that can kill you."

"I didn't need you to come to Zurich to tell me that, Garth. As I recall, I left you a shopping list of subjects to look into. You haven't had time to do any real digging, but now here you are."

"I cashed in a favor, and got somebody to open up the Forty-second Street library all night for me. I had three research assistants, and two librarians to run between the stacks. I found out enough—as much as I was likely to in New York. We're going to get you out of this business, Mongo, but you're going to have to back off and let Veil, Harper, and me take care of business from here on out. You're not going to be hunting anyone, which is what I know you think you're going to be doing."

"Bullshit. I don't need you to tell me what to do; just what you found out about the matters I asked you to look into."

"That's going to take some time, and this definitely isn't the right place. Right now, we have to get you out of this airport. We have reservations at your hotel, which is probably no more dangerous a place for you than anywhere else; the security guards there probably outnumber the guests. We'll go pick up our luggage and then take a cab into town."

"We don't need to take a cab. I've got a car."

"Okay," Garth said, nodding to Veil, "let's get out of here."

Garth and Veil continued to closely flank Harper and me as we went to the baggage area to pick up the luggage of my unwanted visitors. Then we headed to a side exit leading to one of the parking areas. Carlo had the limousine waiting for us at the curb, and he was standing by the open trunk. When he saw us, he hurried over, snatched the luggage cart from my startled brother, pushed it back, and began loading the bags into the car.

"What the hell is this?" Garth asked, turning to me. "You hired a limo?"

"Not exactly. It belongs to Cornucopia. I figured the least I could do to repay Neuberger for throwing me to the wolves was to use his foundation's car and chauffeur."

"Terrific thinking, brother," Garth said in a flat tone as he glanced at Veil.

Veil nodded curtly to Garth, then abruptly strode across the wide sidewalk to where Carlo was struggling to fit the last bag into the limousine's trunk. I started after him, but was stopped by Garth's firm grip on my shoulder. "Whoa, brother," Garth continued in the same emotionless tone. "You stay here."

I watched as Veil walked up to the old man who was my driver. Carlo smiled tentatively as they exchanged words, and then Veil put his hands on the man's shoulders, gently but firmly turned him around, pushed him up against the side of the car. First Veil searched Carlo's pockets, then began to pat him down. As Veil's hands quickly and expertly ran over his body, Carlo turned his head and cast me a plaintive, questioning look.

"Give me a break, Garth," I said, again starting forward, only to be pulled back with even greater force. "He's only a chauffeur, for Christ's sake."

"He works for the man who got you into this mess."

"Not directly. He's just a worker, an employee of the office here. He's harmless."

"Just like you once thought that Emmet P. Neuberger was just a poor, harmless, misunderstood, and bumbling fool, right? This newfound naiveté of yours is not amusing, Mongo. How do you know what your chauffeur's real marching orders are? Even if he's not personally working against you, how do you know the car itself isn't bugged, or that it doesn't carry a transmitter that would allow somebody to follow you? As long as you allow that man to drive you around in this car, it's possible that whoever's trying to kill you knows your every move. And you say you don't need handling? You act like your brains have run out of your ears."

"He saved my life, Garth. He ran down the gunman at the hotel about one tenth of a second before he was able to drop a pound or so of bullets into me."

"So we'll send him a medal. The car could still be bugged."

Harper gently squeezed my hand. "Your brother and Veil are right, Robby. You can't afford to take any chances."

They were right, of course, and I felt more than a little chagrined at the fact that it had never occurred to me, even after it had become obvious that Emmet P. Neuberger had been using me very badly, that it was a risky business to be using Cornucopia's car and driver. While it was true that the car could have been bugged or outfitted with a signal-emitting device without the Italian's knowledge, I had instinctively liked and trusted Carlo, and still did. I was convinced he, at least, meant me no harm, and it made me decidedly uncomfortable to watch him being so rudely—if gently—treated by Veil. I looked away as Veil, having finished with Carlo, steered him off to the side before getting into the car to begin searching the interior.

"You owe your friend over there an apology, brother," Garth said in a low voice, shaking me slightly. "You're being childish as well as naive, and you should be ashamed of yourself."

"Oh, yeah? What do you know about it?"

"Enough to know you owe Veil an apology."

Harper said, "Veil told us about the conversation the two of you had before you left, when he tried to warn you off."

"Did he, now? Perchance, did he tell you what he knows about John Sinclair that he wasn't able to share with me?"

"No. But he did imply certain things."

"Well, bully for him. A number of people are now dead who might still be alive if I'd been more adequately prepared for what I was going to find over here."

Harper shook her head, said firmly, "Veil's not responsible for that, Robby, so stop talking like he is. He knows you, sweetheart, just like your brother and I do. Whatever it is Veil knows or suspects, I'm convinced there wouldn't have been any payoff for you in connection with the reason you came here, and it could have been dangerous information. He didn't want you harmed; he was just trying to protect you."

"I needed information, not protection."

"It wouldn't have helped you. Veil assured us of that, and Garth and I believe him." Harper paused, squeezed my hand.

"Besides, there was another reason he was reluctant to say more to you than he did. He was afraid of your brother."

"That's lunacy," I said, wincing inwardly as Carlo, standing off to one side as Veil painstakingly searched under and behind the seat cushions of the limousine, shot me another pained, questioning look. I again averted my gaze. "They may not get along too well, but Veil is no more afraid of Garth than Garth is of Veil."

"You should listen to Harper, Mongo," Garth said gruffly, "because she's right." He paused, glanced quickly at Harper, then looked back at me. "If you remember correctly, I once tried very hard to kill him. The tension between Veil and me is my fault."

"I remember all too well, Garth," I said quietly.

Garth said to a startled Harper, "Forget what you're about to hear; don't mention it to Veil."

Harper nodded. "You can talk freely."

I started to protest, not wanting the woman I loved to hear things that could conceivably put her at risk one day, but Garth ignored me.

"The reason I tried to kill him," Garth said to me, "was that I blamed him for involving you in the Archangel business and almost getting you killed. I damn well would have killed him, but—thanks to you—I wasn't able to pull it off. Veil could have killed me, and he had every right to after the way I'd gone after him, but he chose not to. And he's never forgotten my rather extreme reaction to his sucking you into that mess; he didn't want to risk creating a similar situation by telling you things that might set you off on various courses of action and get you into trouble. He tried to simply warn you off, but you wouldn't listen. He didn't think anything he could say would be of any help to you, but the information could have proved dangerous. He was afraid I'd find out he'd talked to you, and contributed to any danger you might be in, and that I might come after him again. You're right that he's not afraid of me, Mongo, but he was very much afraid that he might have no choice but to kill me if I tried to lay my 'mad big brother' number on him again, and his killing me might not set too well with you. Veil's a good friend, Mongo, and a very good man—the finest I've ever known, except for you. Like I said, you owe him an apology."

Veil had finished searching the limousine. It was obvious that he hadn't found anything, but it was just as obvious that he wasn't going to let that fact alter his and Garth's determination to get rid of Carlo. He took out his wallet to give the old man some money, but Carlo stiffened, shook his head, and backed away. Veil threw some bills through the open window onto the passenger's seat. Carlo hobbled around to the driver's side, paused with his hand on the door handle, looked at me. Then, in a gesture I found at once faintly ridiculous and profoundly sad, he waved to me. I waved back. Then Carlo got into the limousine, turned on the engine, and pulled away from the curb.

"It may not be so easy to make amends," I said quietly to Garth as Veil came back across the sidewalk toward us. "I said some pretty nasty things to him."

"Oh, I don't really think it's going to be a problem," Harper said brightly as Veil reached us, shrugged his shoulders to indicate he had found nothing incriminating on Carlo or in the limousine. "Now be a good boy and do what your brother says. Make nice to Veil and tell him how sorry you are."

"Right," I said, and proceeded to do so.

• • •

As the waiter brought our drinks to the isolated table at the back of the half-filled restaurant in downtown Zurich where we had gone to eat and talk, Garth took a notebook out of his pocket. He set the notebook down in front of him, but did not open it. "Anybody know how we can get hold of a gun or two around here?"

I looked at Veil, who shook his head. "Not in Switzerland."

"Just thought I'd ask," Garth said with a shrug. He tapped the cardboard cover of the notebook, continued matter-of-factly, "John Sinclair was born in Osaka, Japan, in nineteen forty-six to Henry and Anne Sinclair. The father was a midlevel career diplomat who'd gained a virtually permanent posting in Japan and had a reputation as having gone native, in a manner of speaking. He was a Japanophile. He'd been part of MacArthur's occupying army after the war, and he spent most of the remainder of his life there. According to one of the obituaries I read, the man became deeply steeped in Japanese culture and spoke the language fluently. Both the mother and father died under what were described as mysterious circumstances, when the son was nineteen years old, and there was some speculation that the couple had been murdered as retribution for the father having delved too deeply into the secrets and practices of certain mystical Japanese secret societies.

"John Sinclair's upbringing in Japan is shrouded in speculation and seeming contradictions; accounts differ, and there's a lot of obvious tabloid stuff that's fiction. However, I think we can safely assume that he was educated in the best American private schools there. He learned the language as a child, and so can be assumed to be fluent. Also, we can assume that the father arranged for him to begin learning the martial arts at a very young age. That's where he picked up his fighting skills. He attended graduate schools in both London and Paris and picked up the equivalent of a doctorate from the Sorbonne. His dissertation was on secret Japanese societies in the eleventh and twelfth centuries. He enlisted in the United States Army after he received his degree and was subsequently commissioned.

"Whatever he did in Vietnam is still highly classified, and I didn't want to take the time to try to dig it out, but I think it's also safe to assume that he was involved in intelligence and covert military operations in Laos and Cambodia, like Veil. He was a super-soldier." Garth paused, sipped at his drink. He set the glass down, glanced at the man sitting on his left and my right, continued, "There were two men in that war who received a disproportionately high number of medals for exceptional bravery above and beyond the call of duty. John Sinclair was one of those soldiers. The other was Veil Kendry."

Harper reached across the table and squeezed Veil's hand. She waited until the waiter, who had arrived with our salads, went away, then said quietly, "That's very impressive, Veil. Robby is always talking about your incredible martial arts skills, but he never mentioned that you were a war hero."

There were several good reasons why dear Robby had never

83

mentioned Veil's war record, which no longer officially existed; not the least of those reasons were the circumstances surrounding his dishonorable discharge engineered by the man who had been determined to celebrate an enormous political victory by killing his old enemy, Archangel—Veil Kendry. It hadn't worked out well for him. Although Orville Madison had very nearly killed not only Veil but also Garth and me, in the end it was Madison who died in a hail of bullets in a dusty congressional hearing room in the Old Senate Office Building. Kevin Shannon, President of the United States, had, for his own very good reasons, conspired to cover up the whole affair, and it was not a subject we wanted to talk about ever again, especially not to people we loved. Garth and I exchanged glances, and I was pondering ways to change the subject when Veil managed to at least steer it off into safer channels.

"I wasn't a war hero by any good definition, Harper," Veil said casually. "I was a war lover. Without boring you with too much of my personal history, suffice it to say that I was more than a bit mad back then. I loved the war, because that outlet for sanctioned violence helped me with a certain medical problem I suffer from, which is associated with brain damage I sustained when I was born. I dream vividly. Now my painting resolves the conflicts and enables me to function. But before I learned that I could paint in order to ease the pain, I picked up a lot of decorations in Southeast Asia simply because I usually managed to be where the fighting was; that's where I wanted and needed to be. That's a description of psychosis, not courage. Sinclair was brave, not psychotic—at least not back during the war years. Now . . . well, I suppose there's no way of knowing."

I watched as Veil leaned back in his chair and sipped at his drink. What he had said wasn't true; as far as I was concerned, he *was* a war hero, by any definition. Psychotic or not, he had risked everything to save a village marked for destruction by his controller for political reasons, and it had been that act which had led to his dishonorable discharge and sentence of death. But those facts were hidden away in the larger labyrinth of secrets about Archangel that were best kept that way.

Garth turned to Veil. "How do you know this?"

Veil shrugged. "About Sinclair's head back during the war? I don't know for sure. What I do know is that he had a reputation as a top soldier. I wasn't interested in being any kind of soldier; I was only interested in killing."

Garth grunted, and for the first time he opened the small notebook in front of him on the table, referred to one of the pages. "You certainly got that part right about his being a top soldier. He was the youngest major the United States Army has ever had. Word was that he was being groomed by army brass for an eventual top post in the army after the war. In short, he wasn't exactly considered a loose cannon."

"And then one day he ups and deserts," Harper said quietly.

I nodded. "And the same army that had once considered him General Staff material now sent five Rangers after him with orders to kill."

Harper shook her head. "It just doesn't make sense. What could have happened?"

"I think he found out something he wasn't supposed to know, and then he had no choice but to split; he knew he was marked for death. I think he found out about Cooked Goose."

Garth looked up at me. "The thing you believe was a secret military operation."

"I don't know what it was—or is. I'm just guessing."

"Where did you hear about it?"

"A little bird from the CIA by the name of Duane Insolers dropped that name on me during the course of an Alice in Wonderland conversation we were having. He seemed absolutely convinced I'd come to Zurich on some secret mission of my own that was associated with the hunt for Sinclair. He just wouldn't believe the truth, so he kept trying to cue me with names and information so that I'd trust him—at least I think that's what he was trying to do. The subjects I asked you to look into came out of that conversation."

Garth tapped the notebook with his index finger. "Where's this Insolers now?"

"Beats me. What did you find out about Cooked Goose?"

"Not a thing," my brother replied tersely.

"Did you call Mr. Lippitt?"

"Sure."

"You think he knows?"

"Of course he knows. Mr. Lippitt knows everything. He was the source of information for what I just told you about Sinclair."

"But he wouldn't talk about Cooked Goose?"

"Nope."

"Did he give you a reason?"

"He said I hadn't given him sufficient reason to talk about it and that he couldn't see how the information could do you any good. Maybe you should call him."

"I can't give him a reason why I should know about Cooked Goose until I know what Cooked Goose is."

"He offered to help get you out of the country."

"I'm not ready to leave."

"He also offered some advice."

"Which is?"

"He said we should put as much distance as possible between us and Chant Sinclair."

I turned to Veil. "That advice somehow sounds familiar."

Veil said, "I can tell you about Cooked Goose."

I blinked. "What?"

"Operation Cooked Goose was a decidedly half-baked plan devised by a renegade faction of super-hawks in the CIA to assassinate other American hawks—pro-war politicians, writers, clergymen, and various cultural leaders."

Having delivered this announcement, Veil proceeded to begin eating his salad. I glanced at Garth and Harper. Garth actually looked stunned, which was a remarkable display of emotion for him. Harper looked uncomprehending, and I was sure I looked the same.

I tapped Veil on the shoulder. "Uh, you say hawks were planning to assassinate Americans who supported their position?"

"Right."

"But *why*?"

"To discredit the doves by making it appear that the war had literally come home, just as some of them had openly called for. It was sort of an extension of Operation Phoenix, only in reverse. In addition to killing Vietnamese officials who supported the Viet

Cong and North Vietnamese, they would also begin assassinating American supporters of our war effort. It was in the last stages of the war, seven or eight months before the eventual evacuation of Saigon. By then it was obvious—to the hawks, at least—that it was the ground swell of opposition in the United States that was causing us to lose the war. The renegade CIA planners reasoned that if American public opinion could somehow be turned around, the military could stage one last, massive assault on the Viet Cong and North Vietnamese that might finally win the war. Cooked Goose was supposed to marshal that popular support by making it appear that the North Vietnamese and their allies had sent ninja-type assassination teams into the country. The thinking was that not even most of the die-hard doves would tolerate the fact that the North Vietnamese had sent assassins onto American soil to kill American leaders. Public opinion would shift, total victory would be demanded, and the full force of the United States Army could be unleashed to mount an all out air and ground assault on North Vietnam. That's it."

"How the *hell* do you know this?" Garth asked, making no effort to hide his incredulity.

"An Army Ranger friend of mine told me all about it over drinks at a bar on Oahu. We'd both ended up there at the same time for a little R and R."

I was more than a bit incredulous myself. "How could that be, Veil? This Duane Insolers claimed he didn't even know what Cooked Goose was. He also said it was still one of the most closely guarded secrets this country has."

Veil grunted. "And with good reason, don't you think? The reason this guy talked to me about it was that we were both fighters, not planners, and fighters think differently from planners—it's always the planners of deals like this who are anxious to keep what they've planned a secret, usually forever. As you know, I had a reputation as a stone killer. The guy was drunk, he felt the need to talk to somebody about it, and he trusted me. Also, because of my reputation, he just naturally assumed I'd been recruited and was a part of it. He didn't believe me when I told him I wasn't, and he just kept talking. He thought Cooked Goose was a great idea. He was looking forward to being shipped back to the United States where he'd be an assassin for his country. He liked the idea of killing what he called pinko politicians and folk singers once in a while as a break from killing right-wingers, and he especially liked the idea that none of these people would be shooting back at him. Unfortunately for him, he never got to do any of it. He was one of the five Rangers sent after Sinclair when Sinclair took off. I'll bet five thousand of my dollars to your quarter that all five of those men had been recruited for Cooked Goose."

"Jesus Christ," I said softly as I felt my heart start to beat faster.

Garth pushed his half-finished salad to one side, turned to face Veil. "You say this man assumed you'd been recruited for the operation. Why did he think that?"

"Because of my combat record, but most of all because of my martial arts abilities. Remember that the killings were supposed to look like the work of specially trained ninja assassin teams, not shooters. Weapons of choice would be the garrote, dagger, *shuriken*, or sometimes just hands. I was good with all these things."

"But you hadn't been approached?"

"No."

"Why not?"

"I really don't know, but my guess is that I didn't begin to fit the deeper profile of the kind of men they were looking for. Cooked Goose sounds like the sort of nitwit operation my CIA controller would have been in on, or maybe even helped to dream up, and he'd have told the people in charge of recruiting that I was hell on wheels in a jungle fighting situation, but that I was otherwise psychotic and unreliable—and he would have been right, of course. He knew that I needed violence and the presence of danger to keep myself going from day to day, and that I'd have no use for Cooked Goose, namely sitting-duck, targets. He understood that I was fighting for my own reasons, and these reasons had nothing to do with the political or military aims of the United States. My friend, on the other hand, was a super-patriot type who would not be able to see anything wrong with anything he did, just so long as he had been told by some authority that it was for the good of the country. My guess is that all of the recruits fit that psychological profile. I didn't, which is why I was never approached."

We all sat in silence, thinking, for a few moments, and then Garth said, "The planners approached John Sinclair."

Veil nodded thoughtfully. "I think you're probably right, but there's a big question as to why they'd do so. From everything I've heard about Sinclair, he didn't fit the profile of a Cooked Goose assassin either. He was one terrific fighter, all right, but he was above all else a real *professional* soldier. He would never abide assassinating our own public officials." Veil paused, looked around the table at each of us in turn, and it seemed to me that his glacial blue eyes suddenly seemed brighter. "Not only, in my opinion, wouldn't he have abided such a thing," he continued in a low voice, "but I think he probably would have tried to squash the program in any way he could. That could explain why he suddenly chose to become a deserter, and why five Rangers were sent to bring him to ground before he could do whatever it was he planned to do."

Garth and I looked at each other, and I said, "Yes. He'd somehow found out about it, and the planners were afraid he was going to blow the whistle. That's why they felt they had to kill him."

Veil nodded. "That's quite a scenario. Knowledge of Cooked Goose would still be incredibly explosive, and I think we can safely assume that the planners are still alive, most likely still in positions of power—as Orville Madison would be if he hadn't gotten cocky. These people will do anything to keep him from telling what he knows; by the same reasoning, our enemies would be most happy to provide Sinclair with a forum for doing just that—whether he wanted to or not. It could explain why all the various intelligence types are currently swarming in Switzerland. A lot of people want to get their hands on Sinclair, for a variety of reasons. Sinclair could give the kind of history lesson that would open a lot of old wounds and maybe settle some old scores."

Harper, who had been sitting quietly and following our discussion with rapt attention, suddenly held up a hand. "Wait a minute," she said. "There's something missing here. We know this

Cooked Goose business never came off, because I don't recall reading about any rash of assassinations in the U.S. toward the end of the war. Okay, it was called off because John Sinclair was still alive to tell people what was really going on. But things have changed, certainly for him. Now he's an international criminal hunted by everybody, including the United States. What would be his motive for continuing to keep silent about what happened, about why he deserted in the first place?"

Garth and I looked at each other, then at Veil. Veil shrugged, replied, "Unknown."

"Another question," Harper said. "Veil, you said you believe you were never approached by a recruiter because you didn't fit the profile of a Cooked Goose assassin, and you also said John Sinclair didn't fit the profile any more than you did. Assuming he wasn't approached either, how would he have found out about it?"

"Maybe the same way Veil found out about it," Garth offered. "Somebody already in the program told him about it."

Veil shook his head. "Highly unlikely. That Ranger talking to me in a bar on Oahu was a special situation. He and I were both crazy, in different ways. Not one of those recruits would have breathed a word about assassinating American citizens to a full-bird colonel who had a reputation as a straitlaced military man."

Garth inclined his head toward the other man. "Then maybe the planners did try to recruit him. After all, most of what we're discussing is pure speculation, including what you believe was the psychological profile of the men they wanted in the program."

"I think it's highly unlikely anyone ever tried to recruit Sinclair as a domestic assassin," Veil replied, his tone changing somewhat, becoming more distant. I looked at him. He was frowning slightly, as if another thought had occurred to him.

Harper laughed scornfully. "If the Cooked Goose planners did try to recruit him, it has to rank as one of the classic military misjudgments of all time."

"Unless one of the planners had a hidden agenda," Veil said in a voice that had become even more distant.

"Meaning what?" I asked sharply. Suddenly, I felt excited, although I wasn't sure why.

Veil slowly exhaled, seemed to relax somewhat. He looked at me, smiled crookedly. "I just had a thought, but it's way out in left field."

"Left field? Give us a break. We're talking about an unknown game in a whole different kind of stadium. What's on your mind?"

"I was thinking about what Garth had to say about Sinclair's family, and the possibility that his parents may have been murdered for delving into something that was forbidden. He grew up in Japan, and he later wrote a dissertation on ancient, secret Japanese societies. Well, the same guy who told me about Cooked Goose in the first place also mentioned a rumor going around among the recruits that the CIA had laid out a whole lot of cash to hire, as an advisor, some old Japanese guy who was supposed to have been the world's most highly paid assassin. The way this Ranger told it, the old Japanese was supposed to be the spiritual leader of a secret society of professional assassins—old-style ninjas, if you will."

"It sounds like a ninja bullshit story," Garth said drily.

"Precisely," Veil said, and smiled. "Impressionable martial arts types love to believe and tell what Garth always refers to as ninja bullshit stories, and I laughed when I heard it. I thought it was a ninja bullshit story. Now, when I hear what Garth has to say about Sinclair's family and background, and in light of this discussion, I'm not so sure."

I leaned forward in my chair. "A connection between the ninja advisor and Sinclair?"

Veil nodded. "Or originally between the old guy and Sinclair's father. If both parents were killed because of the father's transgression, why not go after the son too?"

Garth looked hard at Veil. "You're implying that this Japanese guy, if he ever existed, would purposely suggest to the planners of Cooked Goose that Sinclair be approached and told about the operation, knowing full well how Sinclair would react, and knowing that the planners would then decide he had to be killed?"

"Something like that," Veil replied with a shrug. "I said it was out in left field."

Garth shook his head, ran a large hand back through his thinning, wheat-colored hair, sighed heavily. "That scenario requires belief that this Japanese would accept an assignment from the CIA to organize and advise an assassination bureau, while all the time planning to risk sabotaging the entire operation just to disgrace and kill one man." My brother paused, quickly closed his notebook as two waiters finally approached the table with our food. Then he continued in a lower voice, "To use your words, that seems highly unlikely. Sorry, Veil, but it does sound like a ninja bullshit story."

I glanced at Harper, and we both nodded in agreement. Veil looked away, said nothing.

CHAPTER EIGHT

The service at the restaurant was slow, even by European standards, but the food was worth waiting for. The proximity of two waiters and a busgirl throughout the main course made it impossible for us to continue our discussion of John Sinclair without risk of being overheard, and so we talked of other things while we ate. As soon as the waiters and busgirl had retreated after clearing the table and serving us coffee, I leaned close to Veil, said, "Why did you send me to see Gerard Patreaux?"

"What did he say to you, Mongo?"

"He told me a story about Chant Sinclair and Torture Island."

Veil, who was now staring at me intently, nodded curtly. "What specifically did he tell you about that matter?"

"He said Sinclair purposely got himself arrested, knowing that he'd be turned over to the CIA, and betting that the CIA would send him to Torture Island for interrogation. He wanted to avenge the death of a friend of his named Harry Gray. Gray was an Amnesty International investigator who'd been tortured to death on the island. Patreaux kept insisting he was only repeating rumors, but if there's any truth at all to the story—"

"It's true, Mongo," Veil said with quiet intensity.

"Okay," I said, "now I'm thinking that the CIA may have sent him there specifically to find out what he knew, or who he'd told, about Cooked Goose. I'm also thinking that Mr. Gerard Patreaux, distinguished official of Amnesty International, is a close personal friend of the world's most wanted criminal and that it was Patreaux who helped Sinclair pull off that stunt."

"That wouldn't surprise me at all, Mongo," Veil said, and laughed. Suddenly, he seemed much more relaxed, as if some burden had been lifted from his shoulders. He grinned at me. "In fact, I completely agree with your thinking."

"How did you know enough to send me to him, Veil? How did you know about Torture Island, and, if you thought it was so important, why didn't you tell me about it in the beginning?"

"I wasn't sure that it was important, and I still don't know that it is. I knew about Torture Island because I once had a Nicaraguan lady friend who told me about it. Even if I had wanted to tell you about it, Mongo, I couldn't have."

"Why not?"

"In a way, I believe she'd broken a pledge to John Sinclair, or at least gone against his wishes, by telling me the story, and I'd specifically promised her I wouldn't tell anyone else. I knew Patreaux had been a part of it, because my lady friend told me he'd arranged with Sinclair for Amnesty International to take care of the surviving prisoners on the island. Since Patreaux, for whatever reasons, saw fit to share some of that information with you, however he may have put it, I see no reason now why I shouldn't talk about it."

"Who is this woman, Veil?" Harper asked quietly. "And what did she have to do with this Torture Island?"

"Her real name is María González, but we'll call her Feather, because that's what Richard Krowl, the doctor who was the torture specialist on the island, called her. She was involved in the incident that got Krowl drummed out of the academic community, and she ended as one of Krowl's resident torturers—the most effective and most feared."

Harper made a sound of disgust and anger in her throat. I put my hand in hers, squeezed.

"She was a torture victim herself," Veil continued in an even tone, looking directly at Harper. "Feather's a physician, and she served the Sandinista guerrillas in their rebellion against Somoza. She was captured in the field by some of Somoza's soldiers and horribly tortured in ways I won't spoil your meal by describing. The torturers left her for dead in the jungle, but she was found by the guerrillas, and she somehow survived. However, the experience had left her catatonic. She was eventually sent to a Canadian clinic for torture victims that Richard Krowl was associated with.

"No matter how well cared for they may be, victims of severe torture are almost never the same; very rarely do they recover all their faculties. Their physical wounds may heal, but not the psychological ones; they are emotionally shattered. They can't cope with the flashbacks and nightmares that become their constant companions whether awake or asleep. Richard Krowl had his own notions about how to treat torture victims: he believed that revenge was the best medicine.

"Back in Nicaragua, the Sandinistas had come to power, and most of Somoza's torturers were dead or in prison. One of their prisoners was the leader of the group that had tortured the woman. Krowl arranged for the man to be sent to the United States, supposedly to be a participant in a research project Krowl was setting up in a secure facility to study the minds of torturers. He had already brought Feather there. The fact of the matter was that Krowl couldn't have cared less about the man's thinking or motives. He was only interested in how having this man under her complete control would affect María González, who hadn't spoken a word in nearly five years. He offered the man to her as a gift, told her she could do whatever she liked with him. She responded. The arrangement cured her of her catatonia, if not her muteness. She opted to torture her torturer to death, as he had tried to do to her. Her choice of torture instruments was a single feather. She worked on the man for a few hours every day, and it took him six weeks to die."

Veil paused as I rose and leaned across the table to wipe tears from Harper's cheeks. He reached out and touched her hand, raised his eyebrows slightly in a silent inquiry as to whether she wanted him to continue.

"Go on," Harper said in a steady voice. "I'm all right. I'm not crying for the man she killed, and you're not really upsetting me. I was just thinking of the horrible physical and mental pain this woman must have suffered to cause it to change her from a healer to a monster like the one she was killing."

"Precisely," Veil said quietly. "But Krowl was only interested in getting her to function at some level, not in healing her emotionally. This latest experience had not only turned her into a torturer but bonded her to Krowl, whom she now viewed as her savior. When his activities were discovered, he was thrown out of the academic and medical communities, and when he proceeded to set up shop on Torture Island, he took Feather with him. Because of the terrible combination of both pleasure and pain she'd learned how to excite using nothing more than a feather, she became Krowl's most effective interrogator, his chief torturer.

"She was there when Sinclair was brought to the island, strapped into a stretcher on a rack in a helicopter. It was Feather who took the first pass at breaking him down, and on the first night she left him unconscious and bleeding from every orifice in his body. What neither Krowl, Feather, nor any of the student-torturers on that island understood was that everything was going according to Sinclair's plan, and he had come carefully prepared. He'd hidden various tiny lock-picking devices inside his body before his capture, and within a few minutes after regaining consciousness and finding himself alone, he was out of his cell, on the loose, and free to kill—which is precisely what he proceeded to do. He began making a circuit of the island, breaking the necks of the various guards posted around the place. He came upon Feather—who never slept more than a half hour or so at a time—alone, standing at the edge of a precipice and staring out to sea. He probably wouldn't have had any compunction about killing a woman if she were just a torturer, but Krowl had told Sinclair her story before setting her loose on him, and he chose not to kill someone who had been a torture victim herself. Instead, he just knocked her out, reasoning that he'd have taken care of his business and would be in control of the island by the time she regained consciousness.

"On his way to the building where Krowl and his staff slept, Sinclair stopped in Krowl's offices to pick up two things he had come for in addition to the revenge he was exacting: a fortune in black pearls Krowl had amassed by forcing prisoners to dive for him in the shark-infested waters, and Krowl's records."

"I can understand his wanting the pearls," Garth interjected, "but why bother with the records?"

"He was finishing Harry Gray's work for him," I heard myself saying, instinctively sensing the truth of it, but not knowing exactly why. "He planned to shut down Torture Island simply by killing Krowl and the other torturers there, but he also wanted to make sure the names of the governments and organizations that had financed and used it were made public. It was his way of trying to keep another such place from starting up."

"That's correct," Veil said. "However, when he scanned the records and other papers in Krowl's office, he came across information that caused him to change his original plan. A memo he found indicated that in three days a well-known Russian dissident and his wife were being flown there for a little gentle persuasion and brainwashing to get the man to recant certain statements he had spoken and written before he and his wife were sentenced to internal exile. If Sinclair went ahead and put Torture Island out of operation that night, there would be nobody to take delivery, as it were, of the couple, and they would be returned to internal exile—perhaps even death—in the Soviet Union. If, on the other hand, Sinclair were to postpone his plans, if he could manage to somehow survive three more days in captivity until the Russians were delivered, he would also be able to rescue them. Obviously, there was going to be additional pressure above and beyond more torture he would have to endure. There were the dead guards he was leaving behind as evidence that something was seriously amiss; many of the torturers on the island knew him by reputation, and that reputation was such that he'd be suspected even if he were still locked in his cell. There would be demands to kill him outright, and, at the least, additional security precautions would be taken.

"Despite the fact that he was home free if he just continued on that night with his original plan, and despite the certainty of more pain and the possibility of death—certain death if Feather had glimpsed his face before he'd knocked her out—Sinclair headed back to his cell and chained himself up again, just to buy time in order to try to rescue the Russian dissident and his wife.

"Well, he pulled it off, obviously—and the second time he escaped from his cell, he did it with Feather's help. He killed every torturer on that island, freed the prisoners, escaped from the island in a Russian helicopter with the pearls, prisoners, and Krowl's records. He turned the prisoners and half the pearls over to Gerard Patreaux, who was waiting on a hospital ship at a prearranged site off the Chilean coast. Sinclair had saved the lives of all those people, and he had swelled the coffers of Amnesty International by a hefty amount, and all he asked in return was that the people involved not reveal what had happened, not talk about him or what he had done. End of story."

"Maybe a ninja bullshit story," Garth said, and from his terse, dismissive tone of voice I could tell that was exactly what he considered it.

"Maybe," Veil replied easily. "But I've seen the scars left on Feather's body by Somoza's torturers, and those were not part of any fairy tale. Neither was her love for, and total devotion to, Chant Sinclair. Somehow, he managed to heal her soul. Whether that story is true or not, he was a tough act to follow. I loved her, and she at least seemed content to be with me, but my knowing that I was constantly being compared with him is the reason Feather and I are no longer together."

I looked at Harper, who had grown very pale, and said, "That certainly doesn't sound like a man who would sanction random killings, or torture to death a bunch of servants."

Veil slowly turned his coffee cup in its saucer. "I don't believe he did either of those things. The gunman at the hotel was an Asian, and Sinclair always works alone. And he couldn't have kidnapped Neuberger and killed his servants if he's still running around here in Switzerland."

Garth made a derisive gesture with his hand and started to say something, but Veil cut him off. "Extreme violence is certainly Sinclair's signature," he said, speaking directly to my brother, "but I suggest there's more to that signature if you closely examine his behavior and past record." He paused, looked at Harper and me, continued, "Discounting, for the moment, all of the incidents connected with this Cornucopia business, consider who all his victims have been. In every case I've ever read about, his victims were scum of the earth, people whom everyone at this table would agree got what they deserved. Check it out; I have. Sinclair scams corrupt, criminal people and outfits—child pornography rings, drug cartels, terrorist networks, the Mafia, rogue government operations. To a man, the people he's killed have been killers themselves, like the good doctor on Torture Island. He may be a butcher, but his victims have butchered tens, hundreds, even thousands, of innocent people. I read of one incident where his victim was the owner of a Dutch pharmaceutical concern. What Sinclair did to the man and his colleagues got all the headlines, but when you got down to the fine print at the back of the better newspapers, you found out that this man had decided to increase his company's profits a bit by watering down all the medicines he had contracted to deliver to an African nation where a plague was raging. The medicines were worse than useless, because the doctors who prescribed them, and the people who took them, had every reason to belive they would work and that there was no reason to take any further medical action. Before Sinclair exposed the wholesale adulteration scheme, hundreds of men, women, and children had died of disease. These are people who might have lived if the medication they had been given had been the proper dosage."

"How did John Sinclair kill the man?" Harper asked quietly.

Veil smiled grimly. "By forcing him to drink a glass of water contaminated with a heavy concentration of a certain type of microscopic worm that eats its way along the optic nerve into the brain. There is no cure. It was a cruel act, to be sure, but I suggest there was more than a trace of poetic justice to it. Other cases fit the same pattern—victims deserving what they get. It's another reason, Mongo, why I—and presumably Mr. Lippitt—tried to warn you off this one. If Sinclair had targeted Cornucopia for one of his scams, I considered the chances very good that Cornucopia was something more than the paradigm of philanthropic benevolence you obviously believed it to be."

"Well," I said with a small sigh, "I think even the village idiot in our midst can now begin to figure that one out. Assuming Cornucopia distributes any funds at all to the causes it claims to support, which I think it unquestionably does, its primary function has always been to serve as a vast money-laundering operation. Duane Insolers told me money has been continuously siphoned off from the foundation since its inception decades ago, and I have to assume he knows what he's talking about. Neuberger's grandfather set up Cornucopia, but only after he had already made a fortune legitimately. He didn't need to set up any criminal operation, because he certainly didn't need the money."

"Greedy people never have enough money," Harper said.

"You've got that right. But even if the elder Neuberger was the biggest crook who ever lived, I just don't believe Emmet P. Neuberger has the necessities, as it were, to run a big criminal organization. He certainly knows everything that's going on in Cornucopia, but as an administrator I see him straining his talents to the limit just to be a figurehead for the family foundation. You agree, Garth?"

"Yes," my brother replied simply. He appeared thoughtful, and had obviously been thinking about what I said. "The money-laundering operation exists for a person, or persons, unknown. It's probably some crime cartel that's been around for a long time, and that may have bankrolled the grandfather, and performed other services, while he was amassing his otherwise legitimate fortune."

Veil had been listening intently, but also tapping his fingers impatiently on the tabletop. Now he said, "Let's shift the focus back to Sinclair, because he's the puzzle we have to solve. The point I was trying to make is that Cornucopia, it now seems evident, is typical of the kind of organization Sinclair targets. It's corrupt at its core, and that's what made it vulnerable. Torturing to death Neuberger's servants? Yes, he's a killer, and he takes no prisoners, but, again, he's never done anything like that to anyone who wasn't richly deserving of his attention—not to my knowledge anyway."

I grunted, said only half jokingly: "That could serve as a description of both you and big brother here. I'm thinking the three of you might actually get along just fine."

Veil laughed, but quickly turned serious again. "The shooting at the hotel, the murders of the Interpol people and others, appear atypical of Sinclair's usual M.O. I say Sinclair has demonstrated a streak of altruism, although, for some reason, he goes to considerable lengths to disguise it. Consider the story about Torture Island: He got what he ostensibly went there for—revenge and a fortune in black pearls. And he'd already suffered considerably for his troubles. Feather told me what she'd done to him. He could have been out of there in twenty-four hours. He certainly didn't have to subject himself to three more days of torment just on the chance he might be able to rescue the Russian couple; he didn't have to concern himself with any of the other prisoners. He spared the life of his chief tormentor, Feather, because she had once been a torture victim herself. Finally, he certainly didn't have to turn over half the treasure he'd gained with his blood to Amnesty International."

"That could still turn out to be a ninja bullshit story," Garth said in a deceptively soft, even tone. "We all agree he's a killer, and I'm nowhere near ready to concede he's not the one trying to kill my brother."

"As Mongo so perceptively pointed out," Veil replied firmly, "the term 'killer' might well apply to certain other people sitting at this table. And Torture Island isn't a ninja bullshit story; it happened."

I glanced at Harper, then looked back at Veil. "You make him sound like a kind of very bad-ass Robin Hood who pounds on and takes from the victimizers, then gives to the victims—after taking a hefty cut for himself. The ultimate vigilante."

Veil smiled wryly, shrugged. "Actually, that may not be a

101

totally inaccurate description. I've been involved with the martial arts all my life, and I've met with others like myself all over the world. I've been in a position to pick up bits and pieces of information and hear rumors that you don't read in the newspapers. A lot of those things *are* ninja bullshit stories—but not all. Chant Sinclair may be the greatest all-around master of the martial arts who's ever lived, and I freely admit that he's always fascinated me. He operates in the ancient, traditional fashion of the ninja—as an outcast and mercenary. In this case, he's a mercenary who happens to be self-employed. Also in the ancient tradition is the way he relies on mental and psychological skills, on deception, as much as, or more than, he relies on sheer physical prowess. He's a master of tactics and strategy. He's also a master of disguise—and I'm not just talking about the usual wigs, moustaches, and accents. I'm suggesting that even his use of extreme violence may be a kind of disguise designed to keep most people from seeing him as he really is. He may only kill killers and other victimizers, but the manner in which he does it manages to scare the shit out of everyone, and it's what the media always focuses on. He may calculate that this works to his advantage. Why else ask Gerard Patreaux, Feather, and all the prisoners he rescued from Torture Island not to tell anyone what he'd done there?" Veil paused, looked inquiringly at each of us in turn. "It was almost as if he was afraid the truth might ruin his image."

"You are definitely beginning to sound like a fan," Harper said, unable or unwilling to keep a faint note of disappointment out of her voice. "Even if most of his victims do deserve what happens to them, why romanticize a man who makes a living out of terrorizing and butchering human beings?"

"My point isn't to try to romanticize him, Harper," Veil replied easily. "I'm suggesting a different way of viewing John Sinclair, an alternate perception of reality. Mongo's life, and maybe even our own lives, may depend on just how accurately we're able to determine what's really going on here in Switzerland."

"I'm sorry, Veil. I didn't mean to imply—"

"There's no need to apologize, Harper. If what I'm suggesting has any truth in it, then I guess it's fair to say I'm a fan. I've never thought of it that way, but I have followed his career for a long time, and I'm certainly in awe of his abilities. He's a criminal, yes, and a killer, yes, but Mongo's description of him as a kind of ultimate vigilante may also fit. What he does may not be legal, but there does seem to be a concern for justice—"

"That's nonsense," Garth interrupted. "You and I may have had our differences, my friend, but I've never accused you of being silly. That's what I'm hearing now. Where's the justice in trying to kill Mongo?"

If Veil was offended by Garth's words or tone, he didn't show it. "But I don't think Sinclair *is* trying to kill Mongo, my friend," he replied evenly. "Obviously, neither does Gerard Patreaux." Veil paused, turned to me. "Did Patreaux tell you the Torture Island story right away?"

I shook my head. "End of the evening—virtually as I was on my way out the door."

Veil grunted, turned his attention back to Garth. "Patreaux was sizing your brother up, trying to determine if Mongo might be Sinclair's enemy. When he was satisfied that Mongo wasn't, he told him that story as a way of indicating that Sinclair wasn't Mongo's enemy either." He paused, looked at Harper. When he continued, his voice was lower, more intense. "You accuse me of sounding like a fan. Okay. But I am telling you that María Gonzá-lez, Feather, would unhesitatingly lay down her life for this man. I suspect Gerard Patreaux might do the same. The man commands loyalty from decent people who have had dealings with him, Harper. If I'm right, Sinclair may have a whole global network of secret friends and allies, good people who know him as a just man, and who are willing to help him keep his secrets. Some of these friends may be in positions of power and influence. I think Sinclair may even have passed on information to some of these people when it would do some good. That's how he'd come to know Harry Gray and Gerard Patreaux in the first place: he'd been feeding them information on various human rights violations."

"Veil," I said, placing my hand on my friend's arm, looking into his piercing blue eyes, "I have to ask you something. Are you one of those friends? If this network of friends and allies does exist, are you a part of it?"

He seemed taken aback by the question. He looked at me oddly for a moment or two, then replied simply, "No. I've never met the man."

Harper asked, "Would you tell us if you had? Would you tell us if you were a part of his network?"

"You'll have to decide that for yourself, Harper," Veil replied evenly.

Garth, who had been studying Veil carefully, abruptly announced: "He's telling the truth."

I looked at my brother, nodded. Over time, I had become a reluctant believer in his uncanny "nose for evil." His poisoning with a mysterious substance called nitrophenyldienal, combined with some particularly horrific experiences we'd shared while tracking a madman who had, in effect, declared genetic warfare on humanity, had subtly altered not only his personality but also his perceptions and sensibilities. He had become a highly receptive empath, virtually a human lie detector. If I'd followed his lead in refusing to have anything to do with Emmet P. Neuberger, I wouldn't be sitting in a restaurant in Zurich trying to figure out how to avoid being killed. If Garth said Veil was telling the truth, that was good enough for me. But then, I would have believed Veil in any case; he might withhold information, or refuse to speak about something, but I didn't think he would lie to me.

I said, "Let's get back to the role of the village idiot in these proceedings. We know I was set up, but we don't know why. So let's look at what we know now, or are pretty certain of. First, I think we can safely assume that Emmet P. Neuberger is a bigtime crook, if only by association, because his family foundation was set up, from day one, as a very large money-laundering operation. We know it was begun by Neuberger's grandfather, but not whether he did it for himself, out of his own greed, or on behalf of secret backers who may have been pulling his strings. My hunch is that John Sinclair found out that Cornucopia was crooked during the course of some other con job he was pulling; he not only found out that large amounts of money were being laundered and skimmed from Cornucopia, but he discovered the basic mechanism for doing it. He then proceeded to do a little skimming himself, ten million dollars' worth. Does that seem like a plausible theory?"

Garth, Veil, and Harper exchanged glances with one another, and all three nodded their heads.

"It'll do until something better comes along," Garth said. "But now it gets tricky. With all the publicity surrounding Sinclair's theft of the ten million and the killing of the Interpol inspector, Neuberger had to have been aware that there was an extreme risk that Cornucopia's money-laundering function was going to be exposed; even if Interpol and the Zurich police didn't stumble on the truth, Sinclair might leak the information. Now, you would think that absolutely the last thing in the world Neuberger would want would be to have a crack private investigator joining Interpol and the police in poking around over here. There's no better investigator in the world than baby brother here, and yet Neuberger moans and groans and goes through all sorts of emotional contortions in order to manipulate baby brother into coming over here to join the parade. Why increase his risk of exposure? What's the point of the exercise?"

I said, "He never expected me to have time to learn anything. I was sent over here by Neuberger as an expendable stalking horse, a Judas goat to flush out his enemies, and then be disposed of later. The man who approached me outside the hotel had a chance to say something just before he got blown away; he was very upset, and he wanted to know why I hadn't shown up for some meeting. Also, there had been a message, supposedly from Sinclair, left for me at the desk, but that was all part of the setup, to make sure I was neutralized in the unlikely event that I had already learned things I wasn't supposed to know and was thinking of sharing the information with the authorities."

"Why were you supposed to be at this meeting?" Garth asked. "What were you supposed to contribute?"

"I don't know. The man never had a chance to say. However, since I'd come here at Neuberger's behest, I think it's safe to assume I was supposed to be bringing something from him. Maybe a message."

"Or money," Harper said easily. She was resting her elbows

on the table, cupping her chin in her hands, and staring at me. I very much liked the look in her eyes, and found myself very much looking forward to the end of this particular meeting, when Harper and I could repair to more private quarters.

"Okay, I like that. The man thought I was a courier carrying money. At the meeting I was supposed to hand over the money to him and his partners in exchange for . . . uh . . ."

"Try to pay attention, brother," Garth said drily. "Your attention seems to be wandering, despite your dire circumstances, and I can't imagine why. Give him the answer, Harper."

"Incriminating documents proving Cornucopia was a crooked operation. Neuberger was being blackmailed with documents Sinclair stole."

"Thank you, my dear," I said, stroking the back of her hand. "I'm not sure that's as self-evident as you make it sound, but it will certainly suffice until a better answer comes along. Now the big question: Why me? Neuberger could have used anyone as a phony courier, but he did everything but beg on his knees in order to get *me* to go. What's so special about poor, hapless Robert Frederickson?"

There was silence around the table for almost a minute, and then Garth spoke. "You're easy to spot. Neuberger told his blackmailers he was sending a dwarf with their money. How many dwarfs would be landing at the airport that day?"

"No," Harper said with an air of certainty. "Robby wasn't approached at the airport by anyone but his chauffeur. Robby's being a dwarf had nothing to do with it; clothes, a hat, a pink carnation in the lapel, virtually anything could have served to identify a courier. Neuberger was planning to have them all killed after Robby flushed them out and then steal the documents back. But he had to be as certain as possible that the blackmailers wouldn't hold anything back as insurance against a double cross; he had to try to make certain they would have all the documents with them when they went to this meeting, where *they* could be double-crossed and killed. For them to be so trusting as to show up with all the documents, they would have had to have absolute trust in a courier who would keep his word, and wouldn't be a part of any double cross. Robby fit the bill."

Again there was a prolonged silence, and then Veil grunted his approval. "Not too trashy, Ms. Rhys-Whitney. It could very well be that it was Mongo's vaunted reputation as a straight arrow that got him into this mess. Do I take it we're all assuming it wasn't Sinclair doing the blackmailing?"

Garth nodded. "Hell, he didn't need to. He'd already picked up ten million with his original scam; if he'd wanted more, he could have taken it when he transferred Cornucopia's money in the first place. But if not Sinclair, then who?"

"Somebody else who got hold of the documents," Harper said, but her tone had grown more tentative. "But how could that happen? If Sinclair did steal documents along with the money, it was for a reason, even if we don't know what that reason was— since we agree it probably wasn't to blackmail Neuberger. It doesn't seem likely that he'd lose them, or that somebody could steal them from him."

"Damn," I said softly as an answer came to me with sudden, perfect clarity. "Sinclair did take documents along with the money, but he didn't lose them, and they weren't stolen from him. He gave them away, and the person he gave them to was Bo Wahlstrom."

"Yes!" Veil exclaimed, sitting up straight in his chair. He glanced at me sharply, and his blue eyes glinted with excitement. "Oh, yes! That's it!"

Garth, obviously puzzled, glanced back and forth between Veil and me. "Bo Wahlstrom is the Interpol inspector Sinclair murdered right after he ripped off Cornucopia. He burned his eyes out. What are you two talking about?"

"No," Veil said.

"No what?"

"Sinclair didn't kill Wahlstrom."

"Explain."

I said, "The connection between Bo Wahlstrom and Chant Sinclair goes back a long time. It was Wahlstrom who arrested Sinclair and, presumably, turned him over to the CIA. But remember that was exactly the scenario Sinclair wanted. We already know of one highly respected official who worked with Sinclair, and that's Gerard Patreaux. Bo Wahlstrom may have been another friend and ally. If it's true, then other pieces of the puzzle begin to fit together."

Garth glanced at Harper, then looked back at me. "Sorry, Mongo. I'm still not tracking."

"Be patient. Here's another point to consider: The Interpol inspector who originally briefed me never mentioned Torture Island, but I was told that Bo Wahlstrom's full-time assignment was tracking John Sinclair. I'll bet he got that assignment soon after Sinclair's capture and subsequent escape from Torture Island, because it was Wahlstrom who had been given credit for nabbing him in the first place. Well, he never quite managed to catch up with him again, did he?"

"I thought the accepted wisdom was that he *had* finally caught up with him, and Sinclair killed him for his efforts."

"The accepted wisdom is wrong. Wahlstrom never caught up with Sinclair again, because he didn't want to catch up with Sinclair again. But he caught a hell of a lot of other bad guys along the way. That's another thing I learned from my Interpol briefing. While Wahlstrom was supposedly devoting all his efforts to catching Sinclair, all sorts of information suddenly seemed to start coming his way. Sinclair may have continued to elude him, but in the meantime he managed to shut down a lot of other criminal operations. You think that's a coincidence?"

Harper reached across the table and squeezed my wrist. "You think that John Sinclair has been feeding information to Interpol for all these years?"

"Not to Interpol—to Bo Wahlstrom, because Wahlstrom was another friend and ally. Just like Harry Gray and Gerard Patreaux, to whom Sinclair fed information and documents on human rights violations."

"You're beginning to sound like Veil," Garth said in a neutral tone.

I shrugged. "What can I say? It's just a guess."

"I believe it's a good one," Veil said. "But I see a problem with where this is all leading us. Bo Wahlstrom was, from all accounts and in Mongo's scenario, a good man who would have used the documents to shut down Cornucopia and nail Neuberger, not blackmail him."

"It could have been the partner, Nicholas Furie; I was told Furie had only recently been assigned to assist Wahlstrom. Furie may have been corrupt. He would have been in a position to steal the documents from Wahlstrom, and, with partners fronting for him, try to blackmail Neuberger."

Harper frowned. "But it wasn't Nicholas Furie who killed Bo Wahlstrom. Wahlstrom was killed in the same manner as the servants in New York, and then Furie himself died the same way."

"Indeed."

"Then who's doing all the killing?"

Yet again there was a period of silence as each of us sat with our own thoughts, sorting through the information we had, attempting to separate fact from speculation, examining different scenarios, trying to see a pattern. And then what I was certain was at least a leading candidate for the answer to Harper's question slowly rose to the surface of my consciousness. "It could be the biggest and meanest baddies of all," I said quietly. "The people Cornucopia was set up to service in the first place, the grandfather's backers."

Harper nervously ran a hand back through her long, brown, gray-streaked hair. "If that is the case, then why would they kidnap Neuberger and butcher all his servants?"

I thought I had a pretty good idea why, but so did Veil, and it was Veil who answered. "They killed the servants for no other reason than that they were there, and they kidnapped Neuberger because they may have prepared some kind of special punishment for him. They probably hold him responsible for the fact that Sinclair stole ten million dollars from them. Or Neuberger himself may have been in on—or thought he was in on—Sinclair's scam."

"All right," I said, "let's take it from the top and see how it sounds so far. At some point in time during the course of his own mundane, workaday criminal activities, John Sinclair learns that a certain famous philanthropic foundation is in reality nothing more than a huge money-laundering operation for some big-time criminal organization. He also learns how the money is siphoned off, and he sets up his own scam posing as a Montreal entrepreneur."

Garth, obviously getting into the spirit of things, cleared his throat, his way of asking for the floor. "As Veil suggests," he said, "maybe Neuberger thought he was in on the whole thing. Sinclair could have used incriminating information he'd already uncovered to blackmail Neuberger into giving him the technical information he needed to bypass the security codes, and then offered Neuberger a deal to keep him quiet and in place. Sinclair, posing as French-Canadian, could have made Neuberger believe he was going to be a partner in a foolproof embezzlement scheme."

"Whatever," I said, tapping the table. "Sinclair may or may not have implicated Neuberger in the scam, but it plays either way, because Neuberger is in deep shit either way. He'll be held responsible. Sinclair pulls off the scam, and, assuming Neuberger is a part of it, double-crosses his would-be partner in crime. After taking his ten million, Sinclair forwards any information and documents he may have to his friend, Inspector Bo Wahlstrom of Interpol, for appropriate action by the legal authorities.

"But Wahlstrom's new partner gets a look at the stuff before Wahlstrom can get the ball rolling. Maybe Nicholas Furie can't believe Sinclair only took ten million dollars. He knows there's a whole hell of a lot more than that to be had from Cornucopia, and he doesn't see any reason why a hardworking civil servant like himself shouldn't also get a piece of the pie before the bakery is shut down. He takes on a partner or two to front for him. They contact Neuberger and make their pitch: all incriminating documents will be stolen from Wahlstrom and returned to Neuberger, in exchange for a very hefty fee."

"My turn, Mongo," Garth said.

"It's my scenario, so I should get to tell it. But I may let you speak if you raise your hand."

Harper was not amused. "There's one thing wrong with your scenario, Robby," she said softly, horror in her voice and maroon, gold-flecked eyes. "I don't see how you can assume Neuberger might have originally agreed to cooperate in the scheme. If you were this man, would you consider for even one second crossing an organization that exacts revenge by torturing people to death, burning out eyes and brains?"

"Neuberger—this Neuberger—may not have known who he

was dealing with, Harper," Veil said gently. "Cornucopia was founded by the grandfather decades ago and subsequently run by the father for years before control passed to Emmet P. Things probably ran very smoothly for all those years, so no nasty business ever occurred. Now, we have no way of knowing what instructions Emmet P. got from his father. He was certainly told what to do, given instructions as to how to do it, and probably given a stern warning to keep conducting business as usual, or suffer the consequences. But we don't know if Emmet P. had a full appreciation of just what those consequences might be. He may never have had any direct contact with anyone from the organization he was laundering money for. Mongo's scenario doesn't require that Neuberger be in on the deal, but if he was, it was because he'd become complacent. By the time he came to realize the severity of just what could happen to him, it was too late. Sinclair had already double-crossed him, and news of the theft had been made public."

Harper thought about it, shuddered as she nodded her head. "Okay. I guess it could have been that way. You're probably right when you say he would have been held responsible in any case."

"Right," I said. "Now, Neuberger had already been ripped off once, and he wasn't going to let it happen again, especially by a crew he probably sensed were amateurs. So he set up a double cross of his own, using me as a stalking horse to flush them out so they could be killed, and the documents recovered. But it was too late to cover his tracks, if it had ever been possible. By this time the *really* bad guys had gotten wind of what was happening, and they began taking care of business themselves, not only exterminating the would-be blackmailers but also going after anyone at all who might know anything about the details of the scam, along with anybody who might be in the line of fire, like those people at the hotel."

"Enter the dragon," Veil said in a curiously distant tone of voice.

"The dragon at the hotel had been marked with a combination brand-tattoo on his back. Garth, did you find out anything about that mark?"

My brother shook his head. "Not a thing. I began by assuming

111

it was a yakuza, or maybe a tong, marking, but I couldn't find anything in the literature, and the FBI and NYPD couldn't help. Tong marks are usually much smaller, and yakuza tattoos usually much more elaborate than what you described to Veil. Nobody knows anything about a mark combining a brand and a tattoo."

Now it was Veil's turn to clear his throat.

"Not you again," Garth said with mock sarcasm—a rare show of humor from my brother toward a man with whom he was usually extremely guarded. "I see I could have saved myself a lot of time and trouble by taking you out for a few beers instead of spending all night in the library."

Garth's tone had been light, but the implication of his words was clear: left unanswered was the pointed and pertinent question of why Veil hadn't volunteered the information about Cooked Goose, or anything else he knew bearing on my situation, when I'd called him after the massacre at the hotel.

"That's my fault, brother," I said quickly, anxious to head off any renewed tension between Garth and Veil. "I was feeling pissy when I called Veil, and I made it clear that all I wanted, or would accept, from him was for him to deliver my message to you. I didn't want to listen to anything he had to say, and after the things I said to him, I consider it a small miracle that he's here at all, much less that he's willing to help. It was my stupidity and stubbornness that wasted your time, Garth, not Veil's, and I apologize to both of you."

Garth nodded to me, then to Veil. Veil nodded back. It looked like things were all right.

"What I have to tell you could be nothing more than just another ninja bullshit story," Veil said carefully, looking at my brother.

Garth didn't smile. "This is one I'll listen to very carefully."

"Okay. I mention, and underline, that possibility, because that's what I always considered it to be. Now I'm not so sure. What makes me begin to consider the possibility that it's true, Garth, is, first, Mongo's description of the mark on the back of the gunman at the hotel, and second, what you had to say about Sinclair's family background, his upbringing in Japan, his dissertation on medieval Japanese secret societies, and so on.

"The story I heard concerns a very old, and very secret, Japanese organization that calls itself Black Flame. Supposedly, it dates back more than fifteen hundred years, and it's much more than some antique yakuza outfit. Yakuza gangs operate within carefully delineated territories; Black Flame's turf is the world. They are supposed to have begun like the ninjas, as relatively straightforward mercenaries and assassins, but then their rationale for existence took on a more mystical flavor. Black Flame, so the story goes, became dedicated to the pursuit of power and wealth through the conscious and willing embrace and exercise of evil."

"It sounds like Satanism," Harper said.

Veil shook his head. "No. Satan and Satanism are Christian inventions. Black Flame's devotion to evil would spring from Tao and Shintoism, a sense of the duality of all forces in nature, black and white, good and evil. It isn't the worship of an evil force to gain supernatural power, but a willing eagerness to use evil means to accrue very real power and wealth. By evil means, include the spiritual and physical destruction of innocents."

"It sounds horrible."

Veil smiled without humor. "Probably no more horrible than the goals and methods of your average criminal gang—or a lot of corporations, for that matter. Black Flame, if it really exists, is simply less hypocritical about where it's coming from.

"Over the centuries, Black Flame grew in influence, power, and wealth because its members are very good at what they do. In a way, they can be viewed as just a very successful, overachieving yakuza gang. But what sets them apart from other criminal enterprises, and what they would claim is the fountainhead of their special skills, is the spiritual aspect of the group. The legend goes that they are masters of the so-called dark martial arts—what Westerners might, for want of a better word, call sorcery."

Garth grunted. "Sorcery?"

"Hang on awhile, Garth; I don't want to lose your attention just yet. Let's call it the psychological mastery of others: manipulation, intimidation, domination—either through violent physical means or with drugs." Veil paused, looked at me, and raised his eyebrows slightly. "This isn't what most people think of as the martial arts, but the goal is the same: total mastery of a

113

situation. Mongo and I can tell you that all the kicking, punching, and screaming business will only take you so far, for so long. Age takes its toll on roundhouse high kicks."

I said: "Amen."

"Again, according to legend, Black Flame is comprised of individuals who are masters of psychological warfare. Yes, they can break bones and crack skulls with the best of them, but Black Flame members are more likely to do it with clubs than with their hands or feet. Their primary interest is in the total domination of those who come under their influence by the breaking of minds and souls. Black Flame was the Mafia of its day."

I said: "And maybe still is."

Veil shrugged noncommittally. "I know I'm the one who brought the subject up, but it's a little hard to believe that an organization supposedly as powerful as this one wouldn't show up in FBI, CIA, or Interpol files."

"Maybe it has shown up, but the public just hasn't been told about it. It wouldn't be the first time something like that has happened. What else have you heard about this Black Flame?"

"To be a member—to have 'made one's bones' as it were— was to be guaranteed wealth, and so there was never a shortage of would-be recruits. But only young people who were already far advanced in the physical martial arts were ever accepted."

"Like the young Chant Sinclair," Garth said in a flat voice.

"Yes," Veil replied evenly. "Like the young Chant Sinclair. Once admitted as a novice, the recruit was given training in Black Flame's secrets of the kind of sorcery I mentioned—the properties of various drugs and herbs, the mastery of psychological as well as physical disguise."

"Psychological disguise?"

"Forcing other people to perceive you as you wish to be perceived. If you want to be loved, you're loved; if you want to be feared, you're feared. If you want to make yourself invisible, which is to say that you want to be ignored by everyone around you, that's what you proceed to do. Among other things, you learn to be an outstanding actor and mime in the service of your greater goal, which is to manipulate your enemies into doing what you want them to do. If you've mastered the arts of physical and psychological disguise, you can sneak up on your enemy and kill him; you can move in the world as you want."

"Again," Garth said in the same flat tone, "just like Chant Sinclair."

"Perhaps," Veil replied, looking directly at my brother. "Again, it was what you mentioned earlier about Sinclair's youth and upbringing, combined with Mongo's description of the mark on the gunman's back, that made me consider the possibility Black Flame might somehow be involved. But there are many ways in which Sinclair doesn't fit the profile of a Black Flame initiate. The story goes that there was a price to be paid for membership that few understood."

"Explain."

"The price for membership in Black Flame was the loss of personality, of individuality. That was the trap. Centuries ago, supposedly, lots of poverty-stricken families wished for a son to be accepted into Black Flame, in the belief that the family would then share in the resulting wealth and power of the son. If the father had the right connections, and the son the necessary martial arts skills, the father might get the son what amounted to a tryout. But once the son was fully accepted into the society, and the final trial was the gratuitous assassination of some innocent person, that new Black Flame member would no longer be recognizable to his family. Black Flame members were said to have been like zombies; having dedicated themselves to evil, they lost their souls, their personalities. Having been stripped of compassion, they lost the ability to love. They became colorless killing machines with no past they cared to remember. And there was no turning back once a person had been accepted as a novitiate. Another trap: any novitiate who did not live up to expectations, or who was reluctant to carry out the killing that led to full membership, or who displayed any second thoughts whatsoever about joining, was summarily executed."

Garth thought about it, shook his head. "Well, *that* doesn't sound like Sinclair. He may be a lot of things, but you certainly can't accuse him of being colorless, or of not projecting a very powerful personality over the course of the past twenty years."

115

"Maybe part of it does fit," Harper said quietly. "We know a different side to him after learning about what he did on Torture Island. The personality he's been projecting for twenty years may not be his real one. He may be a merciless vigilante, but he's not a terrorist in the way he's always depicted in the media; he's very selective about who he goes after, and he doesn't kill innocent people. He's not, it seems, quite what he appears to be."

"A real possibility," Garth said with a nod to Harper.

"Look," I said, "let's stop dancing around the issue. Veil, what do you think is the possibility that this Black Flame outfit exists today?"

By way of an answer, Veil took a pen out of his pocket, drew something on a napkin, shoved the napkin in front of me. "According to the legend, novitiates who were accepted into the society were branded, and the scar tissue embellished by a tattoo. Does that drawing look anything like the mark you saw on the gunman's back?"

I felt the hairs rise on the back of my neck as I stared at the drawing on the napkin. "It's close enough."

Garth asked Veil, "What do you think are the chances of Sinclair being a member?"

"Nonexistent," Veil answered without hesitation. "A member of Black Flame might have gone off to the Sorbonne, or joined the army, in order to further the aims of the organization, but it's unlikely. If he did, he would operate subtly. Sinclair's been the ringleader of his own three-ring circus for twenty years. He doesn't begin to fit the complete profile of a Black Flame assassin."

"Even more to the point," I offered, "he wouldn't have ripped off ten million dollars from his own people. So there doesn't seem to be much chance—"

"Oh, Jesus," Veil interrupted suddenly. His voice was soft, but there was an air of certainty in his tone.

I turned in my chair, looked into his bright eyes. "What?"

Veil cocked his head to one side, frowned slightly as he stared off into space. I could tell he was far ahead of us now, his mind searching for other connections, answers to questions we had not yet asked.

116

"Veil?"

He glanced at me, Garth, and Harper, and then his gaze came back to me. "He's an *ex*-member."

"I thought you said there were no ex-members; there aren't even any ex-novitiates."

Veil's only response was to slowly shake his head back and forth. He seemed lost in his own thoughts, the vision he had suddenly experienced.

"Go ahead, Veil," Garth prompted quietly. "Just tell us what you're thinking."

"There weren't supposed to have been any members who weren't Japanese," Veil answered distantly. "But now I'm thinking . . . that the key may have been Sinclair's father. Garth, you said the man was totally immersed in Japanese culture. He arranged for the son to train in the martial arts at a very young age, and the boy was a natural. So the son progresses as far as he can go with the standard *sensei*, teaching standard techniques. But the father wanted more. What if—and all I'm saying is what if—the father approached a leader of Black Flame, perhaps through some contact he had made, and offered up his son to them in the ancient tradition?"

Harper sighed. "You're saying the father was willing to put his son in grave danger just so the boy could find work one day as an assassin? I don't think so."

"That wasn't the point, Harper," Veil replied quickly, making no effort now to hide his growing excitement. "The father wanted the son to have the opportunity to become the great martial arts master the father thought he could be. He could have been indulging his own pride, as well. He was an American, so maybe he didn't know, or fully appreciate, the kind of people he was dealing with. Or maybe he was simply betting that his son could break free of them after he'd learned the lessons the father wanted him to have. And that's precisely what the young John Sinclair did. He was accepted as a novitiate, he took their secrets, and then he left."

I winced inwardly. "And Black Flame retaliated by killing his parents. It could explain the mysterious circumstances of their deaths."

"True," Garth said. "But why not simply kill the son? Or at least kill him in addition to the parents?"

"They may have tried, and failed. Maybe John Sinclair was never that easy to trap, even as a young man. There's also a possibility Black Flame considered it even greater punishment to leave the son alive after murdering his parents, allowing him to suffer what must have been considerable grief and guilt."

"God," Harper said, and shuddered. "If it's true, that's so terrible, so sad." She paused, took a deep breath, continued, "Assuming this Black Flame society really does exist, and that the present circumstances and past history are about how Veil describes them, why are these people still hanging around here? If Veil's theory is true, I can understand why they would be interested in killing John Sinclair, but we can assume they've been working toward that goal for years. They've eliminated all people and evidence linking them to Cornucopia. So why don't they just fade away?"

"They want to kill Mongo," Garth answered, once again looking around at all the windows and exits in the restaurant, as he and Veil had been doing all evening. "They feel he's a loose end. They know he came here on an errand for Neuberger, and they're not sure how much he knows about Cornucopia and them. They would still want to kill Sinclair, but they may consider Mongo an even greater threat to them at the present time. For whatever reason, Sinclair has never exposed them; they fear Mongo might know enough to do exactly that."

Harper brushed a strand of hair back from her face. "Given the premises we're operating under, that's fair enough reasoning. But it doesn't explain why John Sinclair is sticking around too— if he really is. What does he want?"

"To destroy Black Flame," Veil said, his tone once again distant. He tapped his index finger once, firmly, on the tabletop. "It sounds like the ultimate in ninja bullshit stories, and yet it just might be true. He wants to finish a duel that began when a young John Sinclair stole Black Flame's secrets and walked away from them, continued with the murder of his parents in retaliation, and may have resumed in Vietnam when a man who may have been a Black Flame leader took advantage of his assignment

118

working for the CIA to try to destroy Sinclair by involving him in Cooked Goose, by feeding him explosive information that the leader calculated would get him killed by his own countrymen."

"I agree that it sounds like the ultimate you-know-what," Garth said in a neutral tone that made it impossible for me to gauge how much, if any, of it he thought might be plausible. He paused, looked at me, continued, "I also agree it just might be true. Some of it anyway."

In the silence that followed I struggled to share Veil's vision, to see things the way he saw them. I tried to imagine a Japan-obsessed father with intimate knowledge of and love for that culture discovering, to his joy, that his son had a preternatural talent for the martial arts, virtually Japan's national sport. Then I tried to imagine that same father learning of Black Flame, or suspecting its existence, and then, perhaps partially to feed his own ego, deciding to test the decidedly dark waters of Black Flame's powers using his own son as a plumb line. The son, of course, would have eagerly accepted the challenge of seeing if he could receive Black Flame training, ingest their secrets, and then escape—spiritually as well as physically—from their clutches.

The son had met the challenge posed by the father, but neither had fully gauged Black Flame's ruthlessness, or its implacable will for vengeance.

Years had passed. Whether Black Flame had truly been unable to catch up with Sinclair, or had simply been biding its time waiting for exactly the right moment to exact a full measure of retribution for what they considered his betrayal, was impossible to determine with certainty, as was any complete scenario. But if there was any truth at all in the scenario we were patching together out of little more than motes of data in thin air, it seemed Black Flame had waited until *after* Sinclair had become a war hero before striking at him. It could mean their strategy had been to disgrace him as well as kill him, to see him branded a traitor by his countrymen before being executed. Involve him, against his will, in the monstrous Cooked Goose.

But Sinclair's physical and mental abilities had continued to grow, perhaps beyond even Black Flame's reckoning. He had escaped that psychological and physical snare; he'd rejected the whole idea of Cooked Goose, as the Black Flame advisor had calculated he would, but then managed to kill his own would-be assassins and walk, unscathed, out of Southeast Asia. This the Black Flame master had definitely not calculated.

However, some of Black Flame's goals had been accomplished. John Sinclair, war hero, had been disgraced, and he was totally alone in the world, hunted not only by Black Flame but also by the CIA, which would go to any lengths to make certain he was never in a position to tell about the agency's aborted plan to assassinate innocent American civilians. But then Sinclair turned the tables once again. Branded a renegade and traitor, he appeared to have embraced the labels, virtually cloaking himself in the vilification heaped upon him. In effect, disguising himself. Tearing a chapter or three out of Black Flame's manual on the use of deception and misdirection to achieve goals, he had merrily embarked on a career path that would bring him, presumably, great wealth, and the kind of power one who is feared by a great many people enjoys. Branded a criminal, he would ally himself with a small band of people who fought crime; branded evil, and going out of his way to encourage that perception, he would labor to correct injustice; if Black Flame was a hole in the world through which evil flowed, he would work to stop it up. The duel continued, on a world stage; he would use the very secrets and techniques he had stolen from Black Flame to fight against them. Viewed from this admittedly bizarre angle, it was almost as if John Sinclair, from the moment he had deserted and gone into business as a globe-trotting extortionist, con man, killer, and all-around bad-ass, had actually been engaged in a kind of . . . spiritual exercise.

I was getting a headache.

"Mongo?"

I looked up at my brother, who had spoken, and found Harper and Veil looking at me as well. "What?"

"You appear to have drifted away from us. A Swiss franc for your thoughts."

"They're not worth it. This whole discussion probably isn't worth a Swiss franc. In the end, all this speculation about secret society mumbo jumbo and what John Sinclair may or may not really be up to probably isn't worth the paper it's not printed on. It's probably all irrelevant. What is relevant is that I'm the monkey wrench Neuberger dropped into some infernal machine, and I—maybe we—are going to get ground up if I can't find the Off switch pretty damn quick. I'm a target. If it's not Sinclair trying to kill me, then it's somebody else, and it doesn't much matter to me whether it's Sinclair or some bunch of loony, evil-worshipping Japanese assassins. Definitely, the man with the answers I need is John Sinclair. I don't care who's after him. I do care about the people at this table, and he may know how to get me out of the cross fire. That's relevant. So I still have to find him, and so far I can't see how anything we've discovered, or mused on, is of any use. So let's cut to the chase. Garth, what could you find out about the R. Edgar Blake that Duane Insolers referred to?"

Garth reached into his pocket and once again withdrew his notebook. He opened it, studied a page for a few moments, said, "R. Edgar Blake, when he was alive, was a very wealthy fellow. *Fortune* magazine ranked him number twenty-two one year. His holdings were many, diverse, worldwide. Two of the business articles I read implied that not all of those holdings were on the up-and-up. He seems to have spent a lot of money trying to keep his name out of the newspapers. He had a ton of business interests in the United States, including a pharmaceuticals plant in Texas. R.E.B. Pharmaceuticals held an exclusive patent to manufacture and distribute a drug called gluteathin, or GTN, a very potent hypnotic drug used to treat certain types of psychosis. He was also the founder of Blake College, now defunct, in New York City. He was very reclusive, and there's a strong implication in the literature that he was not a pleasant fellow."

Garth closed the notebook, looked up at me. "A little item of particular interest, brother. Blake was rumored to have had the world's largest private intelligence-gathering network, and supposedly had strong ties to government intelligence agencies around the world, communist as well as Western. The man played all points of the compass. In short, he was very powerful, shadowy, ridiculously wealthy, and an amoral, first-class son-of-a-bitch." Garth paused, raised his eyebrows slightly. "Oh, there is one other thing. Lest I forget, let me hasten to add that R. Edgar

Blake was the half brother of Emmet P. Neuberger's grandfather."

"Gee, Garth," I replied evenly, determined not to give my brother the satisfaction of seeing any evidence of the jolt he had just given my nervous system, "I'm really glad you remembered that small bit of information. It certainly is an interesting item. Is that it?"

"Well, there's just a bit more. R. Edgar Blake's principal residence was a castle on the shore of Lake Geneva—which, if I correctly recall my high school geography, is not too far from where we now sit. I believe you also requested that I make a note of any 'countess' that might come to my attention in the course of my exhaustive labors. One did. Living in said castle on the shore of Lake Geneva is one Countess Jan Rawlings."

CHAPTER NINE

I watched the Swiss countryside roll by outside the passenger's window in the front seat as Garth drove along the highway to Geneva. Harper and Veil sat in the back; Harper dozed, while Veil kept turning in his seat to look for a pale blue Volvo, or anything else that might be following us.

"Jan Rawlings doesn't exactly have the old European ring of a countess's name to it," I said, turning toward Garth.

"You've got that right," Garth replied casually as he glanced in the rearview mirror. "As a matter of fact she's American, an ex-social worker from New York City."

"A who?"

"I know the feeling. That was my first reaction too."

"The closest living relative to one of the richest men in the world was a New York *social worker*?"

Garth shrugged, again glanced in the rearview mirror. "Maybe Blake didn't share the wealth. Or maybe the woman's just an eccentric. A lot of rich people are, you know. Maybe she enjoyed working for a living. The title could have been bought, or it might be wishful thinking."

"Well, she's certainly in a position now to do a lot of social working."

"Indeed. She not only inherited the castle but Blake's entire estate as well; every last holding, every penny. She's got to be one of the world's wealthiest women."

In the distance, barely visible in the hazy morning, slow-moving shapes that I thought might be helicopters had appeared on the horizon. Helicopters were anything but a rare sight in Switzerland, but for some reason the sight of them made me nervous. There had been no time to try to obtain guns, if guns were obtainable, and this lack of weapons did not exactly generate a feeling of security. I asked, "No other heirs?"

"None that the obituaries mentioned."

The helicopters disappeared into some low clouds, and I turned back toward my brother. "That seems odd, Garth. With that much money at stake, you'd think there would have been third and fourth cousins crawling out of the woodwork to contest the will and claim a piece of the action."

"All I know is what I read. The same obituary that mentioned that Blake and the elder Neuberger were half brothers said she was the sole beneficiary, and the will was uncontested at that time."

"You got anything else on her?"

"Brief articles in a couple of business magazines. It seems she's pretty reclusive herself; she doesn't give interviews. She doesn't flaunt her wealth, doesn't give or go to the usual fancy parties, and generally avoids the social scene altogether. In fact, you might almost say she lives like a social worker. Presumably, she has an army of CEOs and accountants to run her business empire, and she just kind of hangs out in her castle. Rumor has it that she gives away enormous amounts to various charities, but always anonymously."

"Jesus Christ," I said. "Another money-laundering operation?"

"Could be."

"Anything else?"

"Like what? I don't think I did too badly for one night, and I'm still waiting to be properly congratulated."

"Proper congratulations on you. How did Blake die?"

"A bodyguard killed him."

"Interesting. Assassination, or did he abuse the help?"

"Unknown. The obituary simply said he was killed by one of his bodyguards, who was then killed himself."

The helicopters had reappeared on the horizon. Although it was hard to tell with the distance that separated us, it appeared to me as if they might be keeping pace with us. Veil had seen them too. We exchanged glances, nodded. The helicopters were definitely making me nervous. I was, yet again, in violation of a police order to stay within the Zurich city limits; if the helicopters belonged to Interpol or the Swiss authorities, and they were on to my presence in the rented car, I assumed we would already have been intercepted by a police cruiser. I didn't like the presence of the helicopters. I also didn't like what seemed to be my only two options: go back to Zurich and passively wait in hiding for the whole thing to blow over, whatever the "whole thing" might be, before I was blown over, or forge ahead into the unknown in an effort to increase my chances of survival. I was forging ahead. I was naturally worried about Harper, Garth, and Veil, but I had done my best to prevent them from exposing themselves to my peril, and I had to admit I was more than a bit relieved to have them with me.

I turned my attention back to Garth, said, "You mentioned that R. Edgar Blake had a private intelligence-gathering operation."

"The largest. He owned a number of satellites through his various corporations, and probably had a lot of stringers around the world. That's usually how these things work."

"Right. What happened to that business asset? Is the Countess Rawlings running that too?"

"Unknown. She may—"

"Could be company!" Veil said sharply. "Green Saab coming up on the left, Garth!"

We were in the center lane of a three-lane highway. Garth quickly glanced over his right shoulder to see if he had room, then yanked the wheel in that direction, sending us into the far right lane. "How many in the car?"

"Only one that I can see—the driver. Here he comes; he's following. He's motioning for us to pull over."

"Fuck him."

I turned around in the seat, got up on my knees, and craned my neck, trying to see around Veil, who was shielding Harper with his body at the same time as he was looking out the rear window. A short throwing knife with a flat, taped handle had suddenly appeared in his right hand. "He's coming up fast now, Garth. Close on your left."

"Okay. Anything in his hands?"

"They're both on the wheel. But he could have a gun on the seat."

"Right," Garth said evenly as he glanced in the side mirror. "I'm tracking him now. Buckle up, everybody, and hang on. If he comes alongside, I'm going to try to cut him off or ram him. If he does have a gun on the seat, we can't risk letting him get close enough to have a clear shot at us."

"Check," Veil replied calmly. "Get ready to do it now. I think he just put the pedal to the floor."

"I've got him."

I watched through the left side window in the back as the hood of the green Saab appeared, and out of the corner of my eye I saw Garth's fingers tighten on the steering wheel as he prepared to sideswipe the other car. A second later the features of the other driver came into view—pale brown hair and eyes, angular face, wispy moustache. "Hold it, Garth!" I said, grabbing my brother's shoulder. "It's Duane Insolers, the designated big mouth from the CIA."

Garth's fingers remained clenched on the wheel. "Is that supposed to make me feel better, Mongo? Fuck him. He's outta' here."

"No! If he was going to fire on us, he could have done it by now. He's got a clear shot, and the agency probably would have issued him a bazooka if that's what he wanted. He's looking to talk. It can't hurt to hear what he has to say."

Garth tilted his head back slightly. "Veil?"

"All right, we'll have a parley. I'll keep an eye on him; one bad move, I'll stick a knife in his throat."

"Okay," Garth said as he eased the car over to the hard-packed dirt on the shoulder of the highway and braked to a stop.

Veil immediately got out of the car, walked around the rear, and stood close by the window on Harper's side. Both of his hands were hanging at his sides and appeared empty, but I didn't have to see it to know that he had palmed the knife and was holding it ready. We had practiced together a few times, and I knew Veil could plant a throwing knife in the center of a target faster than most people could fire a gun.

The green Saab rattled to a halt just ahead of us, and Insolers got out. He saw Veil, unbuttoned his tweed overcoat, and held it open to show that he wasn't carrying a gun in his belt or a shoulder holster. Then he came forward, ignoring Veil. Veil didn't ignore him. As the CIA operative came up to the car, Veil stepped up to him, abruptly grabbed one of his arms, and twisted it around behind his back, forcing him down over the hood of the car. With his free hand Veil patted him down, searched through his pockets. As Veil proceeded with his business, Insolers looked up and shot me a pained look. I turned my head and looked to my left, out the window on Garth's side. The dark shapes on the horizon had disappeared once again.

"He's clean," Veil announced, speaking to Garth. He and my brother hadn't been kidding when they'd told me I was to be "handled." I was being virtually ignored when it came to security matters.

Garth nodded. Veil released Insolers' arm. I rolled down my window as Insolers straightened his overcoat, then walked up to my door and leaned down close to the window. Immediately, I was aware of the strong medicinal smell the man exuded.

"We have to talk, Frederickson."

"So talk."

"Come to my car."

"You join us. There's plenty of room."

"I have to talk to you alone."

"The fellow standing right behind you is Veil Kendry. This is my brother, Garth, and my friend, Harper Rhys-Whitney.

127

They're handling me, Insolers, and I just don't think I'd be permitted to accompany you alone to your car. We're all in this together."

Insolers shook his head impatiently as he nervously tugged on the ends of his moustache. "You have absolutely no idea what it is you're getting into."

"Insolers, if you've got something to tell me, why don't you just come out and say it? We're just a little conspicuous standing here at the side of the road."

"Either get in the car, pal," Garth said tersely, "or get the hell out of the way." He didn't bother even looking at Insolers. "Decide right now."

Insolers cursed softly, then abruptly opened the rear door and slid onto the seat next to Harper, who wrinkled her nose slightly and moved away from him. Veil remained on watch outside the car.

"You can't go where you want to go, Frederickson," Insolers said with quiet urgency.

"How do you know where we're going? Maybe we're just out for a ride, enjoying the Swiss scenery."

"You're going to the castle in Genève."

"Bingo. What are we going to find there?"

"Nothing of any use to you. But you can't go."

"But we are going. If you didn't want me to eventually wind up at Countess Jan Rawlings' castle, why did you mention R. Edgar Blake and the 'countess' in the first place? You dropped quite a few clues and dollops of information on me the other day in my hotel room. Why? Incidentally, you should be warned that these are trick questions, because I already know the answers. But I wouldn't mind having you fill us in on certain details."

Insolers pressed one hand over his eyes. When he took the hand away, he was wearing another pained expression. "It was just a mistake, Frederickson. A miscalculation. I thought you already knew much more than you did."

"Bong. Wrong answer. Spooks like you who work the field, and there are damn few of you left, don't rise to your level by giving out information to people you think already know it. Are you kidding me? I couldn't get you to shut your mouth."

Insolers' expression grew even more pained. "It's the truth. I couldn't believe you were being honest with me about your reason for coming to Switzerland. It was very important for me to find out who your real employer might be and what your real goals were. At the time I thought we might have common interests, and I didn't want us working at cross-purposes."

"Nope. Wrong answer again. I can see I'm going to have to prompt you. You see, if I'd met you six months from now in some bar in New York and you told me that story, I'd have no reason to doubt you. However, the fact that you are now sitting in the back of this car proves that you have gone to considerable trouble, and probably gone without much sleep, all in order to keep track of my movements and everybody I've talked to since you talked to me. You've obviously been very curious about what I might find out. Now, what does that tell me?"

"You shouldn't take my presence in the back seat of your car so lightly, Frederickson. What it should tell you is that if I can follow you, so can other people."

"That's been true all along. But now, suddenly, you want to call the game off, and *that* I'd really appreciate having you explain to me. It was *after* I'd finally convinced you I was really acting as nothing more than a gofer for Neuberger that you started name-dropping in earnest. You primed me just to see what I would do and what I might find out on my own. You've been trying to run me, Insolers, get me to do something for you that you couldn't do yourself. What? What do you possibly think I can find out that *you* don't already know, for Christ's sake? And why, all of a sudden, do you want me to stop?"

I had been turned around, talking to Insolers through the space between the two bucket seats in front. Now Insolers leaned forward so that his face was very close to mine.

"You've got it all wrong, Frederickson. You've cooked up a fantasy with teeth that could get you all killed."

"Why don't you just say why it is you don't want us to go to Blake's castle to meet the countess?"

Insolers sighed, again tugged at his moustache. He glanced out the side window, as if gathering his thoughts, then looked back at me. "The countess isn't going to talk to you, Frederickson.

I guarantee you that. The countess isn't even a countess. She's just part of a very elaborate cover for a very large and very secret CIA operation."

"Aha. Now we're getting someplace. Did R. Edgar Blake work for the CIA?"

Insolers' laugh had no trace of humor in it. "Hardly. But, as you may already know, he ran his own intelligence-gathering business. It was sort of like a hobby with him, and he was pretty good at it. He had his own company satellites, good economic analysts, and great contacts in business and industry all around the world. Among other things, he housed a multimillion-dollar complex of computer gear in that castle, and he kept elaborate files on all sorts of things, including lots of sensitive information about the many government intelligence agencies he routinely did business with. The CIA often used him as an asset, buying information we didn't have, or sometimes just to verify something we suspected, like crop failure in the Soviet Union. He also did business with the KGB. He was often a useful go-between.

"We were perfectly happy with the arrangement until one day Blake decided to switch from passive information gathering to go into actual operations. He owned a company in Texas that manufactured a drug called gluteathin, or GTN. The drug—" Insolers paused when he saw Garth and me exchange glances. "You already know about this?"

"Just tell your story, Insolers," I said. "So far, you haven't touched on the points that interest me most—why you've been trying to run me, and why you now want me to stop."

"Just listen, Frederickson. Gluteathin is an extremely powerful hypnotic drug used for treating schizophrenia and severe delusional psychoses. It puts a normal person into a deep, drug-induced trance in which the subject is highly suggestible, and the person can be made to forget anything he said or did while he was in the trance. Blake's researchers also came up with a little sweetener that they added to the mix—a chemical compound that amplifies strength, like a continuous surge of adrenaline. Blake figured he had the makings of a pretty good weapons system that was cheap to produce and could bring in enormous profits."

Garth and I looked at each other, and I could see we were both thinking the same thing. "Assassins," my brother said tersely. "Drug a man, plant a target in his mind, and then send him off like a guided missile."

"Or a human lobox," Harper said, horror in her voice.

Insolers' brows knitted. "A human what?"

I said, "Never mind. Blake's people used this drug, gluteathin, to program assassins, right?"

Insolers nodded. "Throwaway assassins. He got his subjects from a phony psychological research program he'd set up at a college in New York he owned. Supposedly, the project's purpose was to study the long-term physical and psychological effects of prison on long-term ex-convicts. The subjects were paid, so Blake got a lot of client referrals from social workers and ex-convict self-help programs. In fact, what he was looking for was a specific psychological profile in men with sociopathic personalities, murderers who would not subconsciously resist a suggestion to kill again. When he'd find a suitable subject, he'd pluck that person out of the research project by feeding him a bullshit story about being selected for a special rehabilitation project. The man would be given an easy job with good pay, under an assumed name, in one of Blake's companies around the world. Naturally, the subject thought he'd died and gone to heaven. But, to use your brother's analogy, he was in reality nothing more than a guided missile, sitting in its silo, waiting to be programmed and fired. When Blake would find a suitable customer who wanted somebody killed, and who was willing to pay a high fee, Blake would take one of the subjects he had in reserve, drug him with gluteathin, hypnotize him, then prime him to kill the selected target. Experts will tell you that anyone at all can be assassinated, just as long as the assassin doesn't mind dying himself; all it takes is someone willing to drive a truckload of dynamite or strap a bomb around his waist. You need a kamikaze. Well, all of these subjects were unwitting kamikazes; drugged and hypnotized, they would walk right up to a victim in broad daylight to put a knife in his heart or a bullet in the brain. If the subject was captured, he would reveal nothing, because he would not remember anything. He would not recall his reasons for wanting the victim dead, because

131

he would have had no reasons. He would not recall working for Blake, and there would be no record of his employment, since he had been working under an assumed name. However, few subjects were ever captured, since they'd been programmed to kill themselves after they'd killed their victim. The police would naturally assume the assassination was merely the work of a crazed killer. If an autopsy was performed on the subject, a pathologist would have to know exactly what to look for in order to find any traces of the gluteathin and strength amplifier. A simple idea, really, given the right human and chemical materials, and very effective."

"Indeed," I said. "It sounds like the kind of program the CIA could learn to love."

"I won't deny it interested us, or that some people wished that we'd come up with the whole program ourselves. But there was no way the agency would have bought one of those zombie assassins from Blake; he already had a lot of bad stuff on us in his files, and we weren't about to put ourselves in a position to be further compromised by him. His real problem with us began when his clients started using those assassins to eliminate some of *our* favored clients. He allowed that to happen once too often, and Langley decided to put him out of business."

"The bodyguard who killed him was a CIA operative?"

Insolers raised his pale brown eyebrows slightly. "My, my, you are well informed."

"I only know what my brother reads in the newspapers. Was the bodyguard your operative?"

"No. You could describe him as an acquired asset. He was a man by the name of Tommy Wing, psychotic, long-term ex-convict originally referred to the research project by his parole officer. Tommy turned out to be so off-the-wall that Blake couldn't resist putting him to work full-time as a combination chief bodyguard, executive of sorts, and exotic house pet. In prison he'd acquired the nickname 'Hammerhead,' because he was a biter; in a fight, he'd use his teeth the way other men would use a shiv. Blake put him in nominal charge of keeping an eye on all his potential assassins. When it was decided that it was time for Blake to retire, it was arranged for Mr. Wing to be snatched for a few hours while he was in this country on one of his supervisory trips. He was shot up with gluteathin, programmed to kill Blake, and then sent on his way to Geneva. First chance he got, he tore out Blake's jugular with his teeth."

"That little tidbit wasn't in the obituaries," Garth said drily.

"We got to Blake's personal and corporate records before anyone else, including his lawyers. We did some fancy legal—illegal, actually—footwork, called in some specialists from other intelligence organizations who were in a position to be helpful and who had reasons of their own to cooperate, used the information in Blake's files to apply pressure on those who didn't wish to cooperate, and took over the whole kit and caboodle. The CIA now effectively controls all of the wealth and other assets that once belonged to one of the world's richest men. This is a CIA operation that not even the President of the United States, much less any congressional oversight committee, knows a damn thing about. It put us in a position to finance off-the shelf operations until doomsday, but we needed a cover. Jan Rawlings was it. The papers reported that she was a social worker, but that's not true. She was a secretary for a company in New York that was in reality a CIA asset, and she was extremely loyal. We cooked up a lot of stuff showing that she had been Blake's mistress for years, and our team of specialists cooked up a will that left her everything. I was one of a number of operatives involved in the operation, so I'll have a lot of company in prison if any of this ever gets out."

"Yeah, yeah," I said impatiently. "It sounds really neat, Insolers, but before the Swiss Highway Patrol shows up, would you mind telling us what any of this has to do with John Sinclair?"

"Absolutely nothing," Insolers said forcefully. "There's no connection between what I just told you and John Sinclair. *Nada*. But what I have just described to you is the most effective and valuable ongoing CIA operation ever mounted, and you are going to make some very powerful and extremely dangerous people very dyspeptic if you go knocking on the door of that castle and start asking questions of any sort. Now, I'm not saying they'll kill you, but I'm also not saying they won't. As for me, my ass will be mulch, and I'll be extremely fortunate if all I lose is my pension. I happen to like my job, and my health is reasonably good; I'd like to keep both—which is why I do not want you going to that castle."

"Look, Insolers, why—?"

"Why did I mention Blake and the countess in the first place? It *was* a mistake. I was very much focused on John Sinclair, and I thought you might be plugged into something; there are lots of rumors in the agency that you and your brother here are wired into all sorts of things, know some top secrets. We know you're personal friends with Mr. Lippitt, the head of the Defense Intelligence Agency, and we suspect you're on more than good speaking terms with the President; some of our people actually think the two of you know things that could get Kevin Shannon impeached and put the whole administration out of business. I really did think you might already know about R. Edgar Blake and our countess, because we have reason to believe Mr. Lippitt knows. More important, I thought you might know about Cooked Goose and how it might be connected to Sinclair. I desperately wanted that information. I thought that by mentioning Blake and the countess to you, it would indicate I could be trusted. That's all, Frederickson. Obviously, I seriously miscalculated, and I suppose you could accuse me of underestimating you. I never dreamed you'd go to the lengths you have to dig into these things, and now you're going way off the tracks. It's the truth, Frederickson. I swear it."

I turned to Garth, who had been studying Insolers intently. "The man swears he's telling the truth, brother. What do you say?"

"He's very good, Mongo," Garth replied evenly. "Also very hidden."

"It's his job to be hidden. What are you reading?"

"Mixed signals. He's giving us a combination of lies and truth, but I can't tell which is which. I think he's hiding something very important."

I turned my attention back to the CIA operative with the medicinal smell. "So there you have it. What very important thing are you hiding, Duane?"

Insolers, looking thoroughly nonplussed, jerked his thumb in

Garth's direction. His face darkened. "Who the fuck is he, Frederickson? Mr. Polygraph?"

"Something like that, Insolers," I replied mildly, "and you just flunked the test. I've got no more time to hang around here, but it was nice chatting with you."

"Get out, pal," Garth said in the kind of low, flat voice I recognized all too well as a danger signal to whoever it was he might be speaking to. "The powwow's finished."

Insolers' next move was snake-quick, fluid, obviously much-practiced. Veil had searched the man thoroughly, but he would have needed a microscope and a few hours to find the weapon the man was carrying. Insolers plucked at the sleeve of his overcoat, and instantly two of the horn buttons popped off to become finger grips for a piano-wire garotte which was placed around my neck, pressed against my jugular. One good tug on the wire, and my head was going to land in my lap.

"Everybody just stay still!" Insolers snapped as Harper cried out and Garth started to raise his hands. "And you outside! Just stay there, and back off! If I even catch a glimpse of you out of the corner of my eye, Frederickson dies. Don't think I'm bluffing."

"If he dies, you die a second later," Garth said, his voice a deadly whisper.

"Big deal. Will that help comfort you at his funeral, big brother? I'm tired of fucking around with you people. We're going to the airport, and you're all going home."

I swallowed hard, trying to work up some moisture in my mouth, and I felt the piano wire press even harder against my flesh as my Adam's apple bounced up and down. "I'm not even supposed to leave Zurich, Insolers, much less the country. The police have my passport."

"Don't worry about it, Frederickson. Your passport and everybody's luggage will be brought to the airport, which is where big brother is going to take us right now. Turn on the engine and head us back, big brother."

"You've got it, Insolers," Garth said. "I'll do what you say. Let's get our friend in here first."

"Leave him. I'll send someone to pick him up, and he'll be on the next flight to New York after yours. Turn the engine on, big brother, or your brother's neck is going to spring a leak."

As Garth reached for the ignition key, I kicked out with my left foot. The toe of my shoe hit the key, breaking it off in the lock. I winced, wondering what it would feel like to have my jugular sliced like a slab of cheese. Nothing happened; the pressure of the wire on my skin increased slightly, but the steel didn't break the skin.

"You must be insane, Frederickson," Insolers said, an almost comic note of incredulity in his voice.

"Yeah, well, I'm also very impulsive," I replied in a croaking whisper, "and my impulses tell me that the people who are trying to kill me won't stop just because you've put me on a flight to New York. I'll be just as dead with a bullet in my brain as—" I stopped speaking when I caught Harper's reflection in the rear-view mirror as, ashen and grim-faced, she moved across the seat toward Insolers. "Don't kill him, Harper!" I added quickly.

No sooner were the words out of my mouth than Insolers grunted in surprise and started. The sudden move caused the wire to bite into my flesh, and I could feel a ring of blood begin to ooze down my neck. The pressure was released almost immediately, but the damage had already been done.

Harper's low-pitched, husky voice didn't quaver as she spoke to Insolers. "Before you put any more pressure on that wire, mister, let me tell you what you feel in your crotch. It's a little wooden box, and inside is a tiny little snake called a krait. It's what I use instead of Mace for solving personal problems of this nature. In Africa they call it the hundred-foot snake, because that's about as far as a man can stagger after he's been bitten by one. One flick of my finger and the lid comes off. The snake will strike immediately, and it's not a pleasant way to die. Take the wire away from Robby's neck. Do it right now."

Garth said, "You don't have to worry about suffering too long, Insolers, because I'll snap your fucking neck about one second after you tug on that wire."

The combination of a poisonous snake pressed to my groin and Garth glowering in my face certainly would have given me pause, and I liked to think that Insolers at least looked a bit

136

pale at the moment, but I had to give the man credit for nerve; I would certainly have been the first to know if his hands started to shake, but they didn't, and his voice was steady when he spoke.

"If you kill me, so be it, but this man is also dead. I *am* going to kill him if you don't do what I say. If you think about it, you'll realize that it makes no sense for you to gamble with his life when all I'm asking you to do is drive to the airport. Now get the car started, big brother. Cross the wires."

I heard the sound of glass exploding behind me, to my right, and Garth's hands instantly came up, grabbing both of Insolers' wrists and pulling them forward. The wire came away from my neck. I gasped, put my hands to my throat, and twisted around in my seat. Veil's arm was protruding through the right rear window, and his hand was gripping Insolers' throat just under the chin, forcing the man's head back. In another moment Insolers' windpipe would be crushed, his neck broken, or both.

I gagged, held up my hands. "Don't . . . don't kill him," I managed to say in a hoarse whisper.

Without loosening his grip on Insolers' throat, Veil ducked down so that he could look at me through the broken window. "Why the hell not?" he asked in a casual tone.

Garth said, "An excellent question, Mongo. Why the hell not?"

I took my hands away from my throat, saw that they were covered with blood. "Two reasons. First, we know he's been lying to us, but we're not sure what the lies are. We don't know what's up ahead of us in that castle, and Insolers could prove to be a useful bargaining chip—but only if he's alive. Second, we still don't know why he tried to run me, or what his game really is. He may yet get around to telling us the whole truth, and it could prove to be information we'll need."

"Whatever you say, Mongo," Veil said in the same casual tone, and cocked his wrist slightly before removing his hand from Insolers' throat.

The CIA operative went limp. A tremor shook his body, and then he was still, slumped in the back seat, his head in Harper's lap. For a moment I thought Veil had gone ahead and killed him anyway, but then I noticed that he was still breathing.

"He'll be napping for a while," Veil continued. "Shall we tie him up?"

Garth, who was examining my neck as he gently wiped away blood with a clean handkerchief, nodded. "We'll use his car, put him in the trunk. Mongo, it's with mixed emotions that I announce my suspicion that you're going to live. The slice is messy, but not deep. If it leaves a scar, it could be a hot topic of conversation at cocktail parties."

Harper got out of the car, opened the door on the driver's side, and none too gently pulled Garth away from me. "You tend to Insolers," she said, her tone leaving no doubt that she was unamused, "and I'll take care of Robby. I suppose you'd have thought it was *really* funny if that wire had slit his throat. Give me Insolers' shirt, and I'll see if I can't make a bandage and scarf out of it."

Garth raised his eyebrows in mock alarm, then winked at me before getting out and going around to the other side of the car to help Veil with Insolers. Harper slid onto the seat next to me, kissed me very hard and passionately, then resumed the job of gently wiping away blood until the bleeding finally stopped. I sighed, rested my head against Harper's ample bosom as I was fitted for a bandage and ascot.

CHAPTER TEN

The castle overlooking the western shore of Lake Geneva came complete with all manner of turrets and spires, and looked big enough to house your average army. It was six stories high, constructed of massive blocks of black stone, and was sitting on what looked to be ten or more acres of land in a country where real estate was so precious that it was sold by the square meter. The structure and its magnificently landscaped grounds were most impressive.

The security if, indeed, this was the CIA's most precious asset—was considerably less impressive. There was a high stone wall around the whole complex, and a massive iron gate at the entrance, complete with television camera and a speakerphone mounted on one of the gateposts; but the television camera was pointed up at the sky, and the gate was wide open. There were no guards at the entrance, at least none that were in evidence. We entered the obvious way, simply by driving in the main entrance; no sirens sounded, and no guards jumped out from behind the bushes to challenge us.

Garth drove slowly up the wide gravel driveway toward the

castle, past carefully tended gardens and lush, thick lawns. There were a number of gardeners at work, but none appeared to be security guard types; indeed, only one of them even casually glanced in our direction. We reached the circle at the head of the driveway. Garth drove halfway around, stopped at the foot of a flight of granite stairs leading up to a set of twelve-foot-high carved wooden doors.

"The CIA runs this place?" Harper asked, a note of incredulity in her voice.

"Sometimes the best way to hide something is to pretend there's nothing to hide," Veil said, and when I turned in my seat, I could see that he was looking all around us. I couldn't tell from my angle, but I suspected he had again palmed his throwing knife.

Garth turned off the car's engine, looked at me. "Now what?"

"I guess I go up and knock on the door."

"Great. You got an opening line?"

"It'll come to me."

"Veil and I will come with you."

"No. Harper, you with me?"

"I'm with you, Robby," she replied, putting her hand on my shoulder and squeezing gently.

"Then I suggest that Harper and I go up to the door. We certainly appear harmless enough. You and Veil make a pretty threatening duo, especially at times like now when you're not wearing your party faces."

Veil said, "Not a good idea, Mongo. The two of you will be exposed and vulnerable when you get out of the car, and Garth and I won't be able to protect you."

"We're exposed right now. This isn't exactly a tank we're driving around in. So far, nobody's come around to say boo."

Garth shook his head. "We don't know what's going to happen when you start asking questions."

"I'll play it by ear. Look, no matter how many people go up there, the folks who run this place will get us all if that's what they want. It's best to start off as low-key as possible."

"Robby's right," Harper declared as she perfunctorily opened the door on her side and stepped out into the driveway.

I got out, took Harper's arm, and together we started up the flight of granite stairs. I looked down to check to make certain there were no bloodstains on my clothes. I had not been wearing my jacket during my joust with Insolers, and that covered my bloody shirt. A bandage and ascot fashioned from Insolers' shirt covered the wound on my neck. I decided I looked quite presentable for a man who'd come close to having his head lopped off a short time before.

"Can I help you?"

We halted on the third step, turned to our right, the direction the voice had come from. There was a large rose garden fifteen yards from the driveway, and now a woman stepped from it through a trellis. She was quite tall and slender, stunningly beautiful, with long brown hair and large, soulful brown eyes. She wore a heavy denim gardener's apron and held a large pair of pruning shears.

"We're here to see Countess Rawlings," Harper said brightly, smiling. She made it sound as if we were no more than neighbors from down the road popping in for a spot of tea. "My name is Harper Rhys-Whitney, and this is Dr. Robert Frederickson, the noted criminologist. We have a matter of some urgency to discuss with Countess Rawlings. Would you be kind enough to inform her that we're here, and ask if she could give us a few minutes of her time?"

The brown-eyed woman set down the pruning shears she had been holding, wiped the palms of her hands on her apron, then brushed back a strand of hair from her face. She glanced uneasily in the direction of the green Saab, where Garth and Veil were watching us intently, then looked back at us. "I'm Jan Rawlings," she said tentatively, her mouth forming a nervous smile. "How can I help you?"

Now, I thought, there was an excellent question, equaled in profundity only by the question of what was going to be the first question I was going to ask. Harper solved the dilemma for me. "We'd like to talk to you about a man named John Sinclair," she said sweetly. "Do you know him, Lady Rawlings?"

The woman's mouth dropped open, and she took a small step backward. She certainly did know him, I thought, and felt my heartbeat accelerate. There was no artifice in the woman; shock—and fear—were clearly evident in her large, expressive eyes. She immediately tried to recover and disguise her initial reaction, but it was an impossible task. She put both her hands to her mouth and turned her head away for a moment, obviously trying to collect her thoughts. Finally, she shoved her hands into the pockets of her gardener's apron, turned her attention back to us. "No," she said in a trembling voice. "I'm afraid the name isn't familiar to me. I'm sorry. Has something . . . happened to this man?"

If her first reaction hadn't given her away, her question surely would have. The fear I had seen in her eyes had not been for herself. I strongly suspected that Countess Jan Rawlings and John Sinclair were something more than just good friends. "Lady Rawlings," I said quickly, suddenly feeling sorry for this woman we had so thoroughly shocked by showing up on her doorstep, "nothing has happened to him that we know of, but a great number of things have been happening to us. It's why we have to talk to him. People have been trying to kill my friends and me. I think John Sinclair knows who these people are, and he may know how to stop them. I promise you we can be trusted. If you want, I'll give you the names of some important people you can call to check up on me."

The woman lifted her chin slightly, sniffed. "I'm sorry, sir, but no purpose would be served by checking up on you. I'm sure you can be trusted, but I have nothing to entrust you with. I can't help you. Please leave."

"Duane Insolers told us to come here," I said, watching her carefully.

Her startled reaction was, if anything, even more pronounced than when Harper had mentioned the name of John Sinclair. "No," she said in a strangled voice. "Oh, no."

"No, Duane Insolers wouldn't tell us that, Lady Rawlings?"

"No, I don't know any such person!" she snapped, clearly angry now. "You all have to leave this minute! If you don't, I'll call the police!"

I looked toward the car, motioned for Garth and Veil to present our calling card. The woman seemed numb. She had placed her hands back on her face, pressed against her cheeks, and she didn't protest when Garth and Veil got out of the car. They went to the rear of the Saab, opened the trunk, and pulled out a thoroughly dispirited Duane Insolers. They removed their belts from his wrists and ankles, and each firmly took hold of one of his arms as they marched him across the driveway to where we stood. Insolers seemed very different now from the man who had defied death in an attempt to get us to turn back; he looked defeated, and he averted his gaze as the woman shot him a fiery, accusing look.

"Duane," Jan Rawlings said softly, "what have you done?"

"Jan," Insolers murmured, "I can't tell you how sorry I am. I tried to stop them from coming here."

The woman's initial shock had turned to outrage and seething anger, which now shimmered in her voice. "Duane, what have you told these people?"

"Nothing. Be careful what you say, Jan."

"Four strangers show up at my home to ask about Chant, they pull you out of the trunk of their car, and you tell me to be careful what *I* say? You've done something terrible, Duane. How could you? He trusted you completely."

I looked at Insolers, who had begun nervously glancing around us, and up at the sky. He, too, had seen the helicopters. "Damn," I said quietly. "So you're a friend of his too, part of the inner circle, just like Bo Wahlstrom, Gerard Patreaux, the Nicaraguan woman, and God knows how many other people in important places. If you'd told me that in the beginning, it would have saved us all a lot of trouble. What the hell are you up to?" When he didn't answer, I turned to the woman. "Is he here, Lady Rawlings? We're not hunting him like the others. We know he's not what most people think he is. We won't betray him, or you, but I have to talk to him. Maybe we can help each other."

"No, he's not here," the woman said coldly.

"Jan—!"

"Shut up, Duane. You've already done enough damage with your mouth, and we're not going to be able to lie our way out of it. I'm not as good a liar as you are."

"Will he be coming here eventually, Lady Rawlings?" I asked quietly, glancing at Insolers, who was continuing to scan the sky.

"I don't know," the woman sighed. "Who are you people? What do you want?"

"It's a long story which I'd love to tell you, Lady Rawlings. I'd very much like to hear your story too."

"They're here, Jan," Insolers said, his voice firmer now, unapologetic, "and they're not going away until they hear what we have to say. It's true that they can be trusted. We all have to talk, and I suggest we go inside. Also, the car should be moved out of sight."

Jan Rawlings sighed resignedly. "I'll have someone put the car around in the back," she said, heading up the stairs and motioning for us to follow her. "Welcome to my home."

·   ·   ·

"I met Chant in New York," the beautiful, brown-eyed woman said as she poured Earl Grey tea into fine blue china cups. After hearing our story, she no longer seemed angry or shocked, but had become warm and courteous toward us. I suspected that Harper, with her decidedly warm and reassuring presence, had more than a little to do with Jan Rawlings' change of attitude. I was glad my snake-charming love was with us. Also, although it could well turn out to be an illusion, I felt safer within the thick stone walls of the castle.

She finished pouring, sat down next to Harper, across from Veil and me, on the semicircular sofa in the center of the castle's massive, two-story-high library that came complete with two walk-in fireplaces. "Of course, he wasn't using his real name. He told me his name was Neil Alter. Even if he had said who he really was, it wouldn't have meant anything to me. I'd never heard of John Sinclair. I'd been working for the city's Human Services Department, and he'd been referred to me for job counseling."

"And you placed him in the psychological research project at Blake College?" Harper asked, sipping at her tea.

Jan Rawlings nodded. "Yes—as an interim measure that would allow him to make some easy money while I tried to find him a job. I would have done that with any client who had a long-term prison record, which was supposedly the case with this Neil Alter fellow. Chant, of course, knew that, which was why he had constructed Neil Alter's identity that way, and why he was in my office."

Veil asked, "To what end, Jan?"

"A Swedish diplomat who was Chant's friend had been killed by one of those drugged assassins Duane told you about, a killer whose services Blake had sold to somebody. Chant couldn't accept the idea that it had just been a random killing by some maniac, so he did some checking. He found out that within the space of a year there had been seven other incidents virtually identical to the one in which his friend had been killed. The killings had taken place in different countries, but all the victims were people of some importance in one way or another; all of the assassins were described by the police as crazed killers, and they had all subsequently committed suicide; all the killers were Americans who had only recently been released from American prisons. He did some more checking and found something else they all had in common: they'd all participated in the program at Blake College. He wanted to get into the project to find out what was going on. He did, through me, but then somebody recognized him."

"Tommy Wing," Duane Insolers said in a low voice that hummed with disgust. "Hammerhead."

We all turned to look at Insolers, who was standing twenty feet away looking out a window near the base of a staircase leading up to a wraparound balcony on the second floor. Now he pulled a heavy drape across the window, turned to face us.

"They knew each other in Vietnam," he continued as he walked over to the glass table by the sofa and poured himself some tea. "Wing was in Special Forces, and he had a very big reputation as a dangerous street fighter who liked to settle arguments with his teeth. He'd never lost a fight. He was a biter who'd absorb terrific punishment from another man's fists simply in order to get close enough for him to chomp down on an ear or nose, or any other part of a man's body he could reach. He and Chant apparently got into a hell of a battle over something, and the short of it was that Chant beat the shit out of him. They both spent some time in the hospital, but Wing was there a hell of a lot longer than Chant, and Chant was clearly the winner. It wasn't long after that when Wing was thrown out of the service on a medical discharge as a psycho. Then he bit a man to death in a bar fight, and he was shipped off to a hospital for the criminally insane. He was eventually transferred to a maximum-security prison and released on parole twenty-two years later. He was referred to the project. Blake had a decided taste for the bizarre, and Hammerhead was nothing if not bizarre. Blake pulled him out of the project and made him a bodyguard and personal aide. In the meantime, with a little help from me, Chant had made it through the selection process into the final stages of the program. That's when Hammerhead showed up one day and made him."

Veil asked, "With a little help from you? How did you get involved with Sinclair?"

"I didn't know who he really was any more than Jan did when she first met him. I was trying to set up a long-term ex-convict by the name of Neil Alter as a CIA asset I could run. You see, this Neil Alter character Chant had constructed had spent twenty years in prison for murder, but his sentence had been commuted when new evidence had turned up indicating he might be inno-cent. Only prison time, not guilt or innocence, was the criterion for getting into Blake's program, but the fact that he had been wrongfully imprisoned made me think he might be a likely candi-date for my mole.

"By this time the agency had a pretty good idea of what Blake was really up to with this project of his. We'd made a link between the assassins and the college program, but we still didn't know exactly how he was transforming his subjects into self-destructing killing machines. It was my job to find out. Chant and I were, in fact, on the same case, but he was way ahead of me; he was actually going into the program. I knew enough about what kind of man Blake was really looking for to be able to feed Neil Alter the right answers to certain questions on a battery of psychologi-cal tests all the subjects were required to take in the early stages. This got him passed through to the final, secret phase of the program where men who would eventually end up as drugged assassins were selected."

"Then Tommy Wing met and recognized him," Jan said, her voice trembling slightly. "That's when the killing started."

Insolers nodded. "Blake and Wing knew the chain of people Chant had used to get into the program, but they didn't know how much any of these people might know."

Jan said, "Assassins were programmed to kill everyone who'd had any contact with Chant as Neil Alter, including me. Chant was to be framed for all of the murders—except, of course, his own. But he escaped from the trap they'd set up for him, and then he risked recapture and certain death to come and rescue me. I stayed with him, because that was the safest place to be; if I'd stayed in New York, Blake would only have sent another assassin after me."

Insolers walked around behind Jan, reached out as if to touch her shoulder, but apparently thought better of it and dropped his hand back to his side. "By this time I'd figured out who Neil Alter really was," the CIA operative with the medicinal smell said. "When I informed my superiors, I was told in no uncertain terms that my primary task was now to track down John Sinclair. While Chant, with Jan, was hunting down Blake, I was to close in on and kill him. Unfortunately, I was the one who ended up being captured by Blake's men, along with Jan. We both wound up in a laboratory at R.E.B. Pharmaceuticals in Texas with glutca-thin dripping into our veins."

"Chant came for both of us," Jan said quietly. "Alone, he infiltrated a secure facility guarded by at least a dozen highly trained men." She paused, glanced over her shoulder at Insolers. "He knew by then that you had orders to kill him, but he saved your life along with mine anyway."

Insolers stiffened slightly, nodded. "That he did. We had to reach a truce, an accommodation, to work together to shoot our way out of there. Afterward, we decided to continue the truce until—and only until—Blake's operation was completely put out of business. We had to trust each other for a limited period of time, but our understanding was clear: when our business with Blake was finished, he would be fair game again—I would be too, for that matter, but he'd never shown the slightest interest in killing me.

147

"He faked me right out of my shorts in the endgame. He dumped me, infiltrated this castle alone, and engineered the neat trick of getting Hammerhead to bite his boss to death. By the time I got there—in fact, he'd summoned both Jan and me—he was in charge of the whole damn place. He'd struck a deal with Blake's overall chief of security, he had control of the computers and all the damning information in Blake's records, and he had me cold." He paused, smiled wryly. "Typical of Chant, he then suggested that he and I cut a deal. He pointed out that we'd learned to trust and work with each other while we were shutting down Blake, and he would take my word on the proposed bargain, if I chose to give it. If, on the other hand, I felt duty bound to decline his offer, he could arrange for me to be shot then and there by the six security guards who were holding guns on me. I decided to accept."

Garth, who had been sitting perfectly still and very attentive across from me on the end of the semicircular sofa, now crossed his legs and spoke for the first time. "What was the deal?"

"I was to get all of the credit for unmasking Blake's assassin program and destroying it. As far as John Sinclair was concerned, he'd simply escaped one more time, and his whereabouts were unknown. However, I was now to act as a kind of super-broker between unnamed—and fictitious—members of Blake's family and various intelligence agencies, including the CIA, around the world. Like I told you in the car, they took care of all the forged documents and legal work that had to be done in order to transfer everything that Blake owned over to Jan. In exchange, they would have access to all of Blake's files in order to remove any items of information they might be uncomfortable with; only minor items of an embarrassing nature would be kept by Miss Rawlings, as a gesture of good faith."

"But Sinclair had copies of everything."

"Sure, but only Jan and I knew that. It made me the guarantor, the watchdog, of the bargain; they got what they wanted, and Jan's inheritance was never to be successfully contested by anyone, anywhere, at any time. And she was to be completely left alone. Needless to say, everyone went for it; as a matter of fact, all of the other parties were ecstatic. They were really anxious to clean out those files."

Garth cocked his head to one side, narrowed his eyelids slightly as he studied Insolers. "And you never mentioned Sinclair to any of these people?"

Insolers laughed. "Are you kidding me? Talk about a deal-breaker! Any one of the parties involved would have bombed the place before they turned it over to anyone at the request of John Sinclair. No. They got what they wanted, and this castle is a free zone as far as all those agencies are concerned. They're not interested in Jan, or the money. That attitude would change very rapidly, to say the least, if they even suspected that this was John Sinclair's principal place of residence. But they don't suspect it—yet. I have to assume that they monitor what Jan does with her power and money, but she's astute; she's done nothing to threaten them, and she's a prime mover behind all sorts of good causes. She is what Cornucopia only pretended to be."

Harper turned to the woman sitting beside her. "How he must love you, Jan," she said quietly.

"And Jan him," Veil said thoughtfully. "Sometimes it takes as much love and courage to accept a great gift as it does to give it."

Jan's only response was to lower her eyes. Harper glanced at me sharply, and I felt my face grow warm. I looked away.

"Obviously," Veil continued, looking at Insolers, then at Jan, "the deal has held up for years. Jan, I have to tell you that Insolers came about as close to dying as a man can get in an effort to try to stop us from coming here. He seems to be a man of his word."

"Which brings us," I said, turning my attention to the CIA operative, "to the question of just why Mr. Insolers is in Switzerland in the first place."

Jan made an impatient gesture with her hand. "It was always clearly understood that Duane had the right to continue hunting Chant. It's his job." She paused to fix her gaze on the rodent-faced man, and when she continued, there was more than a hint of anger in her voice. "But not here; not in our home. Like you said, Duane, it was also clearly understood that this castle is a free zone. You had no right to lead people here, Duane. You have no right to be here yourself."

"I didn't come here to hunt him, Jan," Insolers said evenly. "I came to warn him."

Jan frowned uncertainly, shook her head. "Warn him?"

"I don't have any interest in hunting or killing Chant, Jan, even if it is supposed to be part of my job. You may not know it, but he's been feeding me bits of information over the years, just as he did with Bo Wahlstrom and others. Those bits have proved invaluable, and I might even daresay that the good guys have won a couple of battles because of information he's provided. On paper, if you will, we're enemies, but we're also bound together by the agreement we made. That's all well and good, but the fact of the matter is that I owe the man my life and more, and I know it. Just keeping my part of the bargain isn't enough. Pardon me if I sound less cynical than you've come to expect, Jan, but I came to Switzerland to pay off my debt. I don't want him killed, and I don't want him captured. So I came to warn him."

Jan Rawlings looked decidedly unconvinced. "Of what, Duane?"

"It's an assassin, Jan. The CIA has an assassin in place."

The tall woman's response was to smile thinly, set down her teacup. "Duane, I can't believe you're serious. During the past two decades, when has there ever been a time when Chant *wasn't* being hunted by assassins sent by a dozen different governments, or hit men from criminal organizations like Blake's? Your own employer has an open contract out on him."

"This time it's different," Insolers said in a low, tense voice. "This assassin is different."

Jan looked up at him. "How different?"

"I'm not sure. I don't even know if it's a man or a woman. I do know that I've never seen the top people in the company so confident about their chances of finally bringing him down. They know something. It may be a very special assassin with certain information about Chant, but from hints that have been dropped I'm afraid it's someone in the inner circle, someone he trusts, and may even go to for help—or someone who knows how to reach him. I think the agency is forcing, or paying, a friend to betray him."

Jan stiffened and turned her face away. "I don't believe it, Duane. Chant has never been wrong about the people with whom he's chosen to share his secrets. In more than twenty years, you're the first person who's ever put him at risk."

"I didn't come here to betray Chant, Jan. I came to help him."

I asked, "Why didn't you just call Jan and deliver your message, Insolers? She'd have relayed your warning, and you'd have accomplished your goal."

"Because that would have posed an unacceptable risk. If I'm right about this assassin being an insider, it could mean the person is a servant. I know Jan and Chant have dozens of people working for them, at different residences around the world. I couldn't take a chance that her telephone might be bugged."

"Then you should have written her a letter."

"Same answer; her mail is possibly being monitored, intercepted. And I didn't want to come here to see her; I'm watched, just as I watch other people. I felt I had to contact him in the field because Sinclair is definitely up to something. In the past, after an operation like the scam he pulled on Neuberger, he'd simply have disappeared—quietly come back here, or gone off with Jan to one of their other homes. But he's still out there, and he's leaving tracks all over the place, playing cat and mouse with Interpol and the Swiss authorities, not to mention all the people who want to kill him."

I shook my head. "What kind of tracks?"

"American spy satellites can not only hear a pin drop, Frederickson, they can usually see it—if they're aimed in the right place. Sinclair knows where they're aimed. He's been making telephone calls he knows will be heard, allowing blind mail drops he's used in his business for years to be exposed just so people will think he's trapped and panicking. He's neither. He's doing it on purpose. I think he may be the one doing the trapping, inviting—or sucking in—his enemies, or one particular enemy, for a showdown." He paused, looked at the brown-eyed woman. "Am I right, Jan? Is that what he's doing?"

Jan, now obviously troubled, slowly shook her head. "I don't know. He hasn't been in touch since this all started."

"Can you get in touch with him?"

The woman didn't reply.

"I considered it an unacceptable risk to try to contact you in any way, Jan," Insolers continued. "I did everything I could to keep these people away. I've been trying the best I could to contact him in the field; I was hoping that if I sent out enough signals, he might contact me, and I could deliver my warning."

"Insolers," I said, "you seem to be forgetting the fact that you pointed me here."

"I did not point you here, Frederickson," Insolers replied tersely, impatience and a hint of anger in his voice. "Not intentionally anyway. I was trying to send a signal through you. When you showed up in Zurich, I was absolutely convinced you were a part of his network, a friend who'd come to help him do whatever it is he's trying to do. With your background, you fit the profile of the kind of person Sinclair has crossed paths with, and befriended, over the years. These people are incredibly loyal to him. I wasn't about to swallow what I considered then to be a cock-and-bull cover story about doing donkey work for Neuberger. I was in a hurry to get in touch with Sinclair, and I made a snap decision that the fastest way was through you. I was wrong, okay, but at the time I considered it vital to convince you I wasn't an enemy. That's why I said the things I did. I figured that by mentioning Blake, I'd prove to you that I was on Sinclair's side. I couldn't imagine that you'd dig as deeply and as fast as you did into something that didn't mean anything to you."

"If you were so certain I was Sinclair's friend, how did you know I wasn't also the betrayer you're so certain exists?"

Insolers laughed. "You're not the betraying type, Frederickson. Your reputation truly does precede you. I was just trying to nudge you in the ribs to get you to see that *I* could be trusted. I nudged too hard, obviously, and too often."

"What happens now, Duane?" Jan asked quietly.

Insolers sighed, glanced toward the curtained window. "We have to get out of here. Now. I just hope it's not too late."

"Why, Duane? Do you think you've been followed?"

"I don't know for certain that we haven't. If we were seen coming in here by anybody who may have been following us, they could have put things together. They may be waiting, either for Chant to show himself if he's in here, or, if he isn't, simply to show up. But if they decide to move on us, we could all die."

"Where do you propose that we go, Mr. Insolers?" Harper asked. "You may recall that they're after Robby too."

"I'll take you all to a CIA safe house. You'll be protected there until this business is sorted out. Jan, you'll close down the castle, make it obvious to Chant that you're not here."

"I pass," I said. "I can't afford to go into hiding, because there's nothing to be sorted out as far as I'm concerned. If the people hunting Sinclair can't get to him, they may just fade back into the woodwork and wait for another day. But they know where I live. You can take Har—"

"Don't you dare say it, Robby!" Harper snapped. "Don't you *dare!*"

"We're out, Insolers," Garth said evenly. "But we appreciate the offer."

"Jan?"

Jan Rawlings shook her head. "If you have been followed and there are people outside watching my home, it's doubtful they'll let us leave. If there's nobody watching, I'm as safe here as I would be anyplace else. I won't go anyplace where Chant couldn't find or get in touch with me."

"And if you're being used as bait?"

"Chant will know what to do," she replied, then looked around at the rest of us. "You're all welcome to stay here, if you like. I know you mean Chant no harm, and I believe he'll trust you. I believe he'd want me to extend this invitation. If he does get in touch, then Dr. Frederickson can discuss whatever it is he wants to discuss with him." She paused, again looked at Insolers. "I'll give Chant your message, Duane, but you're welcome to stay too, if you want. I'm sorry I spoke to you the way I did. I know you didn't mean any harm, and Mr. Kendry pointed out that you risked your life to try to keep this secret safe. You don't claim to be a friend of Chant's, but I know that he thinks of you as one. I do too. You've kept your part of the bargain over the years, and I appreciate that. Of all the people Chant has struck bargains with, you're the one who's always been in the best position to betray him. You haven't. Again, I'm sorry for the things I said."

"There's no need to apologize, Jan," Insolers said quietly, "but I do thank you for your words. The reason I came to Switzerland is that I do consider you and Chant my friends. Talking to you is the same as talking to Chant, but I would like to stay a little longer to try to see if there's anyone else hanging around here."

Veil said, "If you wait until nightfall, I'll be able to find out if there are men on the grounds."

Insolers looked at Veil, narrowed his lids slightly. "Are you that good?"

It was Garth who answered. "Oh, he's that good."

Insolers nodded, and I turned to Jan Rawlings. "Lady—"

"Jan, please. In the first place, as you already know, I'm not really a countess at all. Good grief. In the second place, if you're going to be my guests for an indefinite length of time, we may as well be on a first-name basis."

"Then you'd better call him Mongo," Garth said with a wry grin. "He hates 'Robby,' and Harper's the only person who calls him that. But then, she knew Mongo before he was Mongo. There's Harper, Mr. Kendry is Veil, and I'm Garth."

The woman nodded to my brother and Veil, then smiled at me. "Then Mongo it shall be. I believe you were about to say something."

"Actually, I was about to ask something. Jan, I think Insolers is right about John Sinclair purposely using himself as bait to draw in an enemy. It's one enemy, one group, in particular that I think interests him, and it's a bunch of Japanese assassins, possibly all members of a secret society. I believe the ties between them go back many years, and your man may see this as an opportunity to take care of business once and for all. Does what I've just said mean anything to you?"

Jan shook her head. "Chant was born and raised in Japan, as you may know," she answered, looking puzzled, "but I don't know about any secret society of Japanese assassins. But then, I know there are a lot of things Chant hasn't told me. I suppose I really don't want to know. The one incident I was involved in with him was quite enough for me, thank you very much. I still have nightmares about those men."

Her tone had the ring of truth, and she had already demonstrated that she had little skill at hiding her emotions or dissembling, but I looked over at Garth anyway, just to make sure. He nodded slightly. She was telling the truth.

"Jan," I said, looking back into the woman's soft, brown eyes, "does he have a mark on his body? It would probably be on his back, but not necessarily. It would be quite large, a combination of burn scars and a tattoo. It would look like fire burning black."

Jan Rawlings' response was immediate, and as dramatic as when Harper had first spoken John Sinclair's name. Her eyes went wide with shock, and she gave a little gasp. "Yes," she said. "That's exactly right. How do you know that, Mongo?"

"Well, well, well," Garth said quietly. "Bingo."

"Jan, it means—"

I stopped speaking when both Garth and Veil suddenly leaped to their feet. Veil gave a slight shrug of his right shoulder, and I knew that his throwing knife had slipped from the spring-loaded scabbard strapped to his forearm and was now in his palm. I stood up, turned and looked in the direction of their gaze.

To my astonishment, I saw a man who looked to be in his late twenties or early thirties standing on the balcony above me and to my right, casually leaning on the railing. He was looking down at us with what could only be described as a silly grin on his face. He was Japanese and, like many of his generation, quite tall, close to six feet. He was handsome, with piercing black eyes that seemed to have no pupils, black hair, high cheekbones, and smooth skin. He wore black linen slacks, expensive loafers, and a red and gray Harvard sweatshirt.

Veil, the only one among us besides Harper who had a weapon, wasn't waiting for the man to introduce himself. His right arm suddenly came up in a softball fast-pitch motion, and his knife flashed through the air. But the Japanese was just as quick. Without any wasted motion—indeed, without even taking his left foot off the bottom rung of the balcony railing—he merely moved his head an inch or so to his right, and Veil's knife sailed on up past his throat and embedded itself at an angle in the ceiling.

Garth, Insolers, and I moved to protect Harper and Jan, while Veil sprinted toward the narrow stairwell leading up to the balcony. It was a pointless exercise. Six Japanese men wearing expressionless faces and black turtleneck sweaters under steel-gray jumpsuits suddenly emerged from the shadows between the deep bookcases set along the walls around the balcony. Four of the men carried automatic rifles, while the other two held small grenade launchers. One of these fired a grenade at Veil's feet, while the other lobbed a grenade into the center of the sitting area where the rest of us were standing. The grenades exploded with a sound like champagne corks popping, and we were instantly surrounded by a pinkish-yellow mist that had the unlikely smell of sour pickles. There was no time, no place, to run, and Harper and I just managed to find each other in the sour-pickle fog and embrace before the thick mist entered our lungs, and the pinkish yellow around us faded to black.

CHAPTER ELEVEN

I'd been drugged with various and sundry concoctions on more than a few occasions in my life, but I'd never experienced a sensation quite like what I felt upon regaining consciousness. I was sitting, if sitting was the word, about where I'd been before our Japanese guests had arrived on the scene. Actually, it would be more accurate to say I was propped up, my head leaning back against the sofa, my hands resting limp on either side of me. I could move my eyes, head, and mouth, but that was all. I had no sensation whatsoever in the rest of my body. I would have suspected succinylcholine, or perhaps a curare cocktail, but those powerful drugs would have paralyzed my entire nervous system, and I was having no difficulty breathing. Whatever they had juiced me up with seemed to work only on the large, smooth muscles of the body, and I was most impressed with the effects of the drug. I could tell by the way the others were placed on the sofa that they, too, had been drugged. Harper was next to me, but her head had slid over onto my right shoulder. Jan was seated in the curve of the sofa, and Garth, Veil, and Insolers were directly opposite us.

The young man out of uniform in the Harvard sweatshirt was standing at the open end of the sofa, next to the glass coffee table, a few feet to my left. Five of the six other men were standing behind him in a semicircle, holding their weapons at their sides. The young man still had a supercilious grin on his face, and it occurred to me that he might suffer from some nervous disorder. However, the faces of the other men were totally impassive. The most startling feature of all the men was their eyes; I had never seen eyes like them, at least not in humans. There seemed to be no life in them; they were an almost uniform matte black, like the button eyes of dolls, as if something in the men, perhaps their very humanity, had been extinguished.

"You must be a Black Flamelet," I said, rolling my eyes in the direction of the young man in the sweatshirt, confirming to myself that I could speak without great difficulty, even if my words were slightly slurred.

The man's laugh was a giggle, a grating, effeminate sound that didn't reflect at all in his eyes. I decided his disorder wasn't in his nervous system. "That's remarkable," he said in perfect English laced with a strong Boston accent. "Really quite remarkable. How do you know that, Dr. Frederickson? Where did you hear the words 'Black Flame'?"

"Wouldn't you like to know?"

"Yes, I would," he replied casually. "And I will know."

"Who are you?"

He giggled again. "You can call me Bobby, or you can call me Zimmy, but I prefer that you call me Al."

"Whatever you say, Al. Typical Japanese name?"

"What have you done with my staff?" Jan asked in a hoarse, harrowed whisper.

"We've discharged them," the young man said, punctuating the words with a high-pitched bray even more grating than his giggle. "They've all been fired."

"God," Jan murmured, closing her eyes as tears came and rolled down her cheeks. "Oh, my God."

I said, "I don't want to give you any ideas, Al, m'lad, but why haven't you discharged us?"

This time the leader in the sweatshirt merely favored us with a supercilious grin, revealing even, white teeth. "You are all, in one way or another, involved in this matter. You are not innocents. What value is there in simply killing non-innocents?"

"Meaning you have some other use for us."

The smile, which like his laughter had never touched his soulless eyes, abruptly vanished. "You are all bound to each other, or to John Sinclair, by ties of love, friendship, brotherhood, loyalty, trust. It will be my pleasure to destroy those bonds before I destroy you. Before you die, your hearts will be broken, and you will watch as I take John Sinclair's soul from him." He paused, looked at Insolers. "You, perhaps, will be an exception. I sense that you've contributed a good deal of evil to the world, although you're a rank amateur. You could be of use to us in the long term."

"I wouldn't count on it, Al," Insolers replied in a flat tone.

In a most curious gesture, Al slowly raised his right index finger to point at the ceiling, then just as slowly lowered it until it was touching the center of Insolers' forehead. "You are a brave man, and you defy me now even though you are afraid—or think you are afraid. You have no idea what real terror feels like. Whether or not we decide to send you back to your keepers for our future use, be assured that I will teach what real fear is all about." He paused, brought his index finger around until it was pointed at me. "Where did you hear about Black Flame? Who told you about us?"

"I can't remember."

He quickly stepped forward, reached over my shoulder, and put the fingers of his right hand behind my head, tightly gripping the base of my skull. Because of the paralyzing drug in me, I felt his fingers only as a dull pressure. But then I had the sensation that his fingers were slicing through flesh and digging into bone, threatening to lift off the top of my skull. Suddenly, the inside of my body seemed to ignite in fire. My spine, from one end to the other, felt like a white-hot poker somebody had skewered me with, and the intense heat spread like a flash fire through my stomach, then seared its way down into my genitals. I screamed, and he let go.

"Ouch, that really does smart, doesn't it?" Al said as he removed his hand from my neck and put it on Harper's. "Now, would you care to answer my question, or shall I caress the lady's neck the way I did yours?"

"Somebody mentioned it to me. For Christ's sake, it doesn't matter. You don't have to hurt her. You've made your point."

"What is the name of this 'somebody'?"

"I told him," Veil said evenly.

Al turned to Veil. "And where did you hear of us?"

"I'm not sure. It must have been twenty years ago. I just heard some story about you. I didn't believe it at the time, but when Frederickson there told me about the mark on the back of your gunman at the hotel, I repeated the story to him. Now, leave them alone."

"Leave them alone, indeed," Al said, then turned and snapped his fingers in the direction of a doorway to his left that seemed to lead to a small pantry.

The missing sixth jumpsuited Japanese came through the doorway. He was holding a tray on which sat six steaming cups. This mysterious culinary sight did not exactly fill me with ecstasy; I doubted very much that the man called Al was going to allow us a coffee break.

"There are many things I wish to know," Al said, idly patting the Harvard logo on his sweatshirt. "Although I thoroughly enjoy hurting you, in the interests of saving time I think I will give you something that will help you to tell the truth."

The man carrying the tray stepped into the semicircle formed by the sofa, stopped in front of Garth. Al took one of the cups, held it to Garth's lips. Garth turned his head away, and Al put his free hand on the back of Garth's neck.

"Don't do that," I said quickly to Al. "Garth, drink it, for Christ's sake. We can't be in any worse shape than we're in, and you'll end up drinking the shit anyway. Save yourself a lot of suffering."

My brother glanced at me, anger and frustration in his eyes. Al took his hand away from Garth's neck, again offered him the steaming cup. Garth drank whatever was in it, grimaced. The man moved on to Insolers, then Veil.

I was the last in line. The bluish-green liquid smelled and tasted like a burning tire dump, and when I swallowed the thick, greasy brew, I did some grimacing of my own. It left a distinct aftertaste of rotting meat. My stomach immediately began to churn, and I was afraid I was going to be sick. I wasn't, but I remained just at the edge of vomiting, and it was only by concentrating my attention on a shelf of books across the room and taking measured, deep breaths that I was able to keep the contents of my stomach down. From the distressed looks on my companions' faces, I could tell we were all experiencing the same sensation. If the thoroughly nauseating brew was supposed to be some kind of truth drug, I much preferred sodium pentothal.

Al placed a chair in the space between the two ends of the sofa, sat down, and casually crossed his legs. "Now," he said easily, "I believe we're ready to begin our interrogation. Before I ask my questions, let me warn you that the tasty beverage you've just consumed will betray you at once if you attempt to lie. Then you will be punished. However, if you simply relax and answer my questions truthfully, you will be all right. We will begin with . . . you." He turned slightly, pointed his index finger at Duane Insolers. "You work for the Central Intelligence Agency. I would like to know what position you hold, and precisely what it is you do."

"I'm a station officer. I—"

Insolers suddenly stopped speaking and gasped, as if his breathing had been cut off. His eyes went wide, and his face drained of color. He barely managed to turn his head to one side before vomiting onto his left shoulder. He continued to vomit until all he could produce were dry heaves, and then he again began gasping for breath. After he had recovered, Al unhurriedly rose from his chair, stepped close to Insolers, and put a hand on the back of his neck. I turned my head away and closed my eyes as Insolers screamed.

At Al's signal one of the uniformed men went to the pantry, returned a few moments later with a towel, which he used to clean the vomit off Insolers and the sofa. Insolers' head was bowed, his breathing ragged. I doubted very much that he wanted to repeat the experience.

Al touched him gently on the forehead, and Insolers flinched. "You were saying . . . ?"

"I'm . . . deputy director of operations," Insolers murmured.

Now, *there* was a surprise, and a glance at Garth and Veil confirmed that they were as astonished as I was. It seemed absolutely incredible that one of the top men in the CIA, the big spook in charge of all the little spooks, should be off the reservation, traipsing around Switzerland, alone, where he would be fair game for enemy operatives, or jokers in the deck like Al and his glum chums. The position of deputy director of operations was so sensitive that the officeholder's photograph was never even published. Information obtained from Insolers could close down dozens of networks, our own and our allies'.

"Why are you here?"

"Looking . . . for Sinclair. Just like you, you son-of-a-bitch."

"The deputy director of operations is a very important man. Why were you assigned to this?"

"Assigned . . . myself."

"To kill him?"

"To warn him. There's something going on . . . special assassin with special knowledge about him. I thought I would be able to contact him, or that he'd contact me if he found out I was looking for him."

"Why should you take such risks to help this man?"

"I owe him. He's the reason I'm DDO. And . . . he's a good man."

Al giggled. "A good man? How quaint. Does your presence here have anything to do with us?"

"No. I've never heard of you."

Duane Insolers might hold a lot of the nation's most important secrets in his head, but Black Flame—or Al, at least—didn't show any interest at all in probing for them. Al's one and only interest seemed to be John Sinclair, and all of his remaining questions were focused directly on that single subject.

After Al had finished draining the CIA's deputy director of operations of all the information he wanted, he continued around the circle. As with Insolers, all of his questions were focused on the object of his obsession—our relationship to John Sinclair, what we knew about him, and our reasons for being in Switzerland.

162

It didn't take Black Flame's boyish leader long to finish with Garth, Harper, Veil, and me, but Jan Rawlings was another matter. Despite what she'd witnessed when Insolers had tried to lie, she started out by trying to conceal the truth, and immediately paid the price. And then, incredibly, she tried again. She ended her agony exhausted and sobbing, her screams echoing in the vast library, the contents of her stomach spilled into her lap. Finally she broke, and along with Al we learned all of John Sinclair's secrets that had been so artfully hidden for more than twenty years—his residences around the world, the many identities he had assumed, all of the people he knew, and who had helped him in the past. In the end, both Jan Rawlings and John Sinclair had been stripped naked. At a nod from Al, one of his men brought more towels and began to clean the woman. Jan turned her head away and continued to cry.

After ninety minutes or so, the effects of both the paralyzing drug and the brew from hell began to wear off. Feeling came first to my fingers and toes and then slowly returned to the rest of my body. My mouth continued to taste of rotting meat. Six straight-backed chairs were brought into the room, and we were all tied into them—with special attention being paid to the ropes and knots binding Veil. Each of us was allowed, temporarily, to keep one hand free, and, to my surprise, we were provided with hot, invigorating tea—which dissolved the bad taste in my mouth—water, and food. But I knew this was a utilitarian, not humanitarian, gesture. There was no kindness, no mercy, in the doll's button eyes of the man in the Harvard sweatshirt and his men. Al simply wanted our bodies and minds brought back up to speed for whatever other trials he had in mind for us. I did not find that thought comforting.

•   •   •

"John Sinclair's father approached my grandfather," the man who called himself Al said in an easy, conversational tone. He was sitting in the curve of the sofa facing us, his legs crossed, his arms folded across his chest. The other men had left the room, and I presumed they had taken up various positions around the castle to wait for the guest of honor to arrive.

163

"I am told the father was a most remarkable man. For a Westerner, he had a deep and subtle understanding of Japanese culture. I was very young, in a private school here in Switzerland, when these events occurred, so I never met the man; I do not know how he first heard of my grandfather, or precisely what he thought my grandfather could offer his son. My grandfather practiced the art of the chameleon, and wore many masks; different people saw him in different colors. On the face of things, Henry Sinclair wanted Master Bai, my grandfather, to teach his son the way of the ninja, as if there were any one such thing, and he offered to pay a large sum of money. It seemed John Sinclair was exceptionally gifted in the martial arts even as a teenager, and when Master Bai witnessed a demonstration of the young man's skills, he accepted both the money and the youth. It is most unlikely that either Henry or John Sinclair knew that my grandfather was the highest *sensei* of Black Flame, or understood that Black Flame acolytes must pass a final test—murder an innocent—or be killed themselves. Black Flame does not hand out promotional literature or administer written application tests.

"Obviously, Henry Sinclair underestimated my grandfather or misunderstood his life's work. This is not surprising; most Japanese would make the same mistake. Incredibly, it seems my grandfather made the mistake of underestimating the will and strength of the young John Sinclair. It is doubtful that John Sinclair was ever committed to the *act* of assassination; he wanted only knowledge of the assassin's *art*, as taught by the world's foremost practitioner. He not only managed to hide his heart and true intent from my grandfather, but rejected the final test and somehow succeeded in escaping from the immediate wrath of the society. He had stolen my grandfather's secrets and refused to pay the price for that knowledge. In thousands of years, this had never happened before, and it was an act that had to be severely punished. Furthermore, the nature of the punishment would have to be much more terrible than mere death; it would have to be exquisitely painful and prolonged. Master Bai's intention was to force him to kill his parents, but by now, with the training he had received, John Sinclair was not so easy to find.

He had become what we call an 'invisible man.' My grandfather had to settle for killing the parents himself.

"Some years later it happened that my grandfather was wearing a different mask and color, working as a highly paid consultant to Mr. Insolers' CIA, formulating the Cooked Goose operation you've mentioned. When he learned of John Sinclair's relative proximity, and realized his status as a war hero in the American armed forces, he immediately shifted his attention to the most important matter in his life—exacting revenge on the former acolyte who had betrayed and embarrassed him before thousands of years of predecessors. The plan was to have Sinclair engineer his own destruction. He would learn of Cooked Goose, which Master Bai knew he would reject, and subsequently be killed by his own people, cursed by the same nation that had so recently and profusely honored him. My grandfather insisted that Sinclair be approached by Cooked Goose recruiters, and he was. The rest you know, or have guessed. The plan did not work. John Sinclair had not been idle. He had taken my grandfather's teachings and built upon them. His powers, both physical and psychological, were very great. Thanks to my grandfather, he had become a Black Flame *sensei* himself, and yet had still avoided paying the price for those skills he had acquired.

"They would confront each other again years later, in Seattle, after John Sinclair had constructed for himself the images he reflects today: a feared terrorist and extortionist to the world at large, a worshipped hero to a select few who think they understand him and his work—and a continuing insult and deep affront to those of us who understand just what it is John Sinclair is really doing."

"What is he really doing?" Garth asked.

Al's response was a mild shrug accompanied by a thin, enigmatic smile. "Dear fellow, I wouldn't know where to begin. I fear it would be beyond your capacity to understand."

"No?" I said, cold rage welling in me at all the suffering that had so recently taken place in this room. "Well, let me give it a shot, dear fellow. It's all mind games to the two of you. You're both fucking crazy, and you both stink of death. Sure, he's a hero to the people he's helped, but the reason he's an affront to Black Flame is that he turns Black Flame on its pointed head. He uses the techniques your grandfather taught him to obliterate the guilty with the same ruthless dispatch you use to murder the innocent. In a way, you're two sides of the same coin. For years, you people and Sinclair have been playing a kind of spiritual chess game, outside the law, with the world as your board, and with the corpses piling up all around you."

"It isn't like that, Mongo," Jan said, an edge to her voice. "It's not a game to Chant. He's not evil."

Al glanced at Jan, then back at me. Again, his lips curled back in an enigmatic, mirthless smile. "Yes," he said. "Actually, it *is* rather like that, Frederickson. That's perhaps as close as an outsider can come to understanding why Sinclair is such a bother to us."

"He's won even if you kill him," Veil said to the leader. "You're an entire organization, while he's a solo act. For years, he's been rubbing your nose in your failure to stop him from beating you at your own game. But I'm betting that when he goes down, Black Flame goes down. Why has he kept your secrets for all these years, Al? I say it's because it suits his purposes; it's the way he plays this strange game. He's kept a lot of secrets for that reason. But he's certainly made arrangements for a lot of information to come out when he dies. He'll end up even more of a legend, while you folks are going to end up looking like a bunch of boobs. His ultimate revenge will be not only to expose you, at a time and place of his choosing, but to make you look silly."

The smile on Al's face abruptly vanished, and for just a moment I glimpsed in his black button eyes the true depths of his rage and hatred. It chilled me.

"No!" he snapped in a voice that had suddenly grown slightly hoarse. "That is not what will happen. First, he will suffer far more than just his own death. He will be forced to kill the ones he loves with his own hands, and then we will kill all the others who love him. He will know depths of despair and loneliness such as few humans have ever experienced. We may allow him to live to a ripe old age with those feelings as his only companions. We will have his soul. We have learned all we need to know from you people. When we are finished, there will be nobody left alive to testify to the supposed good that he has done, or to his real motives. He will be blamed for all of the deaths here in Switzerland, including your own. John Sinclair will not be perceived as a legend, but as a curse. His story shall be as we wish it to be told; the mask we finally give him to wear will be permanent, and it will burn him to the bone."

I was experiencing a lot of conflicting emotions, the most powerful being a combination of regret and outrage at the probability that the man with a Harvard sweatshirt and no heart was no doubt right. Black Flame certainly seemed now to have the situation under control. And it wasn't only the people John Sinclair loved and who loved him who were going to die but also the people I loved and who loved me. All of Sinclair's sanctuaries had been exposed, and the woman he loved was being held captive. He would certainly come; and even if he didn't, Black Flame was now in a position to carry out the strategy their leader had outlined. I wondered how I might have handled things differently, but suspected there had never really been anything I could have done or not done that would have affected this outcome. I'd never had a chance once I had agreed to come to Switzerland. I'd dropped right into a deadly trap the moment I'd stepped off the plane, and there was no way I could have prevented Garth, Veil, and Harper from joining me, once they were aware of my predicament. That thought tended to refocus my attention on the charming fellow who'd done the dropping.

I asked, "What have you done with my good friend Emmet P. Neuberger?"

The question provoked another of Al's grating giggles. "I believe Emmet has learned his lesson."

"You haven't killed him?"

Al raised his eyebrows in mock astonishment. "*Killed* him? You think we would simply kill him after he tried to steal our money, and almost delivered us into the hands of our greatest enemy? You can't be serious."

"Neuberger was in on the original scam, wasn't he? At least he thought he was. Then Sinclair either tricked or blackmailed him into revealing the electronic access codes he needed, right?"

"Something like that. Actually, Sinclair had learned enough to do what he did without Emmet's help, but he wished to entrap the poor man—and he wanted to leave his footprints for us to find. I'm certain he now regrets that little display of bravado."

"Did Neuberger know who he was screwing with when he tried to slip money out of Cornucopia?"

"He was aware that he had certain obligations that had been passed on to him through two generations and that the penalty for betraying those obligations could be severe. It seems his imagination was not up to the task of conjuring what forms such penalties might take. You Americans use the expression 'cut him off at the knees.' We cut Emmet off at the knees, but we used a chain saw instead of an expression. You people will be killed. Although your corpses will be mutilated for effect, there won't be a great deal of pain for any of you. But then, we're not really angry with you people." He paused to giggle again, and the giggle became a bray. "I wanted to put your minds at rest."

Harper and I exchanged glances, and I saw my own love, longing, and regret mirrored in her maroon, gold-flecked eyes. I looked at Garth. My brother's face appeared blank as he stared off into space, and I knew that he was retreating into himself, marshaling his energy and resources for whatever opportunity might present itself to attack Al and his Black Flame colleagues. I wriggled my wrists and ankles, found my bonds tight. It was all very depressing.

"What happened between your grandfather and Sinclair in Seattle?" Veil asked in an even tone.

"My grandfather and sister died," Al replied without any sign of emotion. "John Sinclair had mounted an operation against a very wealthy and powerful man who had virtually enslaved a community of Hmong—the native people Sinclair had fought with in Southeast Asia. Rather than meet Sinclair's demands, the man hired my grandfather—once again wearing a different mask and color—to kill him. I don't know how the man heard of Master Bai, or how he had managed to contact him, but it's not important; indeed, it may have been Master Bai who contacted the man when he learned of the man's difficulties with Sinclair. This time my grandfather attacked John Sinclair's mind and heart, as well as his body, with a most unusual weapon—my sister, who was an expert in the more sensual of the Black Flame arts. Sinclair should have been destroyed, but he was saved by a Hmong woman who loved him. This woman killed my sister, and Sinclair killed my grandfather. Now it falls to my father and I to—"

Al abruptly stopped speaking when one of his men entered the library from a door at the far end. The man walked quickly across the library to where Al was standing, whispered something in his ear. Al frowned, turned to face the other end of the library, then loudly issued a command in Japanese.

I stiffened as three Black Flame soldiers and their prisoner entered the library. One of the men was carrying a bulky, elaborate array of assassin's equipment—a high-powered rifle equipped with night-vision telescopic sight, and a tripod with gyroscopic stabilizers. The other two assassins were each firmly gripping an arm of their prisoner, a familiar, grizzled figure with thick, silver-streaked black hair, coal-black eyes, weathered flesh, a barrel chest, and a pronounced limp. The servile, eager-to-please air I had come to associate with my ex-chauffeur was completely absent; he was obviously angry and frustrated, but most of all Carlo looked embarrassed.

CHAPTER TWELVE

Another sturdy, straight-backed chair was brought to the library, and Carlo was quickly and unceremoniously tied into it. The business with the paralyzing drug was omitted, and Al went straight to the foul-smelling, nausea-inducing "truth brew." Carlo spat out the first mouthful, and I winced as Al put his fingers on the back of the old man's neck and squeezed, with the predictable result: Carlo screamed long and hard, and after he had finished, he drained the liquid from the cup. His response to Al's first question was apparently a lie, for he vomited all over the front of his green plaid flannel shirt. After vomiting, he slumped in the chair, breathing very rapidly, his soiled chin resting on his broad chest.

"Now let us begin again," Al said cheerfully. "What is your name?"

"Carlo Santini, you little bastard," Carlo answered in a rasping voice. "Who the hell are you, and what's that shit you gave me to drink?"

"You were discovered sitting on top of a hill overlooking this estate with the equipment of a sniper in your possession. What were you doing there?"

"I was hunting pheasant, and my eyesight isn't too—"

I certainly had to give my chauffeur-assassin credit for having guts, if no brains; but courage wasn't going to save the day for him. He proceeded to empty his guts, or what was left of them, onto his shirt front. When his stomach was empty, he continued barking in dry heaves before again slumping in his chair, exhausted and pouring sweat. Now he looked completely spent, beaten.

"That's enough!" I shouted at Al as he once again started to reach for the back of Carlo's neck. "For Christ's sake, he's got the idea!"

Al didn't seem much interested in my opinion, for he went ahead and pressed the nerve cluster at the base of Carlo's skull anyway. Carlo screamed and then passed out. Al ordered that more of the dark, greasy liquid be brought to replace what Carlo had voided. When the old man returned to consciousness, he drank it feebly, without resistance.

"What were you doing on the hill, Carlo?" Al asked, resuming his cheerful tone. "Who was your intended target?"

"John Sinclair," Carlo answered in a rasping whisper that was barely audible.

"And what led you to believe you would find John Sinclair here?"

"The dwarf and his friends are here," Carlo said with a rattling sigh and a weak, desultory nod in my direction. "The dwarf has always been the key."

"Indeed?" Al said, glancing in my direction and raising his eyebrows slightly. "From what he has said, I would not have thought so. Mr. Insolers, and you apparently, misjudged his role completely from the beginning. He knew nothing."

"It didn't make any difference. Whoever you are, you misjudged his role too—but you're here. We're all here because of the dwarf."

This turn of conversation did not please the dwarf. The nausea I was suddenly feeling had nothing to do with any brew Black Flame had concocted, and I turned my head away.

"Elaborate," Al said.

"Why? You know what I'm talking about."

Al placed his hand on the back of Carlo's neck. "Indulge me."

"The CIA has always suspected that Sinclair has friends and contacts in high places, people who are both powerful and influential. The problem is that these people would die before they betrayed him, and they're not exactly loose-lipped; that's why Sinclair gave them the gift of his trust in the first place. The thing was that if just one of these people could be identified, then that person's calls and movements could be monitored in the hope that sooner or later the friend would contact John Sinclair, or vice versa, and we might be able to get the tricky bastard in our sights. When this Cornucopia thing went down, it soon became obvious that something had changed; Sinclair was hanging around and leaving signs, almost as if he were inviting people to come after him."

"He was extending the invitation to us," Al said quietly. "It was a challenge."

"He's hunting you?"

"A decision I'm sure he now regrets."

"Who the hell are you? The CIA never told me—"

"Please continue your story," the young man in the Harvard sweatshirt said with an impatient wave of his hand.

"What story? I was hired to kill Sinclair. I figured it was a good bet that the dwarf would take me to him. I was right, for the wrong reasons, probably just the same as you. You've probably already heard everything else there is to know, so why do you want to hear it from me?"

"It's because he's so goddamn afraid of Sinclair," I said, making no effort to keep the bitterness out of my voice. "He wants to understand the thinking that led everyone to follow the village idiot here, because Sinclair is no fool. He may have anticipated what would happen, or at the least realized what was going on. It's a question of who's trapping who. Our fearless leader is beginning to have second thoughts about his own cleverness."

"That's correct, Frederickson," Al said in a flat tone.

"Chant wouldn't sacrifice us," Jan said with feeling. "Not to

172

save his own life, not even to exterminate an unspeakable creature like you."

I watched Al's face as he studied the woman, and it occurred to me that he agreed with her. But he was still afraid. He turned back to Carlo, said, "If you don't want me to hurt you again, continue your story. You mentioned the CIA's suspicion that Sinclair has influential friends."

Carlo shrugged. "Interpol was keeping very close tabs on every-one of note who began showing up in Switzerland after the Cornucopia thing went down. Frederickson fits the profile of someone who might be connected to Sinclair, so when Interpol told the CIA that Frederickson was coming to Zurich to suppos-edly do something for Neuberger, the agency put me on the case. I was to follow Frederickson to Sinclair, if I could, and then kill him. I managed to latch onto Frederickson as a chauffeur."

"So much for your theory of the insider," I said to Insolers, who had a very peculiar expression of what looked like disbelief on his face as he stared at Carlo.

"You and Mr. Insolers seem to have shared the same notion about Dr. Frederickson," Al said to Carlo. "How interesting."

"If you say so, friend. I don't have the slightest notion about Insolers' notions, and I don't give a shit."

I again glanced at Insolers, who now appeared even more disbelieving. Color was beginning to rise in his cheeks.

Al took a step closer to Carlo. "You must have realized almost at once that Frederickson knew nothing—he had never met Sin-clair and had no interest in the man beyond his immediate assign-ment. Yet you stayed with him. Why?"

"Because I realized something else about Frederickson almost at once, friend: after he got sucked into the whole thing, he was damn well going after Sinclair himself. People were dying, and he was going to take matters into his own hands. Perfect. What I discovered was that people who wouldn't talk to you, Insolers, or me in a million years, namely Sinclair's friends, *would* talk to him. They confided in Frederickson, trusted his motives, trusted him to do and say the right thing. Following a man Sinclair's friends would talk to was the next best thing to following an

173

actual contact. Actually, even better; a friend or contact would never have led us here. It kind of looks to me like we've all been tracking Frederickson while he tracked Sinclair. So now why don't you tell me who you people are? Maybe we can make a deal. Our interests are the same. Since you seem to want to kill Sinclair as much as I do, I say that puts us on the same side."

Al merely grunted, then turned to Insolers. From the expression, or lack of it, on Al's face, I didn't think he shared Carlo's optimistic enthusiasm for teamwork, and I suspected that did not bode well for Carlo.

"Do you know this man, Mr. Insolers?"

"No," Insolers replied somewhat distantly as he continued to stare intently at Carlo.

"Well, well," Al said, sounding slightly amused. "Under the circumstances, I have no doubt that each of you is telling the truth. That leads us to an interesting question, doesn't it? We have here, not only in the same country but actually in the same room, the CIA's deputy director of operations, and a free-lance assassin hired by the CIA. How is it, Mr. Insolers, that Carlo could be sent here without your knowledge?"

It was Carlo who answered. "You're asking the wrong man, junior. Like you said, I'm a free-lancer. Insolers was never in the loop on this deal."

Insolers said, "A renegade operation."

Carlo shook his head, winked and smiled at Insolers. "Wrong, big guy. Not a renegade operation."

"Who tasked you?"

"Your boss. I report to the director."

"Bullshit."

Except for his eyes, which remained lifeless, Al seemed almost amused. "Carlo?" he said easily. "I think you've tweaked Mr. Insolers' personal pride to the point where he's calling you a liar. But I know better. After the sickness and pain you've experienced, and will experience again if you appear less than truthful, I believe you are incapable of lying at this point. How do you explain Mr. Insolers' ignorance of your mission?"

"You still don't get it, big guy, do you?" Carlo said to Insolers.

"Get what?" Al asked sharply.

"The agency knows Insolers is Sinclair's man, junior. He's been in Sinclair's pocket ever since the operation run by the character who owned this castle was shut down. You think anybody at Langley believed Insolers' story that he did it all by himself? Give me a break. He and Sinclair worked together, and a bond formed between them. They cut a deal afterward. The CIA smelled that from day one. The decision was made to keep him in place, and even promote him, on the chance that he might eventually lead them to Sinclair."

"Bullshit," Insolers murmured, but his face had gone pale.

Carlo shook his head. "It's the truth, big guy. Sorry to have to be the one to break the bad news to you, but you haven't sneezed or farted for years without the agency knowing about it. Then they finally came to the conclusion that you weren't really Sinclair's friend; he didn't trust you in the same way he trusted others he'd worked with. You'd struck a bargain, and each of you was holding up your end, but that was it. But there was still a possibility that your knowledge of him might prove useful one day, so they kept you around. I guess you're even good at what you do—but you were always sealed out of the loop on any real play that involved trying to get Sinclair. When you assigned yourself to Switzerland after the Cornucopia thing, the director thought you might finally prove useful by leading them to Sinclair. But what do you do? You go to Frederickson. So much for *your* influence. They wrote you off."

Insolers had proved of no value, I thought with a wave of bitterness. All he had managed to do was set me off like a bird dog on a trail that had finally led us all to this place, probably to die. "You're a fool," I said to Insolers, anger and contempt making my voice crack. "You should have been up front with me from the beginning. If you had, we wouldn't be in this situation."

Insolers frowned and slowly shook his head. His eyes were slightly out of focus, as if he were staring at something far in the past. I could understand his failing to appreciate the irony of the fact that while he was trying to turn me into an unwitting asset and run me, his own employers had been running him, without his knowledge, for years. In one sense, the CIA had been right in keeping him on the payroll, for he had finally betrayed Sinclair, inadvertently, through me.

Finally, Insolers' eyes came back into focus. He looked at Carlo, at me, and then at Al. "I don't believe it," he said in a firm voice.

"Oh, but I do," Al replied, and once again favored us with a giggle. "It's so droll, really. I couldn't be more pleased with the way this is all working out." He looked around the room, an inane grin on his face. His gaze lingered cruelly on Jan, until she finally looked away and began to sob. Then his grin abruptly vanished as he turned to the Black Flame soldier on his right. "Take him out and chop his head off, then all of you return to your posts," he said in English, probably for Carlo's benefit, then repeated the command in Japanese.

Carlo cursed and struggled against his bonds, all to no avail, as two of the Japanese lifted him up in his chair and promptly carried him out of the library.

"That's not necessary," I said to the leader. Despite his deception and attempt to use me, I still had affection for the old man. "He doesn't have the slightest clue as to what this game is really all about. What's the point of killing him?"

"One response might be to tell you that the point is that there is no point. Since he is of no consequence to Sinclair, he has no value to us. Therefore he dies. What do you care? You're all going to die anyway. He simply precedes you."

"Al, you certainly do have a way with words, you silver-tongued devil."

"What happens now?" Garth asked.

Al giggled. "What happens now? We wait, of course."

Jan had stopped crying, and when she spoke, her tone was firm, icy. "He won't come. You're a fool if you think he will. By now, he knows you're here."

"That's precisely why he will come. He knows we're here, and he knows we have you, as well as his old companion-in-arms, Mr. Insolers, as well as these other three men and a woman, who, while strangers, would have helped him if they could. He also knows that if he does not arrive soon, your screaming will begin; we will take you apart piece by piece, one by one, until he does

176

finally choose to favor me with his presence. First, he will contact us and offer to give himself up in exchange for your freedom. Of course, we will accept the terms."

"No. He would know better than to trust you to keep your word; trust goes against everything you believe in. He would know you intend to kill us all anyway."

"Of *course* he knows this, dear lady. But he will turn himself in to us in any case. He will do it precisely because he knows you must die, and he will choose to die with you. Alas, dear lady, he is not only a man of ferocious honor but a hopeless romantic. He will come to us, and then we will begin John Sinclair's final ceremony. We will wait."

•   •   •

We waited; tied in our chairs, we had little choice. Harper and I exchanged frequent glances of love and longing; in the dim moonlight that filtered in through the windows by the staircase I could see tears glistening in her eyes. She would occasionally try to start up a conversation, but I wasn't much into idle chitchat, because I was busy with another matter that required all my concentration, and the breath control I had to employ didn't lend itself to talking.

I looked around at Veil, and from the intense look of concentration on his face, as well as the occasional ripple of muscle across his chest, in his shoulders and thighs, I could tell that he was preoccupied with the same matter. Garth, not the greatest conversationalist to begin with, had again retreated deep into himself, conserving his energy for what he hoped would be at least one shot at our captors. Finally, Harper and Jan ended up talking with each other, often with long pauses between sentences, desperately trying to use words, and the sounds of their own voices, to distance themselves from the terror they surely felt.

Suddenly, the lights in the library came on, and I quickly relaxed, stopped what I was doing, and concentrated on breathing regularly. Al, flanked by two of his men carrying pitchers of water and trays of sandwiches, strode briskly into the room. I looked at Garth, saw his eyes take on life at the possibility that at least one of his arms would be freed to allow him to eat and drink. I was happy to see that was not going to be the case. The two Black Flame soldiers fed us. We ate and drank sparingly; by now, all of us were stained with our own urine, and we didn't wish to make matters worse.

"I have a message for you, Countess," Al announced cheerfully. "John Sinclair wants you to know that he loves you very much."

"You're a liar!" Jan snapped.

"Well, it's true those weren't his exact words during our telephone conversation, but I'm sure that thought was in his mind. Why else bother to call?"

"No!"

"Yes. He promised to be here shortly after dawn to give himself up in exchange for letting you all go. I told him you would all be released after we had him in custody. He agreed. Of course, as you pointed out, he knows better; he's planning to join you in death, which I really find quite touching. But he has no idea what we have in store for him. Before you die, Countess, you will see John Sinclair as a thoroughly broken man begging us to kill him. He will be asked to kill you all with his bare hands, and he will do it. Now, why don't you all try to get some rest? Sleep well."

· · ·

So we waited some more. Clouds had covered the moon, cutting down on the light coming in through the windows. That was just fine with me, because it would further hinder any secret watcher from seeing what it was Veil and I were trying to do.

Garth's low voice rumbled in the night. "Mongo, you awake?"

"Oh, yeah. Keep it down, because we don't know if anyone's listening."

There was a pause, and then Garth spoke in an even lower voice. "I still have the little item Insolers here used on you; it's wrapped around my wrist, outside my shirt cuff. I was hoping to use it to introduce Al to his head, but now I'm thinking I may never get the chance. Maybe if we can hobble our chairs back-to-back, you or Veil can get it off my wrist and we'll see if it can cut rope."

"They'd be sure to hear the chairs scraping on the floor, and

I'm not sure it would work anyway. But not to worry. Veil, how are you doing over there?"

"I'm doing," Veil replied in a matching soft whisper, purposely slurring his words slightly so as to make them even harder to hear and understand. "What about you?"

"Ten minutes, maybe less. Are we coordinated?"

"I'm about a half hour behind you. Considering the fact that I'm supposed to be your teacher, and you always hated to practice this, I find your newfound speed and skill rather embarrassing."

"Well, they paid a lot more attention to you."

"Jesus Christ," Garth said in astonishment. "Are you two—?"

"*Shhh*," Veil and I hissed in unison.

"Right on," Insolers said in a low voice, sounding at once excited and slightly amused. Neither Harper nor Jan spoke, but I could feel their eyes on me.

Garth obediently fell silent for a few moments. When he spoke again, it was in an appropriate whisper, and he slurred his words as Veil had done. "Mongo, are you guys really . . . uh, doing you know what? How?"

"This really doesn't seem like the appropriate time or place to discuss it, Garth. However, suffice it to say that if you hadn't always been such a pisshead when it came to the martial arts, calling just about anything you heard a ninja bullshit story, I might have told you about *muzukashi jotai kara deru*—the art of getting out of knotty situations. Think Houdini. Get it? Too late for you now. I'm thinking of leaving you behind."

"My hero," Harper whispered, and then giggled softly.

"We don't know how many of them there are, or where they are. We have to assume most of them are watching the perimeter of the castle and grounds waiting for John Sinclair to show up. We need to find a fast and simple way to get out of here. If we can get away from here, we may be in a position to intercept your man, or at least show some kind of signal that we've escaped. Any ideas?"

"We must get down to the lower level," Jan whispered. "There's a labyrinth to the west, and if we can get to—"

Suddenly, all of the lights came on, momentarily blinding me. I closed my eyes, fighting back the panic that welled in me. I was very close to slipping the last knot in the ropes that bound my wrists, and there had to be a considerable length of loose rope beneath my chair and behind me. If Al or one of his men saw the rope, they would know what was happening. We'd all be checked. Veil and I would be rebound, probably this time with thin wire, and there was no way we were going to get out of that ever, much less before dawn. I brought my legs together as far as I could, hoping to partially block any sight lines to the floor under my chair. Then I began frantically picking up the loose rope with my fingers, pushing the coils under my buttocks.

I slowly opened my eyes. Al and three Black Flame soldiers I hadn't seen before were standing at the opposite end of the huge library. Al was staring at us intently. I stared back, trying to look nonchalant, desperately hoping that no loose rope was visible on the floor around Veil or me, and that what I was feeling didn't show on my face. It was a very bad time for our captors to come and check on us. I glanced at Veil, who was blinking and yawning, as if he had just been aroused from sleep. There was no rope on the floor beneath Veil or behind his chair.

Apparently satisfied that we were where we were supposed to be, Al raised the walkie-talkie he was carrying to his mouth, pressed the Send button on the side, and spoke rapidly in Japanese. When he released the button, he was answered by static. He repeated the action, with the same result. If I'd had to hazard a guess as to what it all meant, I'd have ventured the opinion that our youthful leader had lost communication with one or more of his men. He was, for sure, not looking as bouncy as he had earlier in the evening. He cursed in English, then threw the walkie-talkie against one of the bookcases lining the wall to his left. He signaled to his men, who fanned out. Two of the men pointed their weapons at the entrances to the library, while the third nervously aimed his up at the balcony ringing the second level.

"Oh, my God," Jan said with a sharp intake of breath. "He's here! Chant's already here!"

That might be true, and all well and good, but the problem was that we were already, still, there too. And Al was showing disturbing signs of being more than a bit perturbed at the whole

situation. If John Sinclair had indeed somehow managed to pene-
trate the ring of Black Flame soldiers and had entered the castle
in order to rescue us, the fact of the matter was that his timing
was as bad as Al's. The rope I had spent hours untying from my
wrists was a painful lump under my buttocks and in the small of
my back. I wondered if the Japanese had an expression concerning
frying pans and fire.

As his men continued to slowly circle, sweeping the area
around and above them with their automatic weapons, Al
abruptly strode the rest of the way across the library, stopped in
front of Harper and Jan. He reached into the back pocket of his
black linen slacks, removed what appeared to be an ornately
carved, rectangular box of enameled wood. He gripped both ends
of the box, pulled. There was a soft, ominous clicking sound; the
box separated to become the handles of two shiny, triangular-
shaped knives. He raised his hands, placing the tip of one blade
an inch or so from Harper's left eye, the other an equally small
distance from Jan's right eye.

"Sinclair!" Al shouted, his voice echoing in the huge library.
"I hope you can hear me, because if you can't, each of these
women is going to lose an eye for nothing! We'll talk! Show
yourself!"

The odds for the six of us surviving this business, which had
seemed fairly good only a minute or two before, were now rapidly
diminishing; the chances that one dwarf, however well motivated,
could overwhelm one man with two knives and three men with
automatic weapons were nonexistent. Any move whatsoever on
my part now would be the ultimate fool's play and would un-
doubtedly obliterate any lingering chances we might have for
survival. As horrible as it was, having an eyeball punctured by
the tip of a knife was preferable to dying. And he was going to
take their eyes, any moment now. Even if I hadn't felt it in my
bones, Al had already provided not only ample proof that he was
not a man to bluff, but clear evidence that he enjoyed such things.
However, without question, the only thing to do was to sit tight,
let him stick the eyes, and then hope the men would leave for a
while so that Veil and I could continue going about our business
of engineering our escape.

181

On the other hand.

Al might be wrong about Sinclair being in the castle. Whether or not Sinclair was in our midst, Al wasn't going to stop with taking an eye from Harper and Jan if the man didn't show up. If there was no response after the initial mutilations, he would take the other eyes, then the ears, and then other parts of their bodies. There was no telling when or where he would stop. And even if Sinclair did show himself and give up, Al had made it clear that we were all going to die anyway. Black Flame had been one step ahead of everybody in this game, and still was.

I now felt the desperation Garth had been feeling all along, and I now had what he had been so desperately hoping for—one clear shot at Al. It was a moment that might never present itself again in our lifetimes, and it was mine. I took it.

As I untied the last knot and slipped the last loop from my wrists, and prepared to drop the rope from my hands, I quickly but carefully examined my options, my angles of attack. There weren't many of either. I had been sitting motionless for hours, with my blood circulation restricted, and my legs were bound to feel rubbery when I abruptly stood up. I might even experience a dizzy spell. Under normal circumstances, I would have had no trouble getting up the speed and momentum I would need to leap to his head, which I needed to do in order to strike a killing blow; but I didn't think I had the necessary spring in my legs now for such a move, and I would only have one chance at him.

Another consideration was the fact that my attack would have to snap his head and torso backward, or the tips of the knives he held in his hands would still puncture the women's eyeballs. That effectively narrowed my options for point of attack down to one, but that was fine with me; it was my preferred option. I must have picked up a case of bad attitude from Al, for I was no longer content to simply kill the young leader of Black Flame. I wanted him to have something—or not have something—to remember me by for the rest of his abominable life, long after I was dead.

I dropped the rope to the floor and sprang to my feet. As I'd expected, my legs were stiff, my knees weak; but the massive amounts of adrenaline pumping through my system galvanized my nerves and muscles, and I shot forward, lowering my head and aiming at Al's exposed back. The three gunmen started, but could not fire at me for fear of hitting their leader. One man shouted a warning, but it was too late. I had already centered my *chi*, imagining all the power in my body focused into a fine point at my forehead. I lunged the last step, hunched my shoulders, drove as hard as I could. The center of my forehead connected solidly with the small of Al's back, directly on his spine. The crunching sound of his spine breaking traveled down through my skull, the bone acting as a kind of amplifier, and I knew that all of Al's nasty doings in the future would be done from a wheelchair. He shrieked in surprise, pain, and anger as his upper body snapped backward. As he crumpled to the floor, I rolled over him and lay flat on the floor, using his body as a shield between me and the gunmen.

Then things got a bit hectic. It felt like I was adrift in a blurred universe of sound, sight, and cascading emotion, with everything seeming to happen at once. As I reached to recover the daggers Al had been holding, I heard the sound of wood cracking, breaking. That, I knew, would be Veil focusing his own *chi*; harnessing the enormous power in his hard, finely conditioned body, he stood up, leaving the chair into which he had been tied in shards on the floor.

But not even Veil could dodge bullets. I doubted that his breaking free was going to do either of us much good, but it did afford me an odd sense of relief, of having company out on the thin, far edge of existence in what I assumed were the final seconds of my life. At least I would die as a free man on my feet, as it were, even if I did happen to be crawling on my belly at the moment.

I took the daggers from the unconscious Al's hands, then raised my head slightly and peered over his chest to see what was going on. Everything seemed a chaotic blend of movement, with Veil diving through the air, executing a shoulder roll, then scrambling for the feet of the closest Black Flame soldier even as all three men swung their guns in his direction. Suddenly, there was more movement on the balcony overhead, off to my right. A headless corpse, naked except for a green plaid flannel shirt, came sailing down through the air. The bloody corpse hit one of the gunmen square in the chest, knocking him backward and off his feet. An instant later a deadly steel star, a *shuriken*, came whistling through the air and planted itself in the center of the second gunman's forehead, splitting his skull and killing him instantly. The man on the floor was dispatched in the same manner. The third soldier did manage to get off a burst of fire, but he was distracted, and his bullets passed over Veil's body as Veil rolled once more, came up in the man's face, and wrapped his hands around the man's throat.

Things were definitely looking up.

I sprang to my feet, went to my right, and began cutting through the ropes that bound Garth, Insolers, Harper, and Jan. When Harper and Jan tried to stand, they both fell. Garth and Insolers supported Jan, while I gripped Harper's hand and pulled her to her feet. She lunged for, fell on, the sofa. She rummaged around the overstuffed pillows on the sofa until she found her purse, opened it, took out the small wooden box inside, and shoved it down the front of her blouse.

"This way!" Jan cried, tugging at both Garth and Insolers as she staggered forward toward the door leading to the pantry.

Veil and I started to go to retrieve the dead men's automatic weapons, abruptly halted, turned, and sprinted after the others as two more gunmen came running through the door at the far end of the library. We darted through the pantry door where the others had gone a split second before twin bursts of gunfire sent a hail of bullets chewing into the wood of the door frame. We found ourselves in a long, narrow pantry with a high ceiling. Garth was standing at the other end, holding a door open and frantically urging us on. We ducked through the doorway, with Garth following, slamming the door shut and bolting it behind us. We clambered down a circular staircase to a narrow stone corridor. Insolers and an anxious-looking Harper and Jan were waiting for us. The corridor was like an echo chamber, and the sound of running footsteps was all around us—but the men seemed to be running in a number of different directions, and there was no sound of splintering wood at the head of the stairs down which we had come.

Twenty yards down the corridor there were three more doors, one on the left and two on the right. We followed Jan through the door on the left, skipped and hopped down yet another steel stairwell into a large wine cellar. A door at the opposite end of the cellar opened into yet another stone corridor, and our footsteps echoed eerily as we ran down it after Jan. I presumed we were heading for what Jan had described as a labyrinth, but to me the complex system of stairwells and stone corridors was a hopeless maze and I wondered how many years it had taken the woman to find her way around this massive complex she modestly called home.

A man suddenly lunged out from the dark shadows of a deeply recessed doorway to my left, grabbed Harper with one hand, and started to raise the machine pistol he carried in the other. Jan was in the line of fire between Veil and Garth, and they couldn't get around her before he fired. I tensed, ready to leap at the man, but Harper reacted first. She jerked free from his grasp, reached down the front of her blouse, and took out the wooden box. As Insolers knocked the gun away, Harper opened the lid of the box, then slapped it against the man's face, just below his left eye. The man screamed, clawed for a few moments at the spot on his face where he had been bitten, then stiffened and crumpled to the stone floor. Veil stepped around Jan and picked up the machine pistol, and I grabbed Harper's arm, helping her to step over the corpse of the Black Flame soldier.

"We're almost there," Jan gasped, pausing just before a sharp bend in the corridor. "The door at the end opens into the labyrinth. I know the way through. It will take us to an apple orchard on a hill overlooking the castle. Chant will know where to find us. Come on."

Jan turned and went around the bend, disappearing from sight for a moment, and then we heard a startled cry. The rest of us hurried around the bend, then came to an abrupt halt, with Veil, Garth, and Insolers quickly moving to screen the women, when we saw what Jan had seen.

The door at the end of the corridor was open, and moonlight silhouetted the black shape of the tall man who filled the door frame. The man's hands were empty, hanging at his sides.

185

"Shoot the fucker," Garth murmured.

Veil shook his head, then handed the machine pistol to my brother. "The sound of gunfire through that open door could give away our position. It doesn't look like he has a gun, which means I can take him out without making much noise. You people stay here."

"I'm coming with you," I said, and fell into step beside Veil as he started forward.

The man's features began to emerge from the moon shadows as we grew nearer, and I felt a little shudder as I recognized him. Carlo was bare-chested, which was understandable since he had wrapped his shirt around the corpse of one of the two Black Flame soldiers unlucky enough to have been ordered by Al to carry him out of the library and chop his head off. It seemed Carlo was anything but a run-of-the-mill assassin, with hidden resources neither Black Flame nor we had imagined; like Veil, he knew more than a little about focusing strength. In the second or two before they died, the men who had carried Carlo from the library must have been quite surprised when the chair they were holding abruptly disintegrated, and powerful hands gripped their throats.

The man who had been my chauffeur obviously knew a few other tricks as well. The features were still those of the man who had introduced himself to me as Carlo, but the bad leg was now straight, as was the spine. I stopped, grabbed Veil's arm just as he was about to leap at the man—a move I suspected might not be such a great idea, even for Veil. Suddenly, I knew who this man really was, even before he turned slightly to reveal the large mark, a combination of scar tissue and black tattoo ink, that ran up the left side of his back.

"John Sinclair, I presume," I said to the still figure.

"I want to thank you for what you did back there in the library, Mongo," the man replied in a deep, resonant voice that might have been Carlo's, except that it had lost all trace of any Italian accent. "You too, Kendry. Things were getting a bit out of hand."

"Chant!" Jan shouted with joy when she heard the man's voice, and rushed past Veil and me into his outstretched arms. "Oh, Chant!"

The man and woman held each other tightly, swaying back and forth slightly. They kissed, and then Sinclair gently pushed her away and turned to the rest of us. "We'll talk later. There's no time now. I just wanted to make sure you were all safe. Jan will lead you through the labyrinth to a safe place, and I'll join you there when I'm finished with the rest of that overgrown delinquent's men. I have to move quickly now, before it gets light."

Judging from his tone of voice and casual manner, he might have been talking about going to the corner grocery store for a quart of milk.

"I'm sorry, Sinclair," Insolers said in a low voice. "I came to help, but I . . . I didn't mean for things to happen the way they did. It's my fault those men found your home."

"Don't worry about it, Insolers," John Sinclair replied easily. "I'd have chosen a different battleground, but this was inevitable. They've been getting closer every year. It's why I chose to make my stand now, to try to draw them to Switzerland. It will work out. They're spread all over the castle and the grounds hunting for me." He paused, then added in a tone that chilled me, "I won't be long."

I stepped closer to Sinclair, looked up at him, said, "I want to go with you. I owe them too."

He shook his head. "Thank you, but no. It's better that I work alone."

"I assume you killed the two who carried you out, but you don't know how many are left."

"Eleven, not counting the pain-in-the-ass kid you put down. It's almost a tenth of their entire membership."

"Let me come with you."

"This isn't your kind of play, Mongo. They will never give up, and so they must be killed, one by one. There can be no hesitation. I think it's safe to say you've never killed a man in cold blood, but that is precisely what is required now. There is no middle way."

"Your blood may be cold right now, Sinclair, but mine definitely isn't. I know how they've tortured people to death, and they've shot down men, women, and children in front of my eyes." I paused, held up the twin daggers I had taken from Al. "I won't hesitate. At least let me come along to hold your coat."

"And me," Veil said, stepping up beside me. "My blood's as cold as yours. I may not be as good as you, but I'd like to think I'm damn close—better than any member of Black Flame. I have no doubt that you can kill every one of the fuckers, but I'm not so sure you, alone, can find them all in the hour or so you have before the sun comes up. When it gets light, things are going to get tougher. You can use the help. I've done this kind of thing before—in Laos and Cambodia."

"I know that, Kendry," Sinclair said with a curt nod. "I'd heard of you in Southeast Asia, and I've heard of you since. As a matter of fact, I own three of your paintings. Your point about time is well taken, and yes, I would appreciate your help." He paused, glanced at me, then looked away. He seemed embarrassed, and I knew what he was thinking. Suddenly, I felt vulnerable, hurt. I felt . . . well, small. "Mongo, I just don't think—"

"He's earned the right, Sinclair," my brother said sharply as he stepped up beside me. "Think about it."

"Well, thank you, mother," I murmured, at once grateful for his support, and thoroughly embarrassed.

Veil said: "I agree."

Sinclair nodded. "All right."

"And I'll come along," Garth said in a firm tone. "As backup."

"If you fire that," Sinclair said, pointing to the machine pistol Veil had handed my brother, "you'll give away our position."

"I understand. I don't pretend to have the killing skills the three of you have. I'll stay back. But it can't hurt to have someone with a gun in case something goes wrong."

Again, Sinclair nodded his assent, then turned to Insolers. "Duane, you know this isn't your brand of fighting."

"No argument," the CIA operative replied. "I'll go out with Jan and Harper, wait for you."

"There's one other thing. If I'm going to totally destroy Black Flame, I need to capture at least one of their members. That won't be easy. No member of Black Flame has ever been taken alive; choosing death before capture is deeply engrained in them. All of them have poison-tipped darts in spring loaders strapped to their forearms, and they can shoot the darts into their own wrists if they choose to do so. Some also have a fake tooth filled with cyanide that can be released if they bite down in a certain way. Killing these men could prove relatively easy compared to capturing one and keeping him alive. That will take planning, coordination, and skill." He paused, reached into his pocket, removed a wooden dowel. The dowel was perhaps three inches long, about an inch and a half in diameter. "This must be placed in the captive's mouth, at the same time as the hands and wrists are immobilized, if we are to be successful."

Veil grunted softly. "That will be the last one we take."

"Al's already on ice," I said. "He's the obvious choice, because he's certain to have all the information you need on the entire outfit. He's paralyzed, and may even still be unconscious. We certainly know where to find him."

Sinclair frowned, looked uncertain. "The problem is that he's on the floor, out in the open, impossible to approach without him knowing it—assuming he's conscious. The moment he sees me, he'll know we've killed his men, and he'll kill himself."

"There may be a way."

"We'll see," Sinclair replied, glancing at his watch. "We must go now. Follow me, and please do exactly as I say."

Garth, Veil, and I followed John Sinclair as he ducked out through the doorway, then moved quickly and silently through the chiaroscuro moon shadows at the base of the castle walls.

·   ·   ·

We moved in the night, through and around the castle, like a four-piece, grotesquely shaped killing machine. Actually, it was Veil and Sinclair who did the killing, with Garth and me bringing up the rear and afforded an opportunity to do little more than offer silent encouragement. John Sinclair, in the guise of Carlo the chauffeur and free-lance assassin, had obviously done a very good job of reconnaissance before sitting himself down on a hillside and waiting to be captured. He knew, if not precisely where each Black Flame soldier was at the moment, at least where they had been, and what zones they were likely to be searching. And, of course, he was intimately familiar with the castle and its grounds; intricate, secret passageways allowed us to move freely and quickly from one site to another, often to see without risk of being seen.

Despite his size, John Sinclair moved with incredible stealth, like some great panther, cloaking himself in night, then rising like a deadly shadow behind some unsuspecting Black Flame soldier; a moment later there would be the faint clicking sound of the man's neck snapping. He and his companion in killing alternated targets. Veil moved with the same stealth, used an identical killing technique, and got the same results. I had been in such awe of the ninja mystique in general, and Black Flame's in particular, that I was initially amazed at the relative ease with which Veil and Sinclair went about their business of dispatching the Black Flame soldiers. Then I recalled Veil's comment about Black Flame's emphasis on the psychological and medical, not the physical, aspects of the martial arts. Veil and Sinclair were among the best stone-silent killers, and a ninja who hears nothing before a garrote slices through his jugular, or a knife blade slips into his heart, is just as dead as the rest of us mere mortals.

With the glow of approaching dawn and four men left to find, we split up. Garth went with Veil, while I tagged along—the only way to put it—behind Sinclair, carefully moving in accordance with his hand signals.

I was ending up more voyeur than participant, and I was feeling increasingly embarrassed. It had been, I realized, the height of presumption for me to suggest that a dwarf, no matter how considerable his physical skills, could be of any assistance whatsoever in a matter like this to a consummate master of the martial arts like John Sinclair. He had permitted me to come along only to spare my feelings, and that made me angry—at myself. Indeed, I was becoming increasingly disgusted with myself for asking in the first place and for allowing Garth—also sparing my feelings— to be so insistent. My only job was a negative one, to be certain I remained quiet and unseen as Sinclair snuffed the lives out of the strange zombie-men who had invaded his home, and who would have killed the woman he loved along with the rest of us. Every once in a while I managed to make myself useful by ghoulishly picking over the corpses Sinclair left in his wake. I took one of the men's machine pistols and recovered a fine throwing knife similar to the one Veil had had taken from him. Once, inside the castle, I managed to catch a dead man's automatic rifle before it fell and clattered on the stone floor, but that was, to that point, my one and only contribution to the entire mission.

As the time approached when we would have to make the crucial decision as to which man to attempt to capture and keep alive, an idea occurred to me, a plan in which I might actually be able to play a useful role. Garth and Veil had rejoined us, and as we approached our last target I pulled Sinclair aside and hurriedly outlined my notion to him, emphasizing the specialized skills I possessed that were the basis for the plan. He listened and, somewhat to my surprise, immediately nodded his assent.

My plan required that we make a bit of a mess, and to that end Sinclair used the knife he carried to slit the jugular of the last Black Flame soldier in our path.

.　●　●

The four of us stood in the shadow of an alcove between two bookcases on the library's balcony as the rising sun sent rays of light through the huge bank of undraped cathedral windows at the eastern end, near the sitting area. The light slowly moved across the floor, finally illuminating the man lying near the open end of the horseshoe-shaped sofa. Al's paralyzed legs were twisted at odd angles, but he had used his arms to push himself over on his back. He was awake. His strange, matte-black eyes were opened wide, his gaze rapidly shifting around as he watched, waiting for something to happen, some sound to emerge from the silence that enveloped him.

Garth pressed the trigger on the machine pistol he carried. The gun chattered, spewing out bullets that tore out a section of the balcony railing on our side, and ripped into the books and bookcases across the way. A moment later, Sinclair staggered out from the shadows and collapsed, his blood-soaked body falling at the edge of the balcony, both arms dangling over the edge. Good show. Now it was my turn. Garth let loose with another

191

burst of fire. I screamed and sent my blood-covered body over a section of railing down closer to the eastern end. I executed what I thought was a rather neat little somersault, managed to land square on my back in the center of the curved section of the sofa, just like it was a safety net. I bounded straight up, did a half roll in the air, came back down on my stomach with my torso hanging over the edge of the left arm of the sofa, my blood-streaked face only inches from the startled Al's. I put on my best glazed-eye, "dead" look for a few moments to let him savor the full range of my acting talents, then smiled at him.

"Top of the morning, my dear fellow," I said, and immediately jammed the wooden dowel I had been palming hard into his open mouth. Then I rolled off the couch behind his head, grabbed both of his wrists, placed my feet on his shoulders, and pulled as hard as I could, extending his arms in order to prevent him from flexing his wrists and sending a poison-tipped dart into him, or me.

Sinclair rolled the rest of the way off the balcony, dropped easily to the floor, then quickly strode over to where I was bracing the hapless Al. As Garth and Veil hurried down the staircase, Sinclair pulled up Al's sleeves and extracted the darts from the spring-loaded scabbards strapped to his wrists. He then hit Al hard, with the heel of his hand, on the right side of Al's jaw, knocking the Black Flame leader unconscious. He removed the dowel from between Al's jaws, probed with his right index finger inside the man's mouth until he found what he was looking for. He yanked loose the cyanide-filled plastic tooth, casually tossed it away. Veil picked up a length of rope from the floor, and he and Sinclair bound Al's wrists tightly behind his back. From the looks of the knots they used, it was going to take Al a considerably longer time to get free than it had taken me, assuming he knew a little *muzukashi jotai kara deru*, and it was time he didn't have. He wasn't going anywhere, crawling or otherwise.

"It's done," Sinclair said quietly. "Good job, Mongo."

"It should be interesting to hear what he has to say. He knows where all the others can be found, doesn't he?"

Sinclair nodded. "He knows everything that's needed to erase the Black Flame Society from the face of the earth." He paused, looked up at us, and smiled. "But he'll wait, and I have certain preparations to make before I begin questioning him. Let's go get the others and clean up. I think we all deserve a good meal. I'll buy."

CHAPTER THIRTEEN

The notion of taking time for what turned out to be an elaborate meal in the huge kitchen of a castle that had been virtually transformed into a fresh graveyard marker didn't seem to bother Garth, Veil, or Insolers any more than it did John Sinclair, and Jan Rawlings was too deliriously happy to have the man she loved safely back with her to let anything bother her. That left Harper and me the only ones feeling tense, not to mention a bit queasy, with the culinary arrangements. I was impatient for the drama to end, whatever the ending might be, and have it all done with.

I underwent a remarkable change of attitude after a steaming hot bath, a long session in a sauna with Harper melting, as it were, in my arms, and then another long, coed soak in a hot tub. Only then, with my nerves and muscles relaxed, did I realize just how exhausted I had been and how much we all needed rest and food. There were still close to a hundred Black Flame soldiers and their leaders left alive, and to totally exterminate a powerful secret society that had festered in humankind's midst for many centuries was going to take some doing. There were still unknown dangers ahead, and there was no hurry to get to them. Our business with Al, like Al himself, would indeed wait.

After our baths and sauna, the others dressed in luxurious silk robes that were a sort of "one size fits all" variety—all, that is, except me. However, after Jan spent about twenty minutes with a pair of scissors and a sewing machine, I, too, had myself a silk lounging robe of deep, rich blue.

We all sat around a huge oak table in the center of the kitchen, drinking hot sake, while Jan and Sinclair busied themselves expertly preparing a Japanese-style meal of rice, stir-fried vegetables, seared beef, and sushi. Actually, it was Sinclair who did most of the preparing, with Jan close beside him, stroking his hair, touching his back, and occasionally resting her head on his shoulder. Out of "costume," John Sinclair turned out to have thick, close-cropped, steel-gray hair, and matching eyes. It struck me how confidently and easily Sinclair accepted the love of this woman, and as I glanced at Harper—who was looking at me in much the same manner as Jan was looking at Sinclair—I found myself fervently wishing I had the confidence to do the same.

Garth and Veil were engaged in quiet but animated conversation, and it occurred to me that now, after years, these two powerful, fiercely independent men who loved me would become friends.

Insolers sat a few feet away from them, across the table from Harper and me, looking more isolated than he really was. He had a somewhat vacant look in his eyes as he sipped at his sake, as if his mind were elsewhere.

"My father loved Japan to the point of obsession," John Sinclair said as he laid out a fresh serving of sushi on a marble slab, poured more sake for each of us, then sat down next to Jan. "For him, Japan was much more a state of mind than a geographical location, a country. His obsession finally cost him his life and radically changed the shape of mine.

"If he knew in his head that a *ganjin* could never be fully accepted by the Japanese, he never accepted it in his heart. He had worked most of his adult life to, in some ways, become more Japanese than the Japanese, in a manner of speaking. I believe he saw in me a way to finally become totally integrated into their society. He began by starting my training in the martial arts when I was five years old, sparing no expense. My early training, along with the fact that I had a certain natural talent, allowed me to excel very quickly. By the time I was seventeen, I was considered by Japanese cognoscenti to be among the top all-around martial artists in the world, and I was invited to enter certain very prestigious tournaments that are usually closed to non-Japanese. As a matter of fact, I never competed in any outside tournaments; they were considered vulgar and low-class by the *sensei* I trained with.

"I assume that you've all found out a good deal about me in the last few days. Perhaps you've heard that my father hired a man called Master Bai to give me advanced instruction in the martial arts. This is not true; a *ganjin* like my father would never have been in a position to even hear of Master Bai, much less to hire him. It was Master Bai, posing as a master teacher—which he was, incidentally, although not in the way that my father, or most Japanese, thought—who approached my father after observing me in a number of these closed competitions. He told my father that he wished to instruct me further, and that he would do it for nothing, in honor of this young *ganjin* who had already learned so much.

"It was, of course, a ruse. It was impossible for a man like my father to see through the deceptiveness of a man like Master Bai to the core of evil within. It was Master Bai's intent to make me a Black Flame acolyte, to erase my personality, and then create in me the mind and soul of an assassin who would do his bidding without question. I suspect he was amused by the idea and wasn't even sure what he would eventually do with me. My father, of course, couldn't have known any of this; virtually no *ganjin* had ever heard of Black Flame, a very old and very secret society dedicated to the amassing of wealth and power through the conscious pursuit of evil."

"Veil had heard of it," I said, nodding in my friend's direction.

If our host was surprised, he didn't show it. The man with the steel-gray hair and eyes merely nodded at Veil. "Mr. Kendry is a most unusual man. Unusual men hear things that are often out of earshot to ordinary men."

196

"But you did go with Master Bai," Harper said. She was leaning forward on the table, listening very intently.

"Yes. I progressed rapidly through the initial phases of training, which consisted primarily of intense studies in natural pharmacology—toxic herbs and plants."

I said, "And that knowledge is what you used to beat Al's 'truth serum.' "

Sinclair nodded. "What you were given, in doses calibrated to your estimated weights, was a plant extract that causes extreme nausea. The effect of the extract is heightened by internal tension. In effect, if administered by someone who knows what he's doing and is good at estimating body weight, it works just like a polygraph. Most people become increasingly nervous when they lie, and this shows up as a blip on the polygraph; if you get nervous when you have the extract in you, you vomit. Simple, really."

Harper shook her head. "But that doesn't explain how you did what you did. You threw up at first, yes—but, obviously, you wanted that . . . thing . . . to know you were lying. But then you lied continuously, and it had no effect on you. Why?"

Sinclair thought for a few moments, then said, "Successful disguise requires the ability to act; acting, if it's good, is really nothing more than a successful lie. You are something other than what you appear to be. A great deal of Black Flame training centers on this sort of psychological disguise. It's not unlike method acting: you try to internalize your role to the point where you can at once *believe* you *are* the character you're portraying, even as you know you're only acting. With the proper training, you can use this technique to exert considerable control over your entire emotional landscape. Playing Carlo, I *was* Carlo, and thus allowed myself to react the way Carlo would react when he lied: he vomited. When Carlo told what was to him the truth, namely that he was a free-lance assassin under contract to the CIA, he didn't suffer the adverse reaction. If you want a simpler explanation, you can simply say that I'm a good liar. It's a talent sociopaths, psychopaths, and Black Flame trainees share in common."

"It's incredible," Harper said quietly.

Sinclair shrugged his broad shoulders. "Not really, Harper. It's just the result of a lot of training and practice, but I appreciate what I take you to mean as a compliment.

"An enormous amount of Black Flame training involves not only poisons but means of deception and subterfuge, techniques for getting close to an unsuspecting enemy or target. As a matter of fact, Master Bai was quite pleased with me; after centuries, I was the only *ganjin* to ever become Black Flame, and he was sure he owned me.

"Of course, at no time during my training was I ever told what Black Flame was *really* all about. But I'd always had a pretty good bullshit antenna, even for a kid, and I had a good idea where Master Bai was coming from even before he told me I would eventually be expected to kill somebody he would select at random from a crowd—perhaps even a child. I went to my father and told him of my suspicions; I told him I wanted nothing more to do with Master Bai. His response was to tell me that studying with Master Bai was a once-in-a-lifetime opportunity; it was an honor that had never before been accorded a *ganjin* and might never be again. He told me I should lie to Master Bai, pretend to agree to anything he wanted until I had received all of my training, and then simply quit. He said I would be breaking no laws, and there was nothing Master Bai could do to me. My father indicated it was very important to him that I do this, because he was sure it would win both of us respect from the Japanese we could not otherwise get. To say that my father seriously underestimated Master Bai would, of course, be the height of understatement. I didn't underestimate Master Bai; I sensed there was going to be a great price to pay, but I assumed I would be the one to pay it. I continued my training up to the point of assassination as a gift to my father. I didn't want to displease him. I was a fool."

"You were seventeen years old, Chant, and you worshipped your father," Jan said in a tone that was at once firm and kind. "It was your father who was the fool."

Sinclair glanced sharply at the woman he loved, but did not disagree. "Yes," he said. "That too. In any case, I did what he asked. I completed the training, with Master Bai assuming it was understood that I would undergo the final test, and I was given the Black Flame mark. But I refused to do the killing. I had intended to run away, but found I couldn't. I went to Master Bai and told him I would not be a member of Black Flame. I fully expected to be killed on the spot, but I had failed to absorb one of Master Bai's most subtle and important teachings—death is rarely the greatest punishment that can be inflicted upon a human being. His response was to shrug, giggle like his grandson in the other room, and send me on my way. Before I arrived home, both my mother and father had been killed in a manner that made it clear Black Flame was responsible—which meant that *I* was responsible. They intended to let me live with my grief and guilt for a time, and then torture me to death at their leisure. But this I anticipated.

"My father had always fostered independence in me, and I had money. Because of his position, I was fairly sophisticated in the requirements of foreign travel and documentation. Because of my Black Flame training, I could forge documents. That's what I did. I managed to escape from Japan, made my way to the United States, and made sure Black Flame couldn't find me."

"My God," Harper said. "And you were only *seventeen?*"

Sinclair smiled. "Well, I was actually eighteen by this time. You do what you have to do, Harper. And you have to remember that I'd had some very specialized training in control and self-discipline from many fine *sensei*. When I felt I was safe, I resumed my own identity. I was able to access my inheritance and certain State Department benefits. I went to college and then on to do graduate work. Then I joined the army."

"Why did you do that?" Insolers asked in a curiously flat tone.

"Because I was an American," Sinclair replied simply. "Living in Japan for so long had only heightened my identification as an American. The United States was my country. My father's death benefits had helped to pay for my education. I felt I had an obligation."

Sinclair paused and stared at Insolers, as if waiting for the CIA operative to say something or ask another question. When the man with the rodent features and medicinal smell remained silent, eyes cast down as he sipped his sake, Sinclair continued, "As a result of my education, I was made an officer, and in the course of events I was sent to Vietnam." He paused, smiled distantly, as if at some private joke. "While I was over there, I began to acquire somewhat of a reputation as an expert interrogator of enemy prisoners. Actually, I owed my skills to a rather unusual technique taught to me by Master Bai—not the plant extract. I'm thinking of trying it out on junior. I think he'll be surprised.

"During my third tour of duty a rather crude attempt was made to recruit me for an insane operation called Cooked Goose, which called for the assassination by U.S. Army personnel of selected civilians in the United States. It was thoroughly crazy, and, in my opinion, traitorous. It was only years later, in Seattle, that I learned I'd been set up by my old friend Master Bai, who was working as a consultant to the CIA, of all things. At the time the only thing I knew was that it was my duty as an army officer to put a stop to Cooked Goose, by any means necessary. I couldn't do that by remaining in that theater. As Master Bai had foreseen, by refusing the assignment, I had become a marked man because of my knowledge of Cooked Goose. If I stayed I would be killed, and so I deserted. Five Army Rangers, Cooked Goose operatives, were sent after me, and I had no choice but to kill them."

Without looking up from the table, Insolers said quietly, "You have documentation on Cooked Goose, don't you?"

"I did have."

"Did have?"

"I managed to extract certain papers from some files before I left, my thinking being that I might need them as proof in order to stop Cooked Goose. As it turned out, the mere fact that I was on the loose with knowledge of the operation in my head caused the planners to abort it. I destroyed the papers when the war ended."

"Why? The CIA has never stopped pursuing you. You could have released the documents and blown a big hole in the side of the whole agency. Why didn't you?"

Sinclair seemed genuinely surprised at the question. "My problem was never with the CIA, Duane, only certain men in it. I didn't want to do anything to damage my country more than it had already been damaged by that war. Vietnam was an aberration, and Operation Cooked Goose was an aberration within an aberration. Release of information about Cooked Goose could have caused irreparable damage, further degrading and humiliating the United States in the eyes of the world and in the eyes of many of its own people. Since I had just gone to considerable trouble, and undergone some personal sacrifice, by deserting and being branded a traitor in order to serve my country by *stopping* the damn project because it was so abominable, why would I then turn around and cancel out all my efforts by publicizing something that never happened?"

"Because the sons-of-bitches were trying to kill you."

"Without much success, as you see. In my eyes, *they* were the traitors and were manipulated by Master Bai. I was not about to serve the interests of Master Bai. After the war, the country was going through an agonizing process of redefining itself. I had done my duty, as I saw it, in order to *serve* my country, and I couldn't see how the public learning of a plot hatched by some of its purported leaders to kill U.S. citizens in order to manipulate public opinion could possibly help the healing process."

For the first time since we had sat down at the table, Duane Insolers looked directly at the man whose life had become so inextricably, and ambiguously, bound up with his own. "Jesus Christ, Sinclair. You really are a goddamn patriot."

"And you're a fool, Duane," Sinclair replied easily, without rancor. "I don't think you quite understand. In the end, I did not release the materials I had, or tell what I knew, because the resulting disruption, bitterness, recriminations, and internal dissent would have pleased, and served the interests of, the group whose leader had concocted the plan in the first place—Black Flame. They have always been my real enemies, and I saw no reason to amuse them at the expense of the United States."

"I don't think the CIA would be very impressed with your explanation, Sinclair, and I know they wouldn't believe you've destroyed the Cooked Goose documents. They believe you're hanging on to them to use to bargain for your freedom if and when you're ever caught."

"Chant doesn't care what the CIA believes, Duane," Jan said sharply. "And he doesn't have to explain himself to them or to you. You talk like somebody who's hunting him."

There was a strained silence. Finally, Veil said, "I'd very much like to hear the rest of it, Sinclair."

The man sitting at the head of the table thought about it. Then he looked at Jan, smiled, threw back his head, and laughed. It was a deep, rich, pleasing sound. "The rest of it? Well, the bottom line was that I was suddenly unemployed, and my future job prospects looked rather grim. I was a military deserter, hunted by CIA assassins, as well as far more dangerous assassins from Black Flame. I decided it was time for a career change. I'd had superb training as both a ninja warrior and a military officer, but what was I going to do with it? I suppose I could have found work as a mercenary, but I was pretty certain I wouldn't much care for the kinds of assignments I'd be offered, and that line of work could leave me dangerously exposed to both Black Flame and the CIA. So I decided to go into business for myself as a kind of self-employed mercenary, selecting my own targets. I set up a one-man shop."

Harper said, "More like a one-man army."

Sinclair smiled at Harper, shrugged. "Any man's effectiveness is enhanced by good training and careful planning. The reputation for violence grew out of the nature of the business I'd gone into; I was dealing, for the most part, with extremely violent opponents, and extremely violent means had to be used in order to get their attention. It was good business practice. Also, this reputation for ruthlessness and violence, which I wanted, was helped along by the various outfits that were hunting me, because it also served their purposes. I wanted my targets to fear me, because it made them easier to manipulate, and the men hunting me found it convenient to have me portrayed in the media as a mad-dog killer. But, despite all that, I've still managed to make a few friends, like Duane here, along the way. And, perhaps, the other people at this table."

"I'm flattered that you should think of me as a friend, Sinclair," Insolers said in a somewhat absent tone.

Sinclair nodded in Insolers' direction, turned back to Veil. "During the course of an operation in Seattle, I learned that Black Flame was still very actively hunting me. That served to put me even more on my guard in the following years."

I asked, "When you mounted your operation against Neuberger, did you know that Cornucopia was a Black Flame front?"

"No," Sinclair replied, his tone suddenly revealing a trace of regret, and perhaps bitterness. "If I had, I never would have involved a friend of mine from Interpol by the name of Bo Wahlstrom. At the time, I knew only that Cornucopia laundered money for *some* big international crime organization, which could have been one of many; it was information I'd picked up as a result of something else I was doing. Ten million dollars, incidentally, was the approximate amount of that week's criminal proceeds, with the rest legitimate funds earmarked for various legitimate projects, so it was ten million I took. After I'd gotten what I wanted, I turned the information and documents I'd obtained over to Bo, as I'd done in similar situations over the years, for appropriate action by Interpol."

"I don't think it was your turning the information over to him that got your friend killed," I said. "It was his crooked partner. I'm almost certain it was the partner who somehow left Bo Wahlstrom exposed when he got hold of the file and tried to use it to blackmail Neuberger. Neuberger thought he was going to straighten everything out by sending me over here as a stalking horse to flush out the amateurs, kill them, and get the file back. But it was too late. The way the partner handled things must have tipped off Black Flame to precisely what was going on, and they were already in the game."

Sinclair said, "Yes. And so was I, because the way Bo was killed told me that Black Flame was involved in a big way. Now I had to take steps to attack as well as defend, because they were too close to home, and there was more than one of them. I decided to kill as many members of Black Flame as I could while I had the chance."

Veil asked, "You felt that with so many of them here, they were overexposed and vulnerable?"

Sinclair nodded. "I hoped so. But I have a lot of enemies besides Black Flame, and there were a lot of people coming to Switzerland because they thought I had tripped up and was vulnerable. I needed to gauge the situation, to try to estimate just how many Black Flame personnel I might be up against and who the other players might be. I needed time to watch and plan, while at the same time staying as close to the action as possible."

"Aha," I said with a wry smile. "This sounds like my entrance line in *your* play."

Again, Sinclair nodded. "I might have approached Duane, since he was already on the scene, but I wasn't sure what assignment he was supposed to be carrying out, and I didn't want to compromise him. Also, I doubted he would have any information I could use.

"Then another friend at Interpol informed me that no less a personage than Dr. Robert Frederickson, Mongo the Magnificent, was coming to Zurich, supposedly to get a progress report to send back to Neuberger. Well, that certainly didn't scan. I didn't know about the blackmail business at this time, but Mongo's imminent arrival told me Neuberger was up to something that could severely complicate matters, and I wanted to find out exactly what it was. That's when I decided to appoint myself as Mongo's chauffeur. It was a way of getting close to the action to see how events would play out. Black Flame was running amok, butchering everybody in sight, and I wasn't sure why at first. Then I realized it was an attempt to discredit me among the people who really knew me. That wasn't going to work, but it wouldn't stop Black Flame from trying, and that meant a lot more innocent people were going to die. I didn't want Mongo to be one of them, because by this time I felt responsible for him. I realized blackmail, or some other crazy business with outsiders, was involved when Black Flame attacked Mongo and the man who approached him at the hotel. I figured they would come at Mongo again, and I made it a point to always stay close. But then they passed up a number of opportunities to attack Mongo while he was driving all around the countryside trying to check up on me, and I realized they were leaving him alone for the time being—probably in the hope that he might lead them to me. Then Garth and Veil arrived on the scene and decided to fire me, which made it a bit tougher to act as Mongo's bodyguard. But I still tried to stay as close as possible."

I asked, "What would you have done if I'd checked with Hyatt

Pomeroy here in the local Cornucopia office to see if he'd really sent you, or if I'd even mentioned your name to him?"

Sinclair shrugged. "Either Pomeroy would have assumed Neuberger had personally made arrangements for a chauffeur from New York, or you would have had to make do without my services sooner than you did. Fortunately, I was able to keep pretty close track of you even after Garth and Veil fired me. By this time I was trying to come up with a plan where I could get all of the Black Flame people who'd come to Switzerland in one place where I could deal with them. I certainly didn't plan on this castle being that place, but it couldn't be helped. Mongo moves fast, Black Flame was monitoring his movements, and events took on a momentum of their own. I deeply mourn the death of our servants, all of whom were our personal friends, but I was powerless to prevent that. Perhaps what happened, with Black Flame finally tracking me here, was inevitable. And it's worked out—for us, at least."

"What now?" Insolers asked.

Sinclair abruptly rose from the table. "Now I think is a good time to change back into our working clothes and see what our young friend Al has to say about his Black Flame colleagues who weren't able to join us."

CHAPTER FOURTEEN

Back in the library, we finally discovered how John "Chant" Sinclair had acquired his nickname. He'd mentioned that, while in Southeast Asia, he'd acquired a reputation for successfully questioning prisoners using unusual interrogation techniques. "Unusual" didn't begin to describe it.

He disappeared into the pantry area for a few minutes. When he emerged, he was wearing another silk robe, this one a solid jet black, and he was barefoot. He carried two tall, slender, black candles in black pewter candleholders. As per his instructions, we stood back against a wall, within earshot, but well away from the sitting area where the paralyzed Al lay on the floor.

"You can't know how to do that!" Al shouted, clearly startled and afraid, as Sinclair set the black candles down on the floor, on either side of the young man's head. "It's impossible!"

"Your grandfather taught me, junior," Sinclair replied evenly. "You and I are going to chat. I'm going to ask you a few questions, and you're going to answer them."

"No!"

"You're going to tell me everything about Black Flame. I want to know where to find your father and every other member of the society. I want to know every business or operation with which Black Flame is currently involved. You will tell me the names and positions of all the nonmembers, like Emmet P. Neuberger, you control. You will tell me where your records are kept and how to access them. Your society has existed for more than a thousand years, junior, but you're going to help me destroy it. Together, we're going to blow out Black Flame."

"It won't work on me, Sinclair," Al said in a voice that was now controlled and defiant. "I can resist it, just as you resisted the herb drink. I'm as good as you are. All you can do is kill me, but my father and the others will find and kill you, and all the people you love."

"We'll see," Sinclair replied easily, and then proceeded to draw the heavy drapes across the bank of windows behind him.

The library was plunged into darkness. A few seconds later the twin flames of the candles flickered to life, and Harper, standing close beside me and clutching my hand, gave a little cry. Sinclair had opened windows, or turned on fans, somewhere for ventilation, for I could feel a slight draft; but despite the flow of fresh air, I could clearly smell the distinct, sourish aroma given off by the candles. I also imagined I could somehow *feel* the scent, for I was growing light-headed. The effect was similar to what I'd experienced one time when I'd walked into a room where people had been smoking hash, and I'd gotten a contact high. My first sensation was dizziness, but that quickly passed, and was replaced by a heightened tactile sensitivity that was hallucinatory; the darkness felt like a rubbery substance pressing against my skin, and the air in my lungs like a heavy liquid, like mercury. Every sensation was highly magnified, including the sound of our breathing. The sensation was neither pleasant nor unpleasant, only distinctly peculiar. I took a handkerchief out of my pocket and pressed it to my nose, but that didn't help.

Around the flames of both candles there was a distinct halo of black.

Sinclair began by asking Al a simple question, in a casual, conversational tone. "Where is your father, junior?"

Al's response was a soft moan. There followed a prolonged silence, and I gradually became aware of another sensation. It began as a slight tugging feeling in the pit of my stomach that made me slightly nauseous; then I realized it was caused by something I was hearing. Sinclair was singing—chanting—in a very soft voice. There were no words, only sounds, syllables, chanted in a minor key. The sound gradually grew in volume. Once again I grew dizzy and had to lean back against the wall for support. Harper was leaning heavily against me, clutching my left arm tightly with both hands.

The sound of Sinclair's voice somehow amplified the hallucinatory effects of whatever ingredients were burning in the candle, for with each syllable I felt a pulse beat in the pit of my stomach. My thoughts raced uncontrollably, and I had vivid compressed images of my life, all of it, flashing, as if on a movie screen, just behind my eyes. For me, the effect was wondrous—but I suspected Al was experiencing something altogether different, for he was moaning in pain.

Sinclair abruptly stopped chanting and asked Al the same question. When Al's only response was a tortured groan, Sinclair began to chant again—slightly louder and higher, in a different key.

I suddenly felt an unutterable sadness and loneliness, and I began to cry.

Al began to scream.

Sinclair stopped after a minute or two, and Al began to talk freely, his words tumbling over one another. No more questions were needed.

All of Black Flame's records—its history, its membership role, accounts of assassination through the centuries, individuals and corporations under its control, and complete financial records— were stored electronically in Cornucopia's computer network, and Al provided the information necessary to access any and all of it.

Emmet P. Neuberger was back on duty, presiding over Cornucopia and Black Flame's business affairs from a wheelchair, since he'd had both legs sawed off.

When Al finished, Sinclair, kneeling, leaned over into the black and golden glow cast by the candles. He put his face very close to Al's and made a loud, barking noise that was like a shout, but at the same time unlike any other sound I had ever heard uttered by a human. The noise made both Harper and me jump, and it echoed in the vast stone, wood, and glass library for what seemed a very long time. The candles went out.

We heard Sinclair's footsteps in the darkness, and then the heavy drapes were pulled back, allowing sunlight to once again stream into the library. The man with the steel-gray hair and eyes opened a window, and the black, greasy smoke from the extinguished candles began to waft out into the morning. My head immediately began to clear. Insolers stepped off to one side to stand in front of a bookcase, while Garth, Veil, Harper, and I walked over to the sitting area, looked down at the still figure on the floor. Al was dead, his face a frozen mask of unspeakable agony.

Sinclair took a crocheted shawl from the sofa and draped it over Al's face. Then he went to Jan, put his arms around her, gently kissed her on the forehead.

"You're going to New York?" the woman asked.

Sinclair nodded. "After we tidy up things here. I owe Neuberger a visit, and the complete records can only be accessed from there. I have to finish it, Jan."

"Yes, Chant. I know."

Suddenly, there was an ominous *click-clack-clonk* of metal hitting metal, a magazine being shoved home, an automatic rifle being cocked. We all wheeled around in the direction of the sound, and I was shocked to see Duane Insolers still standing back across the room by a bookcase. One of the dead Black Flame soldiers' weapons that had been picked up and leaned against the wall was now in his hands. The bore was pointed at Sinclair's chest.

"I want everyone to remain perfectly still and do exactly as I say," Insolers said calmly. "Sinclair and Kendry, I want both of you to *slowly* spread your legs apart, then cross your arms over your chests and squeeze your hands in your armpits. Do it right now. If you hesitate, I pull the trigger."

Veil and Sinclair did as they were told.

"Duane!" Jan cried, anger and sorrow in her voice. "Oh, Duane!"

"Be quiet, Jan," Insolers said without looking at her. He had moved the bore of the rifle slightly, now aiming it at a point midway between Veil and Sinclair. "I'm sorry to have to end up the skunk at the garden party, folks, but it had to happen like this someday, and Sinclair knew it. Our relationship has always been a bit tenuous. I'm only interested in Sinclair, and there's no reason for things to become any more unpleasant than they are so long as none of you tries to interfere with me. But know that I will kill any one, or all, of you if I have to."

"Do as he says," Sinclair said in an even tone.

"Thank you, Sinclair. Now, I want the rest of you to move away from him. Kendry, you make sure you keep your hands in your armpits and feet on the floor and apart. Shuffle. Don't turn your body."

Jan abruptly stepped next to Sinclair, thrust her chin out defiantly, and glared at Insolers. "If you're going to kill Chant, Duane, you may as well kill me too."

"Oh, I will if I have to, Jan. I like you very much, but I'm a professional, and I have a job to do. Tell her, Sinclair."

"Move away, Jan," Sinclair said in the same even tone as he stared back at Insolers.

"Chant?"

"It's all right. If he wanted to kill me, he would have done it immediately, without all this chitchat. Duane has something else on his mind, so it's best to let him get on with it. But he will pull the trigger if you provoke him, or if he feels you're trying to use your body to screen me. So do as he says, please." He turned his head slightly, smiled reassuringly at Jan, who finally stepped back away from him. Then Sinclair looked back at Insolers. "I hate to leave things unfinished. You'll take care of eliminating Black Flame for me, won't you, Duane?"

"For sure. I heard everything the little son-of-a-bitch told you, and I'll pass it on to Interpol, the NYPD, the FBI, and everybody else who needs to know. I personally guarantee they'll be put out of business."

"Thanks. I appreciate that."

"So you really did know all along what you were talking about, Insolers," I said, trying to move just a bit closer to Veil. I wondered why the CIA operative was waiting to do whatever it was he planned to do, but I was in no great hurry to resolve the mystery. "There was indeed a CIA special assassin, an insider who was a real threat—you, you prick." I paused, swallowed, tasted bile. "You weren't trying to run me; you *were* running me right along, using me to get next to John Sinclair, and I delivered him right into your lap. You're a clever man, Insolers, but you're still a fuck. I'm thinking it may be very good insurance for your future personal security if you killed me, pal, because I'm working up a real good mad at you."

Garth said, "Shut up, Mongo."

Insolers nodded curtly. "I'm sorry you feel that way, Frederickson. But you're right. I *did* have to find a way to get close to Sinclair, without making him suspicious and putting him on his guard. Like I said, our relationship has always been tenuous, founded more on mutual interests than real trust. I had no way to contact him, knew he wouldn't contact me, and I could never have called or come here without a very good excuse. That was taboo. I'd like to think not, but he might even have killed me if I ever came here alone or tried to contact Jan. I didn't need him angry with me; I needed him off guard."

"So you made a snap decision and crammed all that information into my head at the very beginning, hoping that I'd do exactly what I did—eventually find my way here, bringing you along with me. But you had to be brought here against your will, kicking and screaming all the way, as a captive. It was the only way Sinclair here would buy your story that you'd come to help, the only way you could hope to get the drop on him like this."

Insolers' response was another curt nod.

"You took a very big chance in the car back out on the highway, mister," Veil said in a deceptively easygoing tone that was tinged with regret. "You were pretty convincing when you had that garrote around Mongo's neck, and you can't imagine how close I came to killing you."

Garth said, "This is what we get for listening to Mongo."

Insolers shrugged. "Big jobs require big risks, and there's no

211

bigger job than running John Sinclair to ground. I simply couldn't think of any other way to do it."

I didn't so much actually see as sense a minute shift in the balance of the spread-eagled man standing next to me. Something was about to happen. And, despite all evidence to the contrary, not the least of which was the automatic rifle in the hands of the man standing across the room, I did not feel Duane Insolers was going to be with our little group much longer—unless I intervened, which I did. I had one big question to ask Insolers, and I wasn't going to get the answer if he was dead. Also, dead men's fingers can twitch, and that was all it would take to kill one or more of us.

I raised my right arm and put the back of my hand against Veil's stomach in what I hoped looked like a casual gesture. It was enough to stop him—for the moment.

"Explain something to me, Insolers," I said quickly. "John Sinclair has the knowledge, training, and mental skills to defeat that tasty truth tea Al gave us, but you don't. When Al questioned you, you *did* say that you'd come to help Sinclair. You didn't toss your cookies when you said it. It means you were telling the truth at the time, which makes it hard to understand what you're doing now. Care to comment?"

Insolers grunted, ejected the magazine from the rifle, dropped both it and the weapon on the floor. "Actually, there's nothing to explain. I was trying to make an impression on Mr. Sin—*Jesus Christ!*"

Veil and John Sinclair had moved as one, taking their right hands out of their armpits and flicking their wrists in a single motion so quick that I perceived the motion only as a blur out of the corner of my eye. An instant later, both the throwing knife I had given to Veil and a steel *shuriken* thudded into the wooden casing of the bookshelf behind Insolers, a weapon on either side of his head, both barely an inch from his ears. The blood drained from his face as he took a step forward, then turned and looked back at the two razor-sharp pieces of steel that could have been embedded in his skull.

"It looks like your luck is still holding, mister," Veil said to Insolers as he and Sinclair exchanged glances and approving nods.

"You can thank Mongo for the fact that you're still alive. That's twice he's saved your life in twenty-four hours. I hope you're going to remember him in your will."

Jan made a hissing sound of disgust, shook her head. "Duane, you're an idiot."

"You look a little shaky, Duane," Sinclair said with a wry smile. "You want a drink?"

The CIA's deputy director of operations shook his head. "No," he said, and swallowed hard. "Let's just all sit down. I have a few things to say to you, Sinclair."

Veil unceremoniously dragged Al's body out of sight behind the sofa. Then we all sat down, with Insolers sitting in a straight-backed chair, and the rest of us on the sofa.

"What just occurred could have happened differently, Sinclair," Insolers continued, "and I'm not referring to the fact that you or Kendry might have killed me. You could have taken a sniper's bullet in the brain while you were standing on your balcony or walking around the grounds. The fact of the matter is that I volunteered to come over here to kill you, because if I hadn't come they were going to send somebody else—somebody who would have gotten the job done. Black Flame wasn't the only outfit gradually closing the distance over the years. The agency has also been getting closer and closer to you every day, to uncovering the truth about a lot of things. After this Cornucopia thing in Switzerland went down, they used a computer to start combing through all your files one more time. This time they were taking another, very serious look at all the manipulations that went into the creation of our countess here, and her inheritance of R. Edgar Blake's castle and entire estate. Before too long, they're going to make all the right connections, and they're going to know that the story we made up to tell them is a lie. They already suspect it, and they strongly suspect a connection between you, Jan, and this castle. They wanted to send somebody over here to set up surveillance of this castle—somebody with expert sniper's skills to blow you away just in case you did happen to saunter into his sights. Like I said, I assigned myself to the job. In other words, Sinclair, the party's over. I can't go back unless I can say I've killed you, and offer some kind of convincing

213

evidence. Otherwise, I'm blown. Now, you can certainly kill me as a partial solution to the problem, but I don't think you want to do that. Besides, they'll just send somebody else. You can close up shop here, but now I think they're going to concentrate on tracing and tracking Jan. If she doesn't go deep underground, which I don't think you want, she'll lead them to you. So if you two want to stay together, Chant Sinclair is going to have to die. I've gone to a lot of trouble, and taken considerable risks, to get myself into a position where I could not only deliver this message but make certain you took it seriously. So you're dead. Got it?"

Sinclair's response was to smile thinly, scratch his head. "You do make a strong argument, Duane. I've got it."

Insolers nodded, relief clearly evident on his face. "You died here last night. You managed to kill off these Black Flame members, but you and Jan died with them. If we blow up the castle with all the bodies in it, there's no reason for the agency not to believe the report I give them. I may even say I blew it up. Whatever. It will work as long as you don't one day decide to go back into business."

Sinclair put his arm around Jan, pulled her close to him. "It sounds like a good plan, Duane," he said easily.

Jan smiled at the man with the piercing gray eyes. "Does this mean we're going to be able to live like normal human beings?"

"It looks that way, my dear. If Duane gets the rest of it right."

Harper said, "Black Flame is part of the rest of it. What about the rest of them, Mr. Insolers?"

"I'll do what I said I would, Harper. My guess is that within a week Black Flame will no longer exist; their operations will be shut down, their members and associates arrested or killed, and their finances confiscated."

I cleared my throat. "I'll want to deal with Emmet P. Neuberger personally."

"You've got it. I'll put Frederickson and Frederickson on the CIA payroll as temporary consultants, and you and your brother can not only take care of your business with Neuberger but watch over my shoulder while I take care of the rest of it. Agreed?"

I nodded. When Insolers looked at Sinclair, he nodded.

"Good," Insolers continued. "Now, it's going to take me some time to make arrangements to bring in enough explosives to blow this place up, so I suggest that—"

"It's already been taken care of," Sinclair said. "There's enough C-5 planted in strategic places in the walls to bring the entire structure down. The wiring is in place as well, and all that has to be done is to connect it to a detonator and timer." He must have seen the surprised look on all our faces, for he paused for a few moments, looked at each of us in turn, then continued, "I always knew I would have to retire someday, and this seems as good a time as any. I also knew that one day somebody might connect me to Jan and this castle. Just as in Duane's plan, the *plastique* was put in place to cover our escape and make it appear as if we'd died in the explosion."

"What will you do now?" Veil asked.

"Whatever we want to, I suppose," Sinclair replied, smiling at Jan.

Garth glanced at me, then turned to Sinclair and Jan. "Well, if you need a job, either as cover or simply because you feel like working, Frederickson and Frederickson can always use a good husband and wife team of investigators. Right, Mongo?"

"For sure."

Sinclair raised his eyebrows slightly. "An interesting thought."

Jan sighed. "God, we're sitting on so much money I literally don't know what to do with it now. As Countess Rawlings, I was always able to put it to good use. With the countess dead, I won't be able to do that anymore."

"Cornucopia," I said to Insolers.

"What?"

"Cornucopia. Once before, you and others phonied up old records and made new ones to create a countess and have her inherit R. Edgar Blake's entire estate. Something is going to have to be done with all the millions in Black Flame's coffers. Black Flame and Neuberger are going to be out of the picture. So why don't you arrange for Jan, under whatever identity she chooses, to manage the fund?"

Insolers looked at Jan. "Would you like that?"

"Yes," Jan replied eagerly. "If I can gain control of Cornucopia, I can roll over everything I inherited from the Blake estate and combine it with the Black Flame holdings to make Cornucopia a real philanthropy."

Insolers grunted. "I'll look into it. You'll both need totally new identities."

"That's my department," Sinclair said as he rose, took Jan's hand, and helped her to her feet. "Give us a half hour or so while Jan and I decide who we want to be for the rest of our lives."

•　•　•

Even from a distance of three miles, the thunderous explosion shook the ground. Insolers pulled our car off onto the shoulder of the highway. The car ahead of us—carrying a totally unrecognizable John Sinclair and Jan Rawlings, in possession of birth certificates, passports, and other documents identifying them as Richard and Elizabeth Commons, of New York City—also pulled over. We looked back as a flame-streaked black cloud of smoke from the ruined castle rose up to stain the azure sky.

"You took an awfully big chance just by coming here, Insolers," I said quietly.

For a moment I wasn't sure whether the CIA's deputy director of operations had heard me, for he continued to stare out the window, seemingly transfixed by the mushrooming ball of flame and smoke behind us. But then he turned around and said in a mild tone, "Why is that, Frederickson?"

"You've got to be kidding. You're the CIA's chief spiderman in covert operations. Your head's a hamper with all the nation's dirty laundry in it, not to mention a lot of other highly sensitive information that could benefit our enemies. Switzerland was crawling with operatives. What would you have done if someone had made and nabbed you?"

The man with the brown hair and eyes and rodent features shrugged, then smiled wanly. He seemed in an uncharacteristically mellow mood. When he spoke, his voice took on a vaguely professorial tone. "Frederickson, I'd hate to disillusion you, or anyone else in this car, but you'd be amazed at how many of any country's so-called top secrets are pretty much common knowledge among members of the higher echelons in the international intelligence community. Cooked Goose was an exception, not the rule. The biggest headache for most of us is trying to keep our citizens from finding out how much bullshit is financed with their money."

"Actually, I wouldn't be amazed at all."

"Even if I had been picked up, I'd probably have been released as soon as the operative's superiors found out about it. If it took a mind to, the United States could totally shut down the intelligence operations of thirty or forty countries within seventy-two hours—maybe less. Being responsible for kidnapping any top ops officer would just create too much of a hassle for everyone, making it too difficult to conduct business as usual."

"You may be right, Insolers," Veil said. "But just suppose you'd been snatched by some rookie terrorist who believed everything he'd just finished reading in his training manual, which had most likely been furnished to him by the CIA. Said rookie ties you up, then goes to work on you with heated tongs and chemicals. Then what would you have done?"

Insolers gave it a few moments' thought, once again smiled somewhat wanly. "Probably tried to hold out until Chant Sinclair came to my rescue. Frederickson, are you and your brother really going to put him to work for you?"

"If it's what he wants."

"I'd pay to see that," Insolers said, and laughed loudly.

"What the hell's so funny?"

Insolers just continued to laugh.

When we heard the distant sound of approaching sirens, Sinclair pulled back onto the highway, and we did the same. Five minutes later we reached the turnoff leading to the airport, and Jan waved goodbye to us through the rear window. We continued on toward Interpol headquarters.